"This is

"You! Get your ass
Buford's voice roared
saw the tired, strained   ...ong. Sam
looked as if he was about to collapse. Jenny
reached down with her left hand to help Wong.

"What the hell do you think you're doing?"
Buford howled as he moved quickly to the base
of the ladder.

Jenny shot a glance at Buford that was pure
contempt and anger. She pulled with all her
might, in a mighty heave, but could not move
Sam Wong. Suddenly, coming down from above
her, a figure appeared at Jenny's side. The mud-
soaked trooper to her left reached down and,
working together, Jenny and the man pulled Sam
Wong up.

"This is Eagle Team," the tall, mud-soaked soldier next to Olsen, Major Travis Barrett, shouted
back to Sergeant Major Buford. "We don't leave
anyone behind."

TALON FORCE

THUNDERBOLT

Cliff Garnett

A SIGNET BOOK

SIGNET
Published by New American Library, a division of
Penguin Putnam Inc., 375 Hudson Street,
New York, New York 10014, U.S.A.
Penguin Books Ltd, 27 Wrights Lane,
London W8 5TZ, England
Penguin Books Australia Ltd, Ringwood,
Victoria, Australia
Penguin Books Canada Ltd, 10 Alcorn Avenue,
Toronto, Ontario, Canada M4V 3B2
Penguin Books (N.Z.) Ltd, 182–190 Wairau Road,
Auckland 10, New Zealand

Penguin Books Ltd, Registered Offices:
Harmondsworth, Middlesex, England

First published by Signet, an imprint of New American Library,
a division of Penguin Putnam Inc.

First Printing, February 2000
10 9 8 7 6 5 4 3 2 1

*People sleep peacefully in their beds at night
only because rough men stand ready
to do violence on their behalf.*

—George Orwell

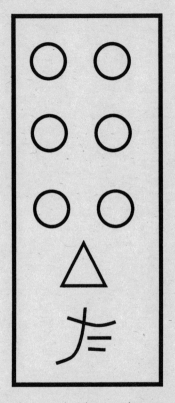

The team acting together is more important
than one person doing something without the group.

—The theme and battle banner of the Seven Samurai

Chapter One

Every American is our enemy.
Every American is our target.
— Yuri Terrek

**March 17, 8:45 P.M., thirty thousand feet
above sea level, 424 miles east of Honolulu
International Airport, Hawaii**

Captain George Gardner checked the cockpit instruments of his Boeing 777. He had 253 passengers aboard, and everything was running smoothly. A knock sounded at his cockpit-cabin door.

"Sir, I've brought your dinner," flight attendant Susie Atworth announced.

Jerry Briskey, the flight engineer, grinned. "About time, I'm starving."

"I swear, Jerry, I've never seen anyone eat as much as you do," Flight Lieutenant Frank Dozois said. Frank looked down at his waistline, which had increased several inches in the past two years, then ran his hand through his thinning, receding hair. He looked at Jerry, who was six years younger than him, had a full head of thick, dark hair, and the sharp, good looks of a college athlete. "How can you eat so much and stay so slim?"

"It's my special diet and exercise program," Jerry offered seriously. "I eat everything I want and never work out. Of course, the key to everything is the sex."

Frank shook his head. "It isn't fair."

Captain Gardner laughed. "Go on Jerry, open the door before I have to listen to another lecture from Frank about the benefits of high-protein diets."

Jerry reached to his right and unlocked the cabin door. Susie Atworth, a pretty Amerasian woman with short black hair, a gorgeous figure, and beautiful dark slanted eyes entered with a tray of food for the cabin crew. "We've completed feeding the passengers, Captain. Mr. Cooper in twenty-one C has had too much to drink, but we have him under control. There's a cranky newborn baby in row forty-four. She's adorable, but her mother's having a hard time with her. Other than that, we're running smoothly and looking forward to three fabulous days in Waikiki."

"Susie, you promised me dinner tomorrow night," Jerry said, lifting his food from her tray. "Afterward, we can go for a swim. The beach is lovely at night."

Gardner reached for a cup of coffee that was on the tray. He knew what was coming, and he was anxious to hear the reply.

"Not on your life, lover boy." Susie grinned, then winked at the captain. "You know I'm married. Besides, I wouldn't go out with a playboy like you even if I was single."

"Susie, I'm shocked," Jerry announced in mocked horror. "I was counting on you. Who am I going to show off the sights of Honolulu to if not you? It's Saint Patrick's day today, and we won't have a chance to celebrate. What do you say?"

Susie shook her head. "Since when did you become Irish, Mr. Briskey?"

"Honey, on Saint Pattie's Day we're all Irish!"

Gardner smiled at the banter, then put down his coffee as he heard a priority message coming over the radio. "This is Control Tower, Honolulu International, with an urgent message for Northwest Flight oh-eight-five."

Gardner picked up the transmitter. "This is November Whiskey oh-eight-five. Send it. Over."

"We've lost Delta two-forty-one and Northwest one-sixteen from our radar. One flight left Tokyo thirty minutes before you, and another left Seoul about an hour and a half before you departed Tokyo Haneda International. Both flights were headed for Honolulu. Have you heard any radio traffic from either aircraft?"

Gardner bit his lip, then looked at Frank and Jerry. Both men shook their heads. This was unusual to lose communications and radar contact with two inbound aircraft at the same time. He knew Captain Mike Iverson, the pilot of Northwest 116. "Negative. We haven't heard anything."

"Oh-eight-five, can you confirm that you have a sky marshal on board?"

A look of dread shot across Gardner's face. If Honolulu was asking for a sky marshal and two aircraft were reported out of contact, it could only mean one thing: Someone was causing aircraft to go down. "Stand by."

Susie looked at the captain and nodded. "Sir, Agent Hartwell is in coach, seat thirty-seven B."

"Roger, Honolulu. Agent Hartwell is on board. What do you advise?"

"Put him on the radio as soon as possible," Honolulu ordered.

Gardner pointed to the door and motioned for Susie to bring Hartwell forward. He leaned over to Frank and said, "I'm taking her down to one thousand feet. If anything happens, I don't want it to happen at thirty thousand feet."

Jerry sprang into activity, plotting a new course at one thousand feet and quickly calculating the fuel required to fly at the lower altitude. His calculations checked out. "No problem with fuel, Captain."

"Jerry, lock that door," Gardner ordered, then pushed the button that activated the aircraft seat belt sign. As Jerry secured the door, Gardner picked up the aircraft intercom. "Ladies and gentlemen, please fasten your seat belts and set your tray tables upright. We're going to be making our descent for landing."

Gradually, slowly, Gardner brought the plane down. He watched his altimeter drop . . . 25,000 feet . . . 23,000.

There was a knock at the door. "Sir, it's me, Susie. I have Mr. Hartwell here."

Gardner nodded to Jerry to open the door. A well-built man in his early thirties with short-cropped hair, wearing a wrinkled, gray sports jacket and dark slacks, came in. "Agent Hartwell. What's the problem?"

Gardner handed him the transmitter as he watched the altimeter. "Honolulu wants to talk to you. It's urgent."

"Honolulu, this is Agent Hartwell on Flight oh-eight-five."

"Agent Hartwell, this is Honolulu. I'm Agent Henry, FBI. We've had two aircraft go down in the last two hours. We don't know how or even if it's an act of sabotage, but we received a telephone warning one hour ago, and we are alerting all U.S. carriers inbound for Honolulu."

Gardner listened carefully as he watched the altimeter . . . 20,000 feet . . . 17,000 feet.

"What do you know so far?" Hartwell asked.

"Not much. We lost both aircraft on routine approach for landing, just one hundred miles out," the FBI agent announced. "There were no radio transmissions from either aircraft. The radar clearly showed Flight one-sixteen breaking up."

"Poor bastards," Frank announced, shaking his head. "You knew Iverson, right?"

Gardner shook his head.

"Well, all seems to be okay here. No suspicious characters that I've noticed," Hartwell said.

Gardner watched the altimeter. The night was clear, and the moon was shining. He could almost see the moon's shimmer in the water. He glanced at the altimeter: 16,000 feet.

"Did the aircraft have anything in common? Did they fly over the same airspace? Could it have been a surface-to-air missile?"

"Negative . . . wait. Yes," the FBI agent announced. "We lost contact with both of them at fifteen thousand feet."

A sense of sheer panic overcame Gardner. He looked at the altimeter. 15,800 feet. It was the last thing he saw.

In the next moment, Flight 085 erupted in a burst of flame as the fuel was detonated by a dozen microexplosives. The tangled mass of burning metal and shattered humanity plummeted to the dark, cold Pacific Ocean, never to be seen again.

Military Must Prepare to Protect the United States Against Transnational Threats

WASHINGTON, D.C., March 27—In the wake of the recent terrorist bombings of three U.S. civilian airliners on Sunday, 17 March—a day which has been named Black Sunday—the U.S. Congress has recommended that the U.S. military expand its role to protect themselves against terrorist attacks by transnational threats.

Black Sunday was the greatest loss of life in a single day to terrorism in the history of the United States. Seven hundred twenty-six U.S. citizens lost their lives that day.

This issue is deemed critical since various intelligence agencies believe that the leading terrorist organizations are moving quickly to acquire the latest chemical and biological weapons.

Broadening the military's role will require legislation that will be passed by Congress this month, a congressional spokesman for the Senate Armed Services Committee reported. Under this new legislation, the Department of Defense will create a new high-tech special operations unit that will be capable of global deployment on a moment's notice.

The Department of Defense estimates that creating the new, high-tech joint force will cost $200 billion in the first six months.

Congress believes that this is a sound investment in America's future in the wake of the horrible terrorist bombings in February. This new special operations unit will be designed to preempt transnational threats before they attack U.S. interests or citizens. This preemption capability is considered a critical aspect of the new organization's role to grapple with the expected chemical-biological terrorist threat.

This new organization, which will combine the best of American technology with the best covert operation warriors in the U.S. military, will be needed to address the growing threat of transnational terrorist threats, the Department of Defense spokesman said.

Chapter Two

I heard the voice of the Lord, saying, Whom shall I send,
and who will go for us? Then said I, Here am I; send me.
—The Book of the Prophet Isaiah, 6:8

**July 14, 0430 hours, at the secret
military training camp in the wilds of the
Big Snowy Mountains of Montana**

Sergeant Major George Buford stood in front of a crowd
of three hundred recruits. Far from being the usual
rookie pukes on the first day of boot camp, they were
almost all players—veteran Special Forces studs in their
own right. Dozens of Navy SEALs, Green Berets, Army
Rangers, Force Recons, PJs, and Delta Force troopers
stood at attention in perfect rows. Many had volunteered
to try out for the U.S. military's newest, most high-tech
special forces outfit, but some had been volunteered by
commanding officers who took pride in sending their best
men and women to the secret training camp in Montana.
There were even a good number of highly qualified civilians, mostly tech people, experts in the kind of cutting-
edge equipment and communications the new TALON
Force would use. For most of the civilians, Uncle Sam
had simply made them an offer they couldn't refuse.

The sun had yet to crest the horizon but the dark night
was lightening to gray. The outline of the rugged, tree-
studded hills that surrounded the secret special forces
camp in the Montana backcountry was clearly visible in
the waning darkness. The neat rows of dark shadows
stood in formation as the dawn approached.

Buford paced in front of the first row of prospective
TALON troopers. He wore the classic flat-brimmed,
high-crowned hat with four indentations worn by drill
sergeants since the Spanish-American War. Civilians

thought of them as Smokey The Bear hats, or state trooper hats. But military people knew to fear anyone wearing one. The hat shouted "drill sergeant" with hot breath inches from your nose. Buford angrily sucked in a vast amount of the thin Montana air, his chest inflating and nostrils flaring as he prepared to hurl invective at the crowd before him.

"Ladies and gentlemen, I see before me a group that represents America's best. That's what I've been told. I am well aware, as no doubt you are, that most of you outrank me, but I have news for you, so listen good. While you are here, under my control, you have no rank. You have no privilege. You have no fancy military academy degree, no pass to let you into the officer's club. *While you are here you are nothing!* Do you hear me? *Nothing!* As far as I'm concerned, as far as Uncle Sam is concerned, you're not America's best until *I* say you're America's best.

"Most of you have already gone through some tough courses and difficult training. Goody for you." Sarcasm and contempt dripped from his words. "Many of you have survived Airborne School, the Ranger course, SEAL training, or the Special Forces 'Q' course at the various special operations academies your Uncle Sam generously operates for you. That's nice. Real nice. But I'm here to tell you, you ain't seen nothin' yet. You're gonna wish you were back there. I am gonna tear you down. I am gonna break you. I am gonna make you beg for your momma. I'm gonna make you cry and suck your thumb. I'm gonna make you want to quit. And I'm gonna enjoy every minute of it. Because if you can survive me and my training course, any enemy you face out in the big, bad world is gonna seem like a puny little sissy by comparison."

Buford was getting into it now, his face glowing red, sparks shooting from his eyes. "Why would I want to make America's best quit? Because if you can't be depended on to go the extra mile now, *how are your team-mates gonna depend on you?* Guess you're not America's best, then. And if you ain't the best, if we send you out on a mission, you'll sure be the deadest.

"Now what I want is the best of the best. And I don't

care who you are. I see some troopers here of the female persuasion. We currently have no female members on any Special Forces teams. Officially, we have no females in the Rangers, or Force Recon, or Delta. But I don't care. This is a new force and we need all type of skills. Everyone here has an equal chance of making the team. I'm a forward-thinking kind of guy. I don't care what kind of troopers we have on TALON Force—red, yellow, black, white, male, female, or Martian. If you can pass muster with me, then you can do the job. Period.

"Before we begin, take a look around you. Don't waste any time remembering any faces, 'cause by the time I'm finished with you, eighty-three percent of you will be gone. Out of three hundred, I will whittle you down to fifty. And the fifty who will survive to the end will become the world's best-equipped soldiers. I'm not going to waste my time telling you about what most of you will never see. All I'll say is, thank the lord you will be on our side. You can quit at any time—all you have to do is tell me or one of my cadre that you have had enough. Okay, any quitters?"

The group was silent. Only the rustling of the wind against the trees disturbed the early morning quiet.

"Let's start right in.

"Everyone down. Push-ups. Fifty. *Now!* One . . . two . . . three . . ." Buford slowly walked through the mass of rhythmically rising and falling bodies, pausing here and there to put a highly polished boot on the backs of a few soldiers. He figured he could weed out the civilians first thing, before the rest of the troopers even broke a sweat. The veteran instructor made eye contact with General Krauss, the commander of the TALON Force, who was standing off to the rear of the formation watching the activities. It was going to be a good five months.

August 28, 1130 hours

Buford surveyed the parade ground under dark and foreboding skies. He was pleased to see that of the original 300 volunteers, he'd whittled them down to 142 in only six weeks' time. He impressed even himself with the kind of tough, realistic training that he'd devised for the wanna-be TALON troopers. Some called the training pure torture—but every second of every day had a purpose planned to it. With the help of the Pentagon's top experts in psychological warfare, he'd devised mental tests as well as physical ones. Sure, there were the usual feats of endurance and strength, though many of them were little more than forcing the mind to tell the body to keep on going. But then there were the hyperrealistic virtual reality simulators, the quizzes, the drills, and what Buford liked to think of as "the crackers."

The volunteers were stressed every minute of every hour of every day. The focus of the first phase of the training was on the mental and physical endurance, emphasizing skill and determination, with none of the sophomoric games you see actors running through in Hollywood films. Survival, first aid, demolitions and weapons skills were tested against a backdrop of fifty-mile marches, hand-to-hand combat training and living off the land. Every day Buford asked who was going to quit. Every so often a few hands went up and the volunteers hustled to Washout Hall. Most of the prima donnas and the Rambos had quit long ago.

Now that the easy washouts were gone, it was time to form the remainders into teams and begin the second phase of training. It was one thing to be outstanding as an individual, but if you couldn't work in a team, you were worthless to TALON Force. Each team was only as strong as its weakest member, as the old saying went, and Buford was out to forge unbreakable chains.

"Attention!" Buford ordered.

Thunder rolled off in the distance, echoing across the Montana hills. The slightly more ragged and scruffy-looking bunch before him had just returned from an overnight forced march over one of the Big Snowy Mountains' tougher climbs, but they snapped to crisp military attention just the same. "All right, you are now going to be divided into teams of approximately twenty troopers each for the next phase of training. Fall out according to your team designation." Buford ran down the alphabetical list of names on his clipboard. The graduates of phase one of training were sent to Asp, Bear, Cobra, Doberman, Eagle, Fox, and Gator Teams.

"Altobelli—Bear," Buford bellowed, checking off names as he yelled them out. "Babcock—Fox, Barrett—Eagle, Benson—Cobra, Bukowski—Asp . . ." On and on he droned until reaching the end of the alphabet. ". . . Weinberg—Gator, Wong—Eagle, Wyznewicz—Bear, Yelberton—Doberman, and Zezell—Eagle. Fall out—now!" The troopers quickly formed into their new teams. Buford looked over his handiwork.

"Now that you've all learned how to walk across the parade ground, I want to make one thing clear. These are your teammates for the rest of training. From now on, you will eat together as a team. You will bunk together as a team. You will shit together as a team. And most importantly, you will train together as a team. Those remaining at the end of the training will know each team member inside and out. You will be able to think like one another, to anticipate each other's moves, to make up the cogs in your team's machine. Each team will become one flexible, unbeatable unit. And if you can't play well with others, you'll be on your way back to your home outfits so fast you'll never believe you were even here."

The winds kicked up, sending dust devils swirling across the barren parade ground.

"You have until 1200 to get organized," Buford ordered. "Dis-missed!"

Major Travis Barrett looked up at the darkening sky then turned to face his new teammates. Some were beginning to drift back toward the barracks in an amorphous mass. He looked back up at the sky. *Well, shit,* he thought to himself, *if nobody else is going to take charge here* . . . "Eagle Team, stand fast. Attention! Double time march to Barracks E, pronto."

The stunned members of Eagle Team looked at the six-foot-two-inch Green Beret. Who the fuck died and left him boss? But Travis never paid their wary faces the slightest bit of attention. He simply picked up his feet and jogged down the middle of two rows of Eagle Team troopers, heading toward Barracks E.

Navy SEAL Stan Powczuk, who knew Barrett from joint maneuvers with the Berets and knew what kind of a solid leader the Army major was, fell in behind him. The big black Marine named Jacques DuBois was quick to pick up on Barrett's move. All six feet five inches of muscle loped along beside the barrel-chested SEAL. A Navy Intelligence Lieutenant named Jen Olsen fell in behind the Marine, and the only other woman on Eagle Team, an Army doctor named Sarah Greene, was right beside her. A good-looking Air Force pilot and PJ named Hunter Blake sighted in on Lieutenant Olsen's tight buns and locked onto their rhythmic bounce, not noticing the little civilian tech nerd named Sam Wong tagging along behind him. The thirteen other Eagle Team members got the hint and joined in the double time march to the barracks.

The troopers on the six other teams just watched and shook their heads at the unnecessarily gung ho move by Eagle Team. Some began to snicker. Some began to mutter that those fuckers were trying to show them up. And then the skies opened up with a tremendous clap of thunder, a blinding bolt of lightning, and fat raindrops coming down so fast it was suddenly like standing inside a car wash. Everyone got soaked to the skin except the twenty troopers in Eagle Team. The door to Barracks E had slammed shut just before the first drops of water hit the ground.

Sergeant Major Buford double-timed over to the mess hall, smiling to himself. He'd just found his first team leader.

Inside Barracks E, Major Barrett faced the members of the newly formed Eagle Team. Seizing the initiative, he gathered them around him in a circle. "Look, we don't have much time before mess call, so let's try to get to know each other a little before Buford runs us through whatever shit he's cooked up for us this afternoon." He looked around at the bunch of new faces. "I'll introduce myself. I'm Major Travis Barrett, U.S. Army. Some of you I've seen before, but the only one of you I actually know is Lieutenant Commander Stan Powczuk. Don't believe it when anyone says Army and Navy hate each other's guts. Stan's a fine SEAL instructor, a real operator, and I'm proud to be on the same team with him."

Short, blocky, and hairy Stan Powczuk stood up to address his teammates. "I'm Powczuk, like Barrett said. I don't know about any of you cocksuckers, but I say we make Major Barrett our team leader. I've worked with Barrett on joint operations, and I'm man enough to say that we couldn't do better than having him as a leader. I'm no expert on parliamentary procedure, but I move to put Barrett in charge of Eagle Team. That is, if you're up for the challenge, Major."

A thin smile curled Travis's lips.

"Well, what do you say?" Powczuk demanded. The other Eagle Team members looked around. Nobody else seemed to come forward to seize the mantle, and as a Major, Barrett seemed to be the most experienced officer in the group. Heads nodded in assent.

The little Chinese guy said, "I'll second the motion."

"Anybody else want the job? No? Then it's done. Come on, Major, tell 'em a little more about yourself," Powczuk said.

"Well," Travis drawled, "all right." He reached into the pocket of his battle dress uniform and pulled out a cigar. He bit off the end and spit it out, then lit up his stogie. "I'm Travis Barrett. If y'all haven't figured it out yet, I'm from Texas. No, I don't remember the Alamo, but I'm fourth generation Army, dating back to my great-granddaddy, who was a tanker with Patton in World War I, and my granddaddy, who was a tanker with Patton in World War II. I was the first in my family to attend West Point. I'm divorced, got a wonderful son and daughter who I miss terribly, and a good ol' hound dog I miss, too. His name, is, however, Alamo." He got a good laugh from everyone.

"I survived Airborne and Ranger schools and fought

with the Second Armored Cavalry in Desert Storm. Went head to head against some Russian-made Iraqi tanks. We could have gone all the way to Baghdad if they'd let us. Became a Snake Eater—Green Beret for you civilians—after the Gulf War, and unfortunately was in Somalia where the Rangers were ambushed. We lost nineteen fine American boys that day. The medals I got won't bring 'em back, though. I also was an observer with the Russian Army in Chechnya, which was another disaster. I'm a lucky son of a gun to be alive. That's enough for right now."

Stan Powczuk stood up. "Travis is too modest to mention he's currently assigned to Delta Force and has done a lot of cross-training with other Special Forces units. And he'll never say it, but this good ol' boy is one hell of a line dancer, so men, keep your wives away from him on the dance floor, and ladies, watch out!"

Travis blushed as Eagle Team laughed.

Stan continued. "If you weren't paying attention, I'm Lieutenant Commander Stan Powczuk. I'm an underwater demolitions expert for SEAL Team Five, and have most recently been a SEAL instructor. I'm from Steeltown, U.S.A., actually a little town in western Pennsylvania called Aliquippa known for two famous sons— me, and Mike Ditka. I had a football scholarship to Pitt, but had to bring in money when my father was killed in a blast furnace accident. Joined the Navy to keep the family afloat. No joke. Went to OCS, then became a SEAL. I also saw action in the Gulf War, doing reconnaissance work in the Persian Gulf. I can pilot any boat you got, from an inner tube to a fucking aircraft carrier. You need something done on or under the water, I'm your man. And if you cross me, I can be your worst nightmare."

"Thanks Stan, that was both informative and friendly," Travis said. He turned to the good-looking blond Air Force pilot with the slicked-back hair next to him. "You're next."

The pilot stood up and coolly eyed his fellow members of Eagle Team, his gaze lingering on the physical attributes of the tall woman across from him. "I'm Captain Hunter Blake, and if it flies, I can fly it. I learned from my father, General Blake, USAF, retired. I've been around planes my whole life, and like Chuck Yeager, I have the right stuff." Eyes rolled at this comment. "I flew F-117 Nighthawk stealth fighter/bombers in the Gulf War, and turned down an offer from NASA to become an astronaut. I spent a few years at Edwards Air Force Base as a test pilot, and at Groom Lake, in Tonopah, Nevada." This comment raised some eyebrows among those in the know. "Yes, that's right, Area fifty-one. Since I figure we all have top-level security clearances here, it's probably okay to tell you that I have even flown a captured flying saucer." Blake looked around the room. Jaws had dropped, and a gasp was even heard.

"No way," Stan Powczuk said. "You're full of shit."

"Yes indeed," Blake countered, then paused for effect. "I'm kidding. But I had you all there for a second. Admit it!

"Most recently, I've been flying with the PJs. We're the Air Force's pararescue squad, and we rescue and recover downed and injured air crews in remote areas, usually under combat conditions. We do some unbelievable stuff, and our motto is 'These things we do that others may live.' Call me an adrenaline junkie, but I have a need for speed, and I like fast cars, fast planes, and fast women, not necessarily in that order."

As Blake sat down on an empty bunk, a suave looking Hispanic officer stood up. He touched his wispy mustache, as if to make sure it was still there. "I am Juan Hernandez, Captain, U.S. Army. But everybody calls me Johnny. I am originally from Puerto Rico, but my family moved to Arizona because Puerto Rico was too hot for them." Everyone chuckled at the soft-spoken captain's joke. "I am very proud to be an American, and I want to do something great to help the country that has been so good to me and my family. I fly Blackhawk helicopters for the 101st Air Assault Division, and provided cover for the action in Mogadishu. We rescued a lot of our boys there, and almost got shot down ourselves, but here

I am. I love to fly, but I'm telling you, all this ground training is wearing me out!"

Hernandez sat down and Jennifer Olsen stood up. She was a blond bombshell, and while she looked as if she should have been on the set of *Baywatch,* she seemed to oddly fit with her surroundings, too.

"For those of you who haven't noticed, and believe me, I know you've noticed, I am a woman," Olsen said, making eye contact with the men in group. "Now that that's out of the way, I'm Lieutenant Jennifer Olsen, U.S. Navy Intelligence. Don't think that just because I'm a woman, I'm soft. I grew up on a farm in northern Minnesota, and I kicked the butts of guys like you my whole life. While this isn't necessarily what my family envisioned for me when I was a kid, I like the Navy. Did the cheerleader thing in high school, dated the captain of the football team, and all that crap. I was going to be an actress, but ended up as a magician's assistant in Vegas instead. I'll be glad to teach any of you escape tricks from ropes, handcuffs, duct tape—all the type of stuff I learned in the act.

"When I was nineteen, I married a Canadian who was a member of the UN Peacekeeping Forces, but while he was keeping the peace, some Bosnian who was carrying on his own war didn't realize he wasn't supposed to shoot and kill Alan. After I became a widow, I drifted for awhile, ending up in Hollywood doing makeup and costume work for Miramax. Got tired of that, did a little singing and dancing with the USO, and finally realized I needed to finish the job Alan had started. I joined the Navy. Turned out my background made the brass think I'd be good at intelligence. I speak a few languages, I'm good with disguises, and I have a way of getting men to tell me their innermost secrets. Trained with the FBI and the CIA. They both wanted me. And though it hasn't been easy—and they gave me no breaks nor have I ever asked for any—I need the Navy. And I'm damn glad to be a part of Eagle Team."

There was silence as Olsen sat down, though a number of the male troopers tried to eye her without being obvious. A shorter woman with green eyes and short black hair stood up.

"I'm Captain Sarah Greene, U.S. Army. I'm a doctor. I have degrees in botany and microbiology. I'm an expert in biological and chemical warfare, so don't borrow any medicines off my nightstand without asking first. I'm from Vermont, and made the Olympic snowboarding team, but I decided to go to West Point instead. My mother, who was kind of a sixties radical hippie feminist, thought I was out of my mind. But when I went to medical school at Hopkins, that made her happy. I was sent to Japan when the Sarin nerve gas attack on the Tokyo subway occurred. I've also been the Department of Defense representative for the Center for Disease Control in Atlanta. If you're sick or get injured in one of our training exercises, come to me first. I may be able to keep you going and keep the team together before you go to the camp doctors."

A short, bullet-headed African-American with a sculpted, V-shaped torso stood up. "Hey there, I'm Sergeant Anthony Jones. I'm from East Saint Louis, Illinois, and I'm an Army Ranger. Been one for a few years, now. I love the Army because it was my way out of the ghetto. My daddy, he served in Vietnam and came back full of pride for serving his country. He always told me and my brothers that he learned the value of hard work and self-sufficiency, and let me tell you, that helped us out when we went through some serious tough times. I want to prove I'm not too old for this stuff. I was involved in the Panama operation against Noriega. So I may be gettin' a bit long in the tooth for the Special Forces game, but I wanted to give it my best shot so I would never say, 'I could have done it if only I would have tried.' "

A slightly built Asian-American stood up. "Hi, my name is Bruce Lee, and I can kill you all with my pinky." Nobody knew what to make of this until he stuck out his pinky and waved it at them. "That was a joke! You must laugh or face the consequences!" He got some laughs now. "All right, so I'm not Bruce Lee. I am really

Arnold Schwarzenegger. Seriously, I'm Sam Wong, and I'm a civilian. I'm a computer geek with the National Security Agency. I'm first generation American, I'm from New York City, I graduated from high school at fifteen, and I hold twenty-five patents. I'm a cryptology expert, code-breaker, and communications specialist. I am also bionic and I can kill the enemy with my powerful brain. I can also riff like this for another fifteen minutes before I run out of material, but since mess is in about one minute, maybe I'll stop here. I'm starving, even for the slop they feed us here!"

"Uh, thanks Sam," Travis said. "Let's go to the mess hall on the double. We'll finish this up after the afternoon's training. Okay with y'all? Good. Let's hustle."

The newly formed Eagle Team bolted out the barracks door, the bonding and team-building process under way.

August 28, 0530 hours

"Go! Go! Go!" Command Sergeant Major George Buford screamed. Fifteen men in battle dress uniforms dropped to the ground and slithered through the oatmeal-like mud on their bellies. The razor wire was strung just a little more than a foot off the ground, and the soldiers quickly pushed through the ooze like snakes chasing a mouse.

The rain fell in sheets, splattering the mud and raising the water level of the worm pit so high that the men had to literally swim through the mud, holding their breath.

The sergeant major and a dozen other stern, hard-looking noncommissioned officers wearing battle dress fatigues and green berets—all special forces NCOs—walked along the narrow paths between the mud pit, throwing artillery simulators, powerful flash-bang explosives, into the pit. Each grenade fell into the mud and exploded with a loud thud, ominously close to the men struggling in the mire. The explosions urged the soldiers on.

Sergeant Major Buford shook his head. The worm pit was a vile, mud-drenched obstacle course that was known by several other names, all of them unprintable. In front of the entrance to the worm pit was a sign: Ye Who Enter Here, Abandon All Hope. It was a mile-long ball-buster consisting of obstacles that tested physical strength and mental determination. Today, for the first time, Sergeant Major Buford wondered if they would also test teamwork.

"I don't give a damn what rank you are or who your momma is!" Buford shouted. His voice was the voice of authority. There was no doubt who was in charge of this piece of God's muddy earth. "Very small forces engaged in high-risk operations . . . cannot afford weak links in people. Go! Go! *Go!*"

The first fifteen troopers crawled through the goo and finally cleared the razor wire. Each individual operated independently, staggering forward, continuing on in spite of fatigue and mental and emotional strain. Then they stood up and rushed to the next obstacle.

At the end of the wire crawl was a long, thirty-foot-high log ladder. The soldiers started to climb that obstacle. One man struggled on the muddy log, unable to make it over the second rung. He reached for the third rung and fell into the goo. An NCO in a green beret ran up to the man lying in the mud, kicked him, and ordered him to run around the obstacle and then repeat the course. If he failed again, he'd have to report to Washout Hall.

Washout Hall was a large prefabricated structure that operated as both office and hotel. Anyone who wished to quit the TALON Force merely headed for Washout Hall. There they were given a shower, a good meal, a medical exam, and a security briefing. The entire process took a couple of hours. When this was completed, they were whisked away by military bus to the civilian airport in Billings, Montana.

Thunder crashed in the heavens and the skies opened up with even more rain. A second group of sixteen troopers arrived at the start point of the worm pit and gained the attention of Sergeant Major Buford. All sixteen were running in place, their weapons at port arms, their fatigue evident, but their determination driving them on. Fourteen were men. Two were women.

"You're too slow. Some damn Chinaman's going to eat you for breakfast on the battlefield!"

"I thought our relations with the Chinese were improving, Sergeant," a thin, pasty-faced Asian-American blurted out.

"Not again," a voice groaned from the far end of the group. All sixteen troopers were running in place in front of the razor wire, splashing in puddles of mud. The lightning flashed as Sergeant Major Buford walked toward the young man. The sergeant major's massive, muscled body stopped in front of Sam Wong.

"Wong!" Buford barked. "Always the wise guy. When will you learn?"

Wong ran in place, not knowing what to say.

"Everyone down and give me fifty!" Buford ordered.

All sixteen soldiers immediately hit the ground in the prone, push-up position with their rifles on the tops of their hands and their palms in the thick, gooey mud.

"One . . . two . . . three . . . Wong, are you getting the message yet? Six . . . seven . . . eight . . . *Wong, will you ever learn?* Eleven . . . twelve . . . thirteen . . . I can do this all day, Wong."

"Sir, I thought we were going to be fighting terrorists, not Chinese!" Wong shot out between gasping for air and swallowing mud.

"Never call me sir, mister!" Buford demanded. "Twenty-one . . . twenty-two . . . twenty-three . . . And you're right, but do you think there are no Chinese terrorists in the world? . . . Twenty-eight . . . twenty-nine . . . And besides," the sergeant major yelled as he knelt next to Sam Wong, "if that bothers you, if you couldn't pull the trigger on a fellow Chinaman, *maybe you should quit!*"

Sam Wong shook his head and continued doing push-ups. It was clear that his strength was failing, as each push-up was more ragged and slower than before.

"You swore to oppose all enemies, foreign and domestic, and don't forget that. Forty-eight . . . forty-nine . . . fifty," Buford finished. Then gazed at the sixteen mud-drenched, exhausted soldiers, belly down in the mud, struggling to catch their breath. "Well? Why are you all still lying here? Hit the deck and get moving through that wire!"

The sixteen troopers dove into the mud. Each wore a standard Kevlar helmet and carried an M-16 rifle. On their bellies, moving with elbows and knees, they slithered through the slime.

Buford knelt behind one trooper whose helmet was caught in the razor wire. He saw that this trooper was a woman. He shouted even louder than before. "Push it, trooper! If you stay here, you'll die. No one stays behind in TALON Force. Everybody fights!"

Buford knew that this was a moment of truth. The more realistic, fatiguing, stressful, and unconventional the methods, the better prepared his troopers would be to make the decisions, risks, and judgments that would allow success in battle. All of Buford's training methods were keyed to stress, exhaustion and, when a mistake was made, a clear consequence.

"Olsen, I have a friend who is one of the nastiest Thai boxers you'll ever see. He fights with strong, vicious kicks, punches, knees, and elbows. His technique is the best. He grapples well, has a head like a rock, and can kick through a two-by-four with his shin. In actual combat with him though, I noticed a lack of aggression when it came to a contest of wills. Before he got into his first fight I wondered whether he had the will for it. It turned out he didn't. He always fell apart in a true test. His great skills and massive training went for *nothing* because of that lack of *will* in the face of such extreme pressure."

Olsen struggled in the mud, gasping for air.

"Do you understand me?" the sergeant major roared. "If you wanna quit, just say the word. It's easy. Just say, 'I can't take it anymore.'"

Jenny Olsen shook her head.

"Come on, you can do it," Buford insisted. "Just say,

'I quit.' It's simple. You'll be back in the showers in ten minutes and on a bus home this evening.''

Jenny Olsen could barely breathe. The mud covered her face as she fought to rise up to gasp for air. She couldn't find anything to push against in the slime. Finally, her toe caught something hard, and she forced herself forward, tearing the camouflage cover of her Kevlar helmet but breaking free of the wire. Raising her head to take a quick gulp of air, she inched forward, just as an artillery simulator exploded off to her right side.

She ducked down, her face completely covered in the foot-deep mud, and pushed through the slime.

"God only knows why we have women in this outfit!" Buford yelled in disgust. He followed Olsen as she made her way under the wire, keeping pace with her and offering his worst insults. "Lady, this is a man's business. What the hell are you doing here? Wouldn't you rather be home right now, all prissied up, getting ready for a night out on the town?''

She had endured the tough, daily physical training, struggled to master a wide variety of pistols and rifles at the weapons ranges, been bruised and challenged in the hand-to-hand combat pits, and passed the dangerous training with explosives and antipersonnel mines. This was her third month of training. She was a volunteer, like everyone here, and she wasn't about to quit now. Jenny cleared the wire and stood up, shaken but still determined. "No, Sergeant Major!"

"Then get your ass up that ladder, damn it, and quit wasting my time bullshitting with me in this God damned rain!''

Olsen stumbled forward. The mud covered her battle dress fatigues like a new, thick, heavy layer of skin. The mud was also inside her clothes, squished inside her boots as she ran, and dripped from her short, blond hair. She reached the ladder and slung her rifle over her back.

The rest of her group, except one—Sam Wong—was already climbing the wet, mud-covered wooden poles that were the horizontal struts in the huge, thirty-foot-high ladder. Each horizontal strut was placed three to four feet apart. The task was to climb up each pole, make it to the top, and climb back down on the opposite side without falling. So far, the "ladder from hell" had claimed three victims in the last five days. All three survived, but the soldiers were cut from the program because of their injuries and sent back to their units.

Jenny slung her rifle over her shoulder, reached for the first log strut and pulled herself up.

"You! Get your ass in gear!" Sergeant Major Buford's voice roared. Jenny looked down and saw the tired, strained face of Sam Wong. Sam looked as if he was about to collapse. Jenny reached down with her left hand to help Wong.

"What the hell do you think you're doing?" Buford howled as he moved quickly to the base of the ladder.

Jenny shot a glance at Buford that was pure contempt and anger. She pulled with all her might, in a mighty heave, but could not move Sam Wong. Suddenly, coming down from above her, a figure appeared at Jenny's side. The mud-soaked trooper to her left reached down and, working together, Jenny and the man pulled Sam Wong up.

"This is Eagle Team," the tall, mud-soaked soldier next to Olsen, Major Travis Barrett, shouted back to Sergeant Major Buford. "We don't leave anyone behind."

The rain poured down. Sergeant Major Buford nodded. Sam Wong and Travis Barrett moved up to the next rung. Jenny took a quick look at the sergeant major before she ascended. She wasn't sure, but for a moment she thought she saw the nearest thing to a grin that had crossed the sergeant major's face since their training started six weeks ago.

September 2, 1830 hours,
somewhere in the Big Snowy Mountains of Montana

A heavy rain greeted the sunset. Sam Wong, wondering why he had volunteered for a life of high adventure, looked at his Casio "G-Shock" watch. He pushed a button to illuminate the face. It was 1830. They had been marching since 0800. Sam knew that they had to be at the rally point by 2230, and he knew that Barrett, his team leader, would not miss the rendezvous. That left only four more hours of marching in the rain.

Sam rested in a one-inch puddle of water, next to his best friend, Jack DuBois. They sat back to back, propping each other up. Both were exhausted from the long march and from carrying heavy field packs, a helmet, and a rifle.

There was no dry place to sit and, with the rain falling in buckets, it really didn't matter. Tired and soaked to the bone with rain, Sam wondered what he had gotten into. The twelve members of his team—they had lost another four in the past two weeks—were sprawled out on both sides of a narrow Montana road. A few talked, but most rested, too tired to waste the energy in conversation. They waited for the word to move again.

Jack DuBois and Sam Wong made a strange pair. Jack was one of two Marines in the group. He was usually very quiet and serious. Standing six feet five inches, he was one solid chunk of muscle, and made most of the rest of Eagle Team look puny. Standing next to Sam Wong, they looked like products from the opposite ends of the evolutionary line. "What did you do in the Marines, Jack?"

"I led a company in the Marine Force Recon," Jack DuBois replied.

"What's Force Recon?"

"Sam, sometimes you're such a civilian that I'd like to bitch-slap you," Jack DuBois replied. "But I'm just too tired. Force Recon is the baddest bunch of Marines you will ever meet. They conduct preassault reconnaissance in support of landing forces. That means we are always on our own, behind enemy lines, making do with what we have. It also means that we run in the sand a lot, jump from planes and helicopters, and do much of the same thing we're training on here."

"Then this must be easy for you," Sam complained.

"Easier," Jack replied. "But only because I understand why we are doing this."

"So why are we doing this? To teach us to be pack mules?"

"Hell no," Jack replied. "To cut the men from the boys and girls. To see who will quit."

"What do you do for fun, Jack? I mean, when you're not out chopping enemies in half or killing bad guys on some distant beach."

"I like to read," Jack DuBois said. "I don't drink much and I don't smoke, but I do study the great military strategists like Sun Tzu, Napoleon, Carl Von Clausewitz, George Patton, and Robert Leonhard."

"Sounds like a lot of fun. You're kidding, right?"

"No. I'm serious. Sometimes I go to the movies or rent a video."

"What's your favorite movie?" Sam asked.

"The Seven Samurai."

"You're kidding! That's my favorite movie!" Sam said.

Jack turned his head to look at Sam. "So what's your second favorite movie?"

"Army of Darkness," Sam beamed proudly.

"Never heard of it."

"Oh, man, you're missing something! It's this great horror spoof with this army of skeletons and a book with magic incantations. . . . It's a cult classic!"

"Still never heard of it," Jack said.

After a moment of silence, Sam asked, "Do you think we'll make it?"

"Do you really want to make it?" Jack said.

"Sure. Of course. I didn't come this far not to make the team."

There was another short silence between them.

"Jack, who do you think will make it?"

"You and me, for sure," Jack said. "I promise you that. I never let my friends down."

"Thanks. What about the others?"

"Major Barrett is as hard as they come. He'll make it. He's one of the best team leaders I've ever met. He's molding us into a fighting unit. And then there is Lieutenant Commander Powczuk and Captain Blake. They are both solid."

"What about Hernandez, or Griffith? How about Murray, or Harris, or Davidov. And what about the women?"

Jack didn't answer.

Thunder resonated through the heavens. A powerful storm, atypical for this time of year, was battering Montana. The rain poured from the clouds like water rushing out of a fire hose. Wong had never seen such rain back in Flushing, New York—but then again he had never vacationed in the Big Snowy Mountains. For that matter, who would?

"Okay, break's over. Let's go," Travis Barrett's voice shouted to the nine men and two women sitting on the ground. "Make sure you have all your gear. The sooner we get moving, the sooner we'll be done."

A collective moan arose from the Eagle Team as they struggled to their feet. Wong tried to sit up, but the pack on his back was too heavy. He rolled to his side and pushed up on his knees. The heavy rucksack bit at his shoulders and held him down. Jack DuBois offered a hand and helped him up. The weary troopers shouldered their packs and checked their M-16s and assorted gear.

"Hey man, give me a hand," Johnny Hernandez pleaded.

Sam Wong, now on his feet, reached out for Hernandez and pulled him up. The momentum of the move almost knocked him over, but he balanced himself with his left foot just in time.

"Let's go, people." The voice of authority, Travis Barrett, sounded. "Move out, Eagle Team. Pick up a five-meter interval."

On order, they marched forward. Thin and standing five feet six inches, Wong weighed only one hundred thirty pounds dripping wet. In this rain, and carrying his rucksack, M-16 rifle, and combat gear, he felt like he must weigh at least two hundred. His legs, still unaccustomed to long foot marches, felt like heavy weights.

"We sure do a lot of walking," Hunter Blake's voice

in the dark shouted cynically. "Hell, I knew I joined the Air Force for a reason."

"I'm with you Blake," Jenny Olsen offered.

"Any time babe," Hunter Blake cracked.

Slowly, Sam shifted the weight of his heavy rucksack and walked over to his place in the column. All around him, the others were doing the same thing. Helo pilot Johnny Hernandez suddenly sat back down on the ground, his pack weighing him down like a turtle lying on his shell. *"No mas,"* he groaned. TALON training had claimed another washout.

The muddy road splashed with the falling drops of rain. The deluge was so constant that half an inch of running water covered the road.

Sam walked to the right side of the road and painfully put one foot in front of another. He could feel the blisters growing on the soles of his feet. The rain poured down, soaking his uniform and filling his boots with water. They squished with each step.

He tightened the strap to his rucksack. Eagle Team was quite a group—a select group that was getting smaller all the time. *Tonight,* Wong chuckled to himself, *Drenched Chicken Team might be a more appropriate name than Eagle Team.*

"Why is it always raining?" someone muttered aloud.

The thunder cracked again, followed by bright bursts of lightning striking the trees in the mountains on both sides of the narrow road that the company marched along.

"All right, knock it off," Major Travis Barrett replied. "If we don't make it to the rally point on time, we'll all be cut. Save your energy for marching."

Lightning split the heavens, followed by the crashing roll of another volley of thunder. The celestial fireworks added emphasis to Barrett's orders. The weather was still warm, but in this rain, everyone was soaked to the bone.

"Hey boss," Hunter Blake asked. "What if I get hit by lightning?"

"Then we'll use your head as a lightbulb to guide the way, Blake," Travis barked. "Don't worry about the lightning. Just keep moving, we've only got a few more miles to go."

The tired soldiers, drenched and burdened with packs made heavier by the rain, trudged on through the dark night. The rain poured down in sheets as lightning lit the dark sky in mad flashes, searching for something to touch. Thunder, mimicking the blast of artillery, echoed in the hills.

Wong's blisters grew to the size of nickels. The rain was making the march much more difficult. As Eagle Team carried on, Sam grew more determined to make the distance. He wasn't going to let anyone see him quit. More importantly, now that he had a good friend in Jack DuBois, he swore that he would never let him down.

September 22, 0900 hours, at the secret military training camp in the Big Snowy Mountains of Montana

"At ease," Sergeant Major Buford ordered. He threw a stern glance at the men and women who stood in ranks before him. He caught the confidence in their eyes, he saw the strength in their physiques, and he knew the mettle of their hearts. He was proud of his handiwork and strode up and down the ranks as he talked.

Forty-nine TALON Force troopers were assembled in a large hangarlike building. Racks of special uniforms, looking somewhat like black space suits, were displayed in groups marked for each team. Special new rifles and pistols hung from holders in arms lockers that had been opened for all to see. A small army of technicians in civilian clothes and lab coats hovered protectively around the assembly of high-tech gear.

"Congratulations. You have made it. You have taken the worst I can dish out. Pending your certification in thirty days, you are all accepted into TALON Force. That means you have progressed to the point where you're ready for your new equipment. But never forget, whether you have all the high-tech weapons in the world or just a spoon, what matters is your will to win. It's the fighter that counts, the person behind the rifle, not just the weapons you carry."

Travis Barrett stood to the right of his six troopers, two women and four men. As commander of the Eagle Team, he had watched each of them pass every challenge. Eagle Team had started with twenty-one candidates. Only seven had made the final cut. The team had finally jelled, he thought.

"We started off with three hundred volunteers, and now we have forty-nine," Sergeant Major Buford announced. "I don't expect to lose any more of you."

The troopers stood at rigid attention, each a model of cold, hard, military discipline.

"But I'll ask you once again. Does anyone want to quit?"

No one stirred. No voice was raised. Everyone had sacrificed too much to get this far.

"Good. Let me introduce the man who will outfit you with your new gear. Mr. Rossner is the TALON Force technical team leader. He'll explain your equipment."

Jerry Rossner, looking like a sheep surrounded by wolves, addressed the forty-nine troopers of America's newest direct action antiterrorist force. "TALON Force, as most of you know, is an acronym. It stands for Technologically Augmented Low Observable Networked Force."

The troopers stood silent, watching. They had waited a long time to receive their new equipment. For three months Sam had studied the technical manuals that described the high-tech equipment in great detail. Now it was time to learn what it could really do.

"The TALON Force Battle Ensemble is the heart of the TALON Force technology concept," Rossner continued, like a teacher addressing a high school science class. "The Battle Ensemble is a 'brilliant suit' that provides full-body armor protection, immediate and automatic medical trauma aid, a body heat or body cooling capability, communications—voice, digital, and holographic—thermal, ranging, laser designating, high-powered optical sensing, and a stealth mode 'brilliant camouflage,' or Low Observable capability."

Rossner nodded to the technicians behind him. "At this time, I want you to move to your team area, and we will suit you up."

Sergeant Major Buford ordered, "Fall out on your gear!"

The troopers moved quickly to their respective areas. A dozen technicians in white coats received them and issued each member a precision-crafted suit that fit the exact specifications of each individual.

"These things look hot," Sam Wong said. "I think I'm in love."

"Don't worry," a technician announced, misreading Sam's infatuation for a statement of fact. "Once it's turned on, each suit is climate controlled for environments up to a high of one hundred fifteen degrees and as cold as minus twenty degrees Fahrenheit."

"You mean this thing is air-conditioned?" Jack DuBois asked.

"Not really air-conditioned," another technician replied. "Microfiber temperature controlled."

"The suit is charged up before missions and has a normal power capacity of seventy-two hours without recharging," the technician continued. "If you read your manuals, you'll know that the Low Observable Suite can only run continuously for six hours in stealth mode before draining the Battle Ensemble's charge. The ensemble is linked by proximity wave transmission to biochip sensors and transmitters embedded just beneath the skin of every TALON Force trooper. The ensemble monitors life functions, regulates body temperature, and weighs only sixteen and a half pounds. Wearing this ensemble, a trained soldier becomes an enhanced fighter with extraordinary battlefield awareness, lethality, and survivability."

Sam Wong was the first to be fully suited up. He even held a new, high-tech XM-29 rifle in his hands. He turned to the technician and asked, "How do I turn this on?

The manual said that I would activate it with a voice command."

"Each suit is specially designed to respond to the exact harmonics of your individual voice, after I activate your system," the technician answered. He lowered Sam's face visor then placed a key in Sam's belt power pack and turned on Sam's suit.

"Stealth," Sam ordered. Immediately his brilliant suit shimmered with colors and shades to match the nearest background.

Jack DuBois shook his head as he stared at the ghost-like outline of Sam Wong. "Sammy, you never looked so good. All I can see are a pair of glasses floating in midair! And you forgot about your rifle."

Everyone looked at Sam and burst out laughing. A disembodied rifle appeared to float in midair.

"Stealth off," Sam ordered, raising his face shield. "Very funny. How do I stop that from happening?"

"All of your weapons have a stealth sheath," the technician said. "You simply hook up the power cord to your power belt, and even your weapons will be invisible. He was joking about the glasses. Your face shield covers your face and glasses—so not to worry."

Captain Sarah Greene, the biomedical expert on the team, put her helmet on. "Can every team member read the team biomedical reports of each individual trooper?"

"Yes. Every team member is networked by RF and HF radio transmissions on your own, personal Internet," the technician said, turning to the dark-haired beauty to his left. "The Battle Sensor Helmet acts as ballistic protection, communications suite, and computer network station. Communications with Joint Task Force Headquarters, and between members, is routed by proximity burst to the communication biochips embedded under the skin near the right ear of every TALON Force trooper. Communications are directed skyward—what we call straight-up communications—to a constellation of thirty-six satellites. Straight-up communications enables unlimited communications, position location, and digital data transfer, regardless of terrain and line-of-sight restrictions. This capability provides for continuous, practically unjammable communications and data transfer anywhere on the planet."

"But will the helmet stop a bullet?" Stan Powczuk asked.

"The helmet is made of light but extremely tough microfibers," the technician answered, nodding. "Yes, it'll stop or deflect everything up to seven point six-two millimeters."

"Not bad," Jack DuBois added.

"You hear that, Sam?" Jenny Olsen added. "You better remember to lead with your head."

"Is this how I get on line?" Sam Wong asked, disregarding the verbal jab by Olsen. With his helmet on his head, he pointed to an attachment on the helmet that folded down in front of his left eye.

"Yes. The Battle Sensor Device—BSD—folds down from the Battle Sensor helmet over the left eye like a monocle. The device generates a laser pathway that paints images into the eye of the trooper, using his retina to produce the illusion of holographic images," the technician said. "This holographic capability can be used to display status reports, maps, and battlefield telemetry from distant locations. Linked by the Battle Sensor Helmet's communications system via satellite, the TALON Force trooper is interconnected as well as internetted. With his BSD, each trooper can see what other troopers, unmanned air vehicles—UAVs—or sensors, and satellites can see in realistic, three-dimensional holographic images."

Travis Barrett buttoned on his chest armor. "The BSD also acts as a laser range finder to determine the range to and the location of a target," he said. "The BSD can laser-designate targets and has a thermal viewing capability that will allow us to see in the dark and through smoke and haze."

"Yes sir, you are correct," the technician replied. "This Microbiochip Transmitter/Receiver implant is a voice transmitter and will allow you to use the Battle Sensor Helmet Communications system to talk to Joint

Task Force Headquarters and members of your team without the need for an external microphone. The Microbiochip Transmitter can also transmit and receive on its own, using line-of-sight transmissions, within a range of one thousand meters, when the Battle Sensor helmet is turned off, damaged, or missing. This communications system is called the com-net."

"Anything else we need to know?" Jenny Olsen asked as she fiddled with the small, rectangular device on her left forearm.

"Yes. Please be careful with that! This is your Wristband RF Field Generator. It's a nonlethal weapon that uses a short, intense burst of directed high-energy radio frequency energy, which forms the acronym HERF, to disable electronic devices. The Wristband RF Field Generator is woven right into the fighting ensemble and is activated by voice command via the Microbiochip Transmitter. The range of this wrist generator is about two hundred meters, depending on intervening obstacles, and must be aimed by pointing the left arm at the target."

"How effective a weapon is this?" Hunter Blake asked. "Will it stop an airplane?"

"If you're close enough," the technician replied. "The radio frequency waves from this generator will not penetrate thick metal plate, as that of a tank, armored personnel carrier, or most fighting ships, but it will fry the ignition on an unarmored automobile or motorcycle and can short-circuit most electronic devices, including computers. The Wristband RF Generator is ideal for stopping ground vehicles, disarming computer-aimed weapons, and turning off computers, radios, radars, and unprotected electronic devices. A poorly aimed burst will also blank out a TALON Force Trooper's Battle Sensor Helmet and Low Observable Camouflage capability for one to two minutes, depending on the charge level left in the ensemble. Electromagnetic Pulse safeguards in the TALON Force ensemble protect each trooper from catastrophic electronic failure."

"So when can we try out all this superhero shit?" Stan Powczuk asked.

The technician looked at Powczuk with complete contempt. "Commander Powczuk, I'm glad to see that you are so eager."

Sergeant Major Buford walked up to the group, having heard the conversation. "In one hour, Major Barrett, Eagle Team will move out on its first full-equipment training mission. Report to General Krauss in the briefing room in twenty minutes for a mission brief."

"Wilco, Sergeant Major," Travis Barrett replied.

General Krauss stood at the podium in the briefing room, his forty-nine TALON troopers sitting in seven rows of aluminum folding chairs. Sergeant Major Buford was at the back of the group. "You've completed the basics and now you're going to test out your new toys with a simple training exercise. No more of the grueling forced marches or obstacle courses or mind-fucking. We're moving on to a new phase of training, and we're going to develop tactics with the new equipment. This will be a learning process for us as well as for you. While our engineers and designers tried to come up with every possible way to use and abuse your technologically enhanced weapons and defenses, we know that there's nothing like a field test to see how it really holds up. We also know that some of you will come up with things we never even considered—but we need to know the equipment's uses and limitations, as well as your limitations with it so we don't order you to do the impossible.

"What we're going to have you do today may bring back childhood memories of a little game called capture the flag. Except we're going to throw in a twist. To make the odds more realistic to what you'll face out in the field, we're going to have Eagle Team opposed by the other six teams. Six to one—sounds pretty bad. But to even things up a little, the other six teams will not be able to use the stealth features of their suits. The other teams can use all the other equipment, though, including the Unmanned Aerial Vehicles, HERF guns, and three Wildcat armored cars."

General Krauss turned to a large map of the training area mounted on the wall behind him. He pointed with his prosthetic hand. "Eagle Team will parachute into Training Area Whiskey with their stealth camouflage activated. Eagle Team's mission is to move to the objective on foot and capture one of the command bunkers by infiltration and stealth. The exact bunker will be designated in your battle plan. The mission for the rest of the teams is to prevent Eagle Team from achieving their objective. That's it. Either Eagle Team will succeed, or they'll fail. We'll debrief after the exercise to learn what went wrong and what went right, and then we'll try it again in a different area with a different team. Any questions? Good. Move out to your staging areas."

As the TALON Force troopers left the briefing room, General Krauss approached Sergeant Major Buford from the back of the room. "George, a word?"

"Sir," Buford replied.

"I want to let you know that Eagle Team will be in for a little surprise. I didn't want to tell you because I know you think they're the best team going so far—not that I don't trust you to keep a secret, but this is good. I've had the techs preprogram power failures in several of Eagle Team's battle suits. I want to add the friction of war to test Eagle Team's reactions. I want to see how well they learn to adapt, improvise, and overcome the opposition."

Buford smiled. "That's fine. I think they'll show you what they're really made of today."

Travis reviewed his battle plan. The typical tactics that the TALON Force had developed over the past few months were called Swarm Tactics. Operating in small, dispersed units, TALON Force teams were so well internetted that they could rapidly coordinate, coalesce, and then disperse. Initially, individual TALON Force troopers would scatter throughout the battle area and occupy key positions. The troopers would then call in accurate air, artillery, and missile fire on targets that they identified in their areas. At the time and place of their choosing, the teams would converge and mass to engage in direct combat. Knowing the exact location of every friendly force trooper, and receiving up-to-the-second reports on enemy locations—and with all this information depicted graphically on their three-dimensional, virtual battle maps through their BSD screen—made a TALON Force team thirty to fifty times more effective than regular, unconnected commandos.

Travis planned for Eagle Team to execute a HALO jump. The high-altitude, low-opening jumps were dangerous, but they were a necessary means of avoiding detection. After parachuting in, Eagle Team would march thirty kilometers—far enough away to avoid immediate detection by the enemy teams—then infiltrate enemy lines to capture the bunker Sam had waggishly codenamed Archie. At the same time, the other six teams of the TALON Force—each seven troopers strong and composed of some of the best special operations troopers in the world—would do their best to stop the Eagle Team. The defenders were designated as the Red Force. Although the Red Force defenders did not know which bunker the Eagle Team had to penetrate, with only five bunkers in the area of operations, it wasn't hard for them to guard all five and still have enough personnel left to conduct roving patrols in their Wildcat armored vehicles.

To add realism to the exercise, each team was armed with laser stun rifles. The lasers wouldn't kill anyone, but when a TALON Force soldier was hit, the electrical discharge would knock the trooper over and disable his or her equipment. After several hits in vital areas, the suit would turn off and the player would be "dead." These demanding force-on-force training exercises gave the TALON Force teams on both sides valuable battle experience and allowed members of the TALON Force to hone their fighting skills without risking actual casualties.

Travis knew that the Red Force was eager to capture the Eagle Team. The tall Texan planned this mission like the true military professional that he was. Every member of the Eagle Team knew exactly what to do, and their internetted communications provided them with instantaneous situational awareness that allowed members to adapt and improvise as needed.

Barrett's plan was simple. As Jack DuBois said, quoting

his beloved military philosopher, Sun Tzu, "All warfare is based on deception." While DuBois and Wong caused a diversion at one of the two far bunkers—code-named Edith and Meathead—to draw the enemy toward them, Barrett planned to seize the objective with the rest of the force. Sam Wong and Jack DuBois would occupy a hill between Edith and Meathead and set up a false electronic signature that would order the defenders to rush to Meathead Bunker. According to the plan, this would leave Archie Bunker relatively unguarded and easy prey for Eagle Team to assault the objective.

The tricky HALO parachute insertion went like clockwork and was completely trouble-free. Even Sam Wong was getting to be a HALO expert. The thirty klick march was easy, too, for troopers who'd been put through Sergeant Major Buford's version of hell for the previous few months. When they reached Area Whiskey, the plan went into effect. Sam and Jack climbed the hill and sent out the false signal. Sam used his skill at computer codes and created fake voice and internet transmissions of the commander of the defending force while he blocked the enemy's transmissions for ten minutes. Ten minutes was all that Travis thought his assault team would need. But, as the old soldier's dictum goes, no plan survives first contact with the enemy.

"Well, that ought to do it," said Sam as he finished transmitting the counterfeit message. "You think maybe we'll get a night off, Jack?"

"Uh, no, actually," Jack said.

"Why not?" replied Sam.

"Because we have a tiny little problem. I can see you."

Sam waved his hand in front of his helmet. "Oh no! I can see me, too! I've lost my stealth function. Stealth on," Sam said, trying to activate his suit's voice command. Nothing happened. Then, before Sam even had a chance to activate his auxiliary power pack or run the internal diagnostic on his suit, Jack's camouflage faded, too. Suddenly, instead of blending in with the rocks on top of the barren hill, Sam and Jack stood out like two targets with large bull's-eyes painted on them. They quickly scrambled to the back side of the hill, but it was too late; their position had already been compromised.

"Major Barrett, sir? DuBois here. We have camouflage malfunction on my Battle Ensemble and on Captain Wong's Battle Ensemble. We have been spotted. Repeat, our position has been located. We will hold off the Red Force as long as possible to give you time to take Archie Bunker. DuBois out."

"Roger, DuBois. Gain us five minutes, and we're in. Barrett out."

"Okay, Sammy, any suggestions?" Jack asked.

"Well, we can set up motion sensors to warn us when the Red Force is approaching," Sam said.

"Good. I'll do that and send up a UAV to give us advance warning. Why don't you send out another false transmission. Even if they don't fall for it, if it makes them take another fifteen seconds, that can mean the difference between victory and defeat." Jack removed the Dragonfly, a palm-sized unmanned aerial vehicle, from his cargo pocket. It could only fly at low altitude and only had a thirty-minute flight time, but it was more than enough for this situation. He sent it out to patrol the area from one to three kilometers in a fan-shaped area in front of their hill. Then he scooted around the hill and placed three motion detectors about a hundred yards out. That would give them enough advance warning to prepare for the showdown.

Meanwhile, Sam sent out contradictory orders to the enemy teams on the Red Force command frequency. He monitored the Red Team's radio net, copied a few transmissions from their leaders, then quickly manufactured a short series of orders in the leaders' own voices. As Jack had predicted, it took at least thirty seconds for them to untangle the conflicting messages, and by then, Jack and Sam only had to "survive" two and a half minutes more. In another fifteen seconds, the Dragonfly UAV sent back images of a Wildcat armored car bouncing over the rocks and gullies, heading for their hill. Forty-five seconds later, the Wildcat's engine signature was picked up by the motion detectors.

"All right, Sam, this is it," Jack said. "Shoot to kill. We know that we're not going to actually hurt anyone with these laser stun rifles, but that doesn't mean we should let ourselves be taken. Eagle Team has a reputation to uphold, and exercise or not, no one is going to keep us from achieving our objective, even if that means we're going to be the sacrificial lambs."

"I got you Big Guy. Just like in *The Seven Samurai.* Teamwork, baby! Banzai!" Sam screamed.

"Banzai!" Jack repeated at the top of his lungs, just as the point men for the Red Force crested the hill.

Zap! Sam let a charge fly from his laser stun rifle, scoring a direct hit on a Red Force helmet, instantly putting the trooper out of the fight. "Got one!"

Zap! Jack took down another point man. Two up, two down.

And then it got crazy. Eighteen Red Force troopers poured up the hill. Earlier, while they waited for the enemy to appear, Sam had managed to reprogram his rifle to emit a steady stun charge. It emptied his laser rifle faster, but he didn't need to hold off the enemy that long, anyway. When the Red Force became silhouetted on top of the hill and paused to take aim with their stun rifles, Sam let it fly. He scored hits on arms, legs, and torsos, sending troopers flipping ass over teakettle back onto the other side of the hill, bowling over some of their own troops who were in the process of charging up the hill. "Banzai!" Sam screamed, a look of intense satisfaction on his face.

The clock was winding down—only thirty seconds to go. Jack crawled around the side of the hill to catch the Red Force in a ninety-degree crossfire as they regrouped for a second attack. Just as they reached the top, Sam let fly with a charged stream, while Jack sent out deadly accurate laser bursts. More Red Force troopers started dropping out of the battle entirely, until there were only ten of the original twenty left from the first wave. Then Sam's rifle discharged completely and the return fire began in earnest.

While Jack continued to score hits, Sam began to run

in a serpentine pattern for the woods, screaming, "Banzai," jumping over logs, ducking under branches, and leading the Red Force on. He took a hit to the back, then to the right elbow, then to the buttocks, and finally to the left foot before going down. Jack yelled, "Go, Sammy, go!" while he kept up a steady stream of fire. He took out two more Red Force troopers, and then he received a direct hit to the chest, knocking him backward and sending him sprawling. He, too, was down for the rest of the exercise. The remaining eight troopers from the Red Force began to surge forward to flush out the rest of Eagle Team when a message was received by everyone's BSD. "Eagle Team has accomplished its mission and taken the bunker. Repeat, Eagle Team has defeated the Red Force. The exercise is now concluded."

Sam and Jack jumped up and yelled, "Wooooo! We did it!" Jack jogged over to Sam. They high fived each other, and Jack picked up Sam and gave him a bear hug.

"Easy, Jack, don't squish me!" Sam squeaked. They had put up a heroic resistance, stunning twelve of the twenty attackers before they were "killed." Their sacrifice, which came to be known throughout Eagle Team as Wong's Last Stand, was not in vain. While Sam and Jack engaged the Red Force, Barrett and his assault force entered the bunker, disarmed the single Red Force defender left behind to guard Archie Bunker, and captured the flag. Even though they sacrificed themselves in the act, Sam Wong and Jack DuBois were the heroes of the day.

Sam bragged to Jack that everything he knew about fighting he'd learned from his favorite movie, *The Seven Samurai*. Since Jack was also an expert on the classic Japanese film, he took the bait and asked the question: "What lesson was that?"

Sam replied proudly, "In *The Seven Samurai*, individualism is looked down on. The team working together is more important than one person doing something without the group."

It was a lesson in teamwork learned by all.

Chapter Three

Come not between the Dragon and his wrath.
—Shakespeare, *King Lear*

November 10, 5:00 P.M., Rome, Italy

A big, hard-faced man in a white shirt and dark slacks sat in a chair on the second-story balcony of a dingy, rented apartment. The man's sleeves were rolled to the elbow, revealing a pair of dusky blue dragons tattooed on his muscled arms. The man sat alone, preoccupied with his thoughts, contemplating the dark task that was on his mind.

The weather was cool but pleasant, especially for Rome in mid-November. Earlier this morning, it had rained. Now, shortly after noon, the air smelled crisp and clean. The sunlight bounced across the slanted rooftops, making the brown tiles glow like gold. But the man sitting in the chair on the second-story balcony could not see the beauty that was Rome. His eyes were fixed on something else; his heart, if he had one, did not register anything outside his immediate orders.

The rented apartment where he sat on the balcony overlooked the ancient *Amphitheatrum Flavium,* the Colosseum of Rome.

The Colosseum was a massive structure. In its prime it could seat 45,000 spectators on its marble benches. In those days, the very top edge of the outside wall was ringed with wooden masts that supported canvas awnings to shade the spectators from the hot Roman sun. Inside, the Colosseum had been a marvel of human engineering. Tunnels, cages, gladiator training areas, animal pens, and caverns filled the inside arena. Today, the floor timbers were gone, revealing the heart of this intricate setting. In its prime, however, thousands of slaves were required to manipulate the fantastic spectacles that had become the staple of Roman entertainment and showcase of power.

Centuries ago, this arena had housed the bloodiest games in ancient Rome. Inside this amphitheater, slaves called gladiators had fought each other to the death to the delight of cheering, bloodthirsty crowds. That the massive walls still stood after all these years was a great engineering achievement, an elegant tribute to the power of Ancient Rome. But the Colosseum also represented something much more sinister. It was a monumental memorial to man's cruelty to man. Because of this, it became a fitting backdrop to the first act of a new, violent contest.

I am a gladiator, he thought. *Someday, I will be a master.*

The man in the white shirt reached for the glass of dark scotch liquor that was resting on a table. The half-empty bottle of spirits indicated that he had waited a long time. He sipped the scotch slowly, then raised a pair of binoculars to his eyes.

He scanned the road in front of the Colosseum, then glanced at his watch and frowned. His quarry was late.

"Hey, are you gonna sit out there all day?" a woman's voice asked in Italian from inside the room. "I get paid by the hour, you know, whether you do it or not."

The man looked back at the naked hooker who lay on top of the queen-sized bed inside the small apartment. The woman was on her belly, her shapely tan legs swinging above a firm, tight ass. She was a looker, no denying it, the man thought, and the tight pearl choker necklace around her dainty neck gave her that sexy look of an experienced professional who loved her trade.

She is a minx, all right. Must be at least twenty-four, the man thought. *Big tits, gorgeous face—just the way I like them.* But she was his cover, not his recreation, and he doubted whether he would have time for her.

"Come on, big man, I'll make it worth your while."

"Just shut up and lay there," the man replied in broken Italian. "I'll be there when *I'm* ready."

He took another swig of scotch and leaned back on his chair. A black laptop computer lay on the table next to the bottle.

"I'm bored," the pretty young woman moaned in a voice that was a mixture of longing and frustration. "Wouldn't you rather come over here and play?"

The man shot her a glance, a look that made her heart freeze. He turned away and looked back at the Colosseum, and in that moment, he decided about the girl.

He brought the binoculars to his eyes again and scanned the area to the left of the Colosseum. A man with a video recorder on his shoulder was patiently pointing his camera at the entrance to the Colosseum, just as the plan indicated.

"What can be more interesting out there than me?" the girl teased. "At least tell me your name?"

"Ratchek," he answered, realizing that it wasn't necessary for him to hide his identity anymore.

"Ratchek, you must be a body builder. I love to make love to athletic men. Come over here, and I'll give you a real workout."

Ratchek shook his head and fixed his gaze on the Colosseum.

Then, like unsuspecting lambs to the slaughter, his prey arrived. Three buses, one following the other, slowly turned the corner and stopped in front of the ancient structure. Ratchek checked his watch again. The three buses were twenty minutes late, but they had arrived, and that was all that really mattered.

Like a hunter in a deer stand who has just spotted a prize buck, Ratchek sprang into action. He opened the black case on the table and lifted the screen to the laptop computer. The screen contained an image of a green and red button.

Men, women, and children poured out of the buses, massing in front of the Colosseum to the urgings of their tour guides. The tourists, Ratchek knew, were almost all Americans. Through his binoculars he looked with satisfaction at the innocent mixture of young and old, children and grandparents, milling about. Most had cameras slung around their necks. Some carried purses, books, or small packs.

Ratchek focussed his binoculars on a pretty young woman in a short dress on the outskirts of the crowd. The girl was wrapped in the arms of a young man. Ratchek grinned again, a sick, sinister smirk. *They are probably on their honeymoon,* he thought.

"Well, if you are not going to do anything, I'm going to put my clothes on and leave," the naked Italian girl on the bed announced.

Ratchek put down the binoculars and moved the computer mouse so that the cursor was centered on a red button in the center of the screen. "We who are about to die, salute you," Ratchek said quietly in perfect Latin, mimicking the motto that the gladiators of ancient Rome would pledge before they entered into combat.

The hooker looked at Ratchek, thinking that he had intended that comment for her. A puzzled look, inspired by Ratchek's weird response, covered her face.

But Ratchek couldn't see the girl's face; his eyes were focused on the buses. Ratchek, the executioner, Ratchek the destroyer, looked again at the mouse on the screen and the red button and double-clicked.

A tremendous explosion rocked the apartment building. Outside the room, in the courtyard, a huge fireball of black smoke and orange flame erupted in the center of the two buses. A flash of light and heat hit the balcony and swept into the room like a wave. The young, naked woman rushed to the window, screaming. "Oh Mother Mary! Oh my God!"

The sound of the tremendous blast echoed across the city of Rome.

A bomb had detonated directly in the center of the mass of tourists. The girl looked at the mangled burning hulls of the buses and stared at the black cloud of smoke as it mushroomed to the heavens. As the smoke cleared, she saw the burning, jagged, and flattened outline of the buses. All around the burning debris she saw hundreds of bodies or the smoldering pieces of human bodies scattered all over the plaza in front of the Colosseum. Not a single person from the tour group was standing. Then, in terror, she turned to the man who was now at her side.

She saw the wild, cruel glee in Ratchek's cold, brown eyes as he witnessed his deadly handiwork. She saw the scar that marked his left cheek and forehead. Suddenly she realized that he never intended to have her, that she was just a prop to justify the use of the room. Quickly she tried to turn to run, but the man caught her.

Ratchek's strong right hand grabbed the girl by the chin. In a quick move he pushed her back against the wall of the apartment, knocking over the small table. She looked at him with wild, scared eyes, her chest heaving with fright as he pinned her to the wall.

"I want you right now, dearie. I'm always aroused for a good killing."

The girl tried to move, but Ratchek was too powerful for her. "Please," she cried. "Don't . . ."

Ratchek smiled a cruel smirk and looked into the young terrified brown eyes of his captive. He pulled her to him and forced her to the bed. Holding her down with one hand he unzipped his pants and mounted her. The woman struggled. He struck her several times across the face and pinned her arms behind her head. Then he entered her. In a few moments it was over, but he stayed on top of her, looking into her terrified eyes.

"Please, let me go!" she pleaded. Ratchek just smiled and held her head in his big hands. With a quick twist of his powerful hands, he snapped her delicate neck as easily as breaking a chicken bone. The pearl necklace that was wrapped around her pretty neck broke as Ratchek twisted her thin neck. The pearls fell to the bed and bounced across the hardwood floor. Ratchek released her, and the girl fell limp against the sheets, dead before she could register the pain.

Ratchek looked down on her for a second, then stood up from the bed. He zipped his pants and turned to complete the business that had brought him to this room. He moved toward the window, heard screams in the courtyard and the wail of police sirens, and picked up the laptop computer. Turning, he grabbed his leather jacket, opened the door and, without a second glance at the bed, walked out.

The war against America had begun.

1500 hours, US Military Training Camp, TALON Force Base 4, in the wilds of Montana

Pain. Throbbing pain shot up from Sam Wong's ankles to the calves of his legs. He reached for his glasses on the government-issue wooden nightstand, put them on, then hobbled over to the sink on sore, blistered feet and opened the medicine cabinet.

Sam wondered what he was doing here, how his life had taken such a strange turn. He took a bottle of Extra Strength Tylenol and a tube of muscle ointment from the medicine cabinet.

He looked in the mirror and smiled. He knew the answer to his own question before he had asked it—but he half-expected a reply. In spite of the pain that he felt from his aching, tired muscles, he knew exactly why he had joined up. The fact was that sometimes it made him feel good to complain, even if he was only complaining to himself.

Sam flipped open the top of the Tylenol bottle, took out two white pills, and placed them in his mouth. After swigging them down with a large glass of water, he slowly hobbled back to his bed.

He opened a tube of muscle ointment and rubbed the medicinal-smelling salve over his legs. The last two weeks of tough, demanding field training had taken a toll on his lean body. He had done his very best to keep up, but of all the members of his seven-person team, he was the slowest and the weakest. No matter how hard he tried, he just could not compete with the other military-trained members of the TALON Force. In fact, even the women had outpaced him, and that hurt his self-image more than anything else did. It was one thing if Major Barrett or Lieutenant Commander Powczuk never

seemed to tire. They were trained professionals, seem-
ingly born to be soldiers. Everything appeared to come
easy to them. But when Jenny Olsen and Sarah Greene,
the two female members of the team, offered to help
him carry some of his gear on the last fifty-mile march,
his personal humiliation was too great, and he drove himself even harder.

Before the march was over, however, Jenny and Sarah
had both carried some of his gear.

Still, in spite of sore, bloody feet, and aching muscles,
he had made the cut. He was a member of the Eagle
Team of the TALON Force, and every member of the
team had congratulated him on his drive and determination. He had proven that he could pull his own weight
and get the job done. He had completed the difficult
training and was now recuperating from the exertions of
a training regime that would make quitters out of even
the most dedicated athlete. No, it was something more
than just mere physical strength that kept him from quitting. He felt a new, unique feeling. He was a respected
member of a team, and the sense of belonging that came
with that was an emotion that he relished.

He heard a knock at the door. Hobbling across the
cold tile floor, he opened the door to see Jack DuBois
standing there in a bright red Marine Corps T-shirt,
sweat pants, and sneakers. Jack held a six-pack of beer
in his powerful left hand.

"I thought that you might need some company," Du-
Bois offered with a grin. "I brought you a little present."

"Come on in!" Sam said, returning the smile. "Take
a seat."

Jack opened a can of beer and offered it to Sam.

Sam grabbed the beer and took a swig. "You know,
my parents taught me to be proud of my Chinese roots
and appreciate the customs and traditions of the old
ways. But I never seemed to fit into their world or the
world of the kids I went to school with. All my life,
except for now, I've felt like an outsider."

"One swig of beer and you're getting philosophical on

me?" DuBois kidded. "I can't wait to hear our conversation after you down this six-pack."

Sam Wong smiled. "Jack, I'm serious. I need to tell you something. My parents taught me a lot. They came to America with nothing. They escaped Communist China for freedom and made a home here. They taught me to appreciate America as a place where the rights of the individual meant something, but I never really appreciated their lessons. Now, I understand. For the first time in my life, I am part of an important team and, for you and me, our team and our country is something worth fighting for."

"I thought all you wanted to do was make money," Jack replied. "You can use your skill at computer programming and your passion for games and codes to make a fortune. Why did you sign up?"

"I grew up in Flushing, Queens, in a household that spoke almost no English," Sam answered. "It's such an Asian neighborhood I've heard it referred to as Flu-Shing. My family, including all four grandparents, still live in the crowded house that I grew up in. But despite all the noise and the cramped house, school was always easy for me. I skipped three grades in grammar school and junior high, then aced the entrance exam to Stuyvesant High School. You've probably heard of it—it's one of those math and science magnet schools. I was a senior at fifteen, and I won a Westinghouse Science Award for a computer chip that I designed. Got a patent on it, too!"

"That's my point," DuBois said. "Why join the TALON Force? Why not leave the rough stuff to knuckleheads like me?"

"You're no knucklehead, Jack. You are one of the brightest guys I know. I wish I was like you."

"Like me? Why? Do you know how hard it is to be a Marine and still be disciplined enough not to drink like a fish?"

Sam laughed. "Look Jack, I won an academic scholarship to Stanford and breezed through all four years. But all I know is computers. That's it. There is a world out there, and I'm missing it. You may not be able to tell, but I'm kind of shy and insecure in social situations, particularly with women. Don't let my jokes fool you. I may be a bruiser behind a keyboard, but I'm a wimp in front of any member of the opposite sex."

"Don't you worry 'bout that at all," Jack said with a wide, toothy grin. "Black Jack DuBois can square you away on that account. I know where we can spend quality time with some very nice ladies and have one helluva ball. You know what I'm saying?"

Sam laughed and took another swig of beer. "Do you really want to know why I joined up?"

"Sure," Jack said, opening a can of beer for himself.

Sam downed the contents of the first can and took a second from Jack. "I'll never forget the first day I arrived in Palo Alto after graduating from Stanford. Being near Silicon Valley all those years was too great an attraction to ignore. I rented an apartment, set up a computer I designed and built myself, and immediately sent out my résumé to every computer company in a five-hundred-mile radius. I started developing software for a small, independent company two days later. But the work was too easy, and after six months, I wanted a new challenge."

Jack finished his beer and reached for another.

"Then, my life changed. Right before my twentieth birthday, while going to a job interview with Steve Jobs at Apple Computers, I was . . . hmmm, how can I put this tactfully . . . I was arrested by federal agents. A couple of weeks earlier, I had hacked into a Top Secret Department of Defense computer system. As a prank. On a dare, you know? I was immediately taken into custody, interrogated, debriefed, and tested. They gave me a code to break. It wasn't hard, and I gave them the answer in, like, two minutes. Then they tested me again. When I cracked a problem that had been haunting the National Security Agency for years, I was offered a choice: work for the feds or go to jail. If I took the job, all charges and the possible thirty-year jail sentence would be dropped."

"Wow. Sam, that's some heavy shit. So you really don't want to be here?" DuBois said.

"No, that's just it. Although the stuff I do at the NSA is kind of boring, I wouldn't change the way things worked out if Bill Gates offered to switch places with me. I'm deadly serious. When this TALON Force thing was formed, it sounded cool, so I put my name in the hat. I've never been a gung ho type, but I've lived more in the past four months than I have the rest of my entire life."

"I understand," DuBois said. "Virtual reality, after all, is virtual."

"Exactly. I guess I always dreamed of being a man of action, not just a computer geek. As a kid I must have watched *The Seven Samurai* a million times."

"Yeah, you mentioned that before," Jack said. "*The Seven Samurai* is one of Kurosawa's best films, and one of my favorites, too. I've seen it several times."

They started to recite the plot to each other, about the small farming village that is periodically raided by brigands. The peasants of the village are tired of having their produce and women stolen by the brigands and seek a solution. After a town meeting, the villagers decide to consult the town elder. He suggests that they hire samurai. The idea seems good, so four men go to town to hire samurai to defend them. Their attempts to find a suitable and desperate samurai fail, until they happen to come across one who believes in their cause. This one, named Kanbei, finds a friend to join. But Kanbei decides that he and his protégé are not enough, and they need a total of seven to defend the village properly. The search ends up with five samurai, a student, and one who has no real name or credentials.

"Yeah, and then the samurai prepare the village and the villagers for the brigands," Sam added. "The village is prepared, and when the brigands come, they attack the village and suffer losses at the hands of the samurai-led villagers. The brigands try several other strategies, but nothing works. But remember, four of the samurai are killed in the fighting. Even though the brigands have guns, the samurai finally win and completely wipe out the brigands. The remaining samurai, paid only with food and shelter, then return to the wandering lifestyle they left."

"Sad, but heroic," Jack said, envisioning the characters in action. "So you joined up because of the seven samurai?"

"Sounds pretty crazy, huh?" Sam answered. "I'm tellin' ya, Jack, in the past four months, I've experienced a sense of belonging and pride that made all the pain and hardship worthwhile. I wouldn't give it up for anything in the world. And you know what the kicker is? I never did have my interview at Apple!"

Suddenly, Sam's Battle Sensor Helmet beeped. He looked at Jack. "And look what I get in the bargain. I have a direct link to the most sophisticated computer system on the planet. How awesome is that? I was surfing the net just before you came in. Looks like I have a priority message."

"Go ahead," Jack said. "Check it out."

Sam leaned over to the nightstand and took the Battle Sensor Helmet that was sitting next to the table lamp. As the communications-computer specialist for Eagle Team, he was authorized twenty-four-hour use of his computer. His helmet provided a portal to the NSA's supercomputers and was a special, more sophisticated helmet than those of the other members of Eagle Team. As long as he could acquire a satellite communications uplink, Sam could communicate with the NSA's supercomputers from almost anywhere on the planet.

When he was wearing his helmet, the special microchip implanted behind his left ear gave him personal access to a vast array of sensitive information and programs.

"What was the NSA's motto again?" Sam said with a wry smile. "At the NSA, the direction is forward."

DuBois shook his head and offered Sam another beer.

Sam declined the offer and placed the helmet on his head. He lay back on the bed and headed forward into cyberspace. He was immediately transported to a three-dimensional virtual world where everyone and everything he saw was generated by the computer in far off Fort Meade, Maryland. Initially he scanned his mail, but was quickly interrupted by the priority message traffic. His personally designed intelligence search program received information updates on terrorist activities from around the world. Quickly, he saw a pattern emerging as video feed from the bombing at the Colosseum in Rome was displayed through his Battle Sensor Device that projected images directly onto the retina of his eye. What he saw horrified him.

Wong scanned for the locations of his team members. Every member of Eagle Team, except himself and Jack, were on pass, scattered across the country, taking some well-earned time off. Now, however, he knew that something horrible was about to happen. He explained what he thought would emerge from these incidents to Jack.

Jack placed his huge hand on Sam's scrawny shoulder. "Sam, you've got to get in touch with Major Barrett, pronto."

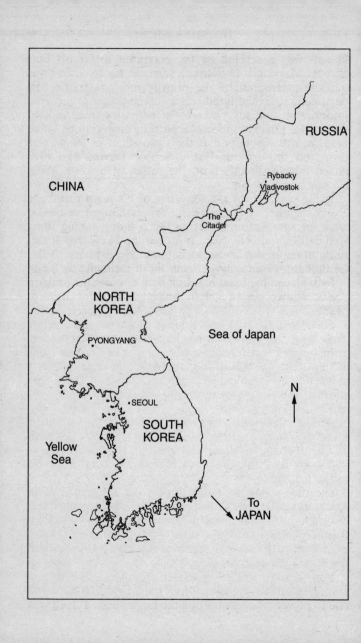

Chapter Four

. . . the struggle for power changes when knowledge about knowledge becomes the prime source of power.
—Alvin Toffler

November 11, 1000 hours local time,
at the Citadel, near Aojin, North Korea

General Cho Chong Sik sat at his desk reviewing the stack of reports that he was preparing to send to the General Staff Headquarters in Pyongyang. The room was filled with smoke as the result of Cho's chain-smoking one Japanese cigarette after another.

The office was cold and austere, with concrete walls, a wooden desk, two metal filing cabinets, and a floor lamp. Two telephones sat on the wooden desk to the left of his papers. A threadbare rug lay on the floor in front of the desk. The desk faced the door, the one entrance to the office. Behind General Cho, the only thing that adorned the bare concrete walls was a large white, red, and blue North Korean flag.

Cho smashed out a cigarette in the ashtray, and pulled a Top Secret report from the stack of papers. A thin trail of smoke from the dead butt rose up to join the cloud that hung near the overhead fluorescent lamp attached to the ceiling.

The report was the latest dossier on the man that he was responsible for. Yuri Terrek was a mad genius and the leader of an international terrorist network called the Brotherhood. He was also a man who Cho knew that he must control or at least restrain. But how? Cho studied the report carefully.

Yuri Terrek: leader of the Brotherhood, the largest criminal/terrorist organization in the world. His meteoric rise to power started with humble beginnings. Terrek was born in 1969 in Vladikavkaz, North Ossetia, in the Caucasus. His father was a Russian oil engineer and his mother a local Ossetian. At age five, Yuri's brother Doku was born. Yuri's father was killed in an oil rig accident when Yuri was six. His mother was not allowed to receive his father's pension because she was not considered a Russian citizen. At the age of ten he was involved in a criminal gang. At eighteen he was drafted into the Soviet Army. At nineteen he was recruited for the elite Spetznaz special operations unit of the Soviet Army. In 1991 he killed an officer and deserted the Russian Army.

He traveled to Georgia and then to Chechnya. By the age of twenty-five, he led the largest Mafia organization in the Caucasus. In 1993 Terrek visited the United States to set up his brother in a gang in New York, dealing in drugs and prostitution. During this time he established the Brotherhood as one of the most successful criminal groups in the Northeast United States.

After five months in the United States, he was arrested after a gun battle with police. His brother Doku was killed resisting arrest. Yuri was charged with the murder of two New York police officers during the arrest and was held in prison pending trial. While being transferred to court, Terrek escaped with the assistance of members of his Brotherhood. Terrek killed two guards and his lawyer in the process. With the help of the network of contacts he developed in the Brotherhood, he returned to Chechnya. In 1995, during the Russian-Chechen war, he made millions selling guns to the Chechens and information to the Russians.

By 1998, Terrek ran the largest and most powerful Mafia organization in the Russian Near Abroad. The Brotherhood expanded and established an international presence in many countries. By 1999, Terrek owned a major piece of the Caucasus oil trade, several legitimate businesses in Tajikistan and Turkmenistan, and a portion of the Burmese heroin trade. By 2000, Terrek had accumulated several billion dollars in assets and led the largest crime-terrorist organization in the world. Terrek's drug peddling operation became the number-one crime syndicate in the United States.

In February 2000, intelligence services in United States located Terrek in a mountain retreat in Ossetia. A secret Joint U.S.-Russian raid to arrest Terrek was mounted to put an end to his criminal empire. The raid failed and Terrek escaped, but not before Russian soldiers killed his wife and children in their attack on the stronghold in Ossetia. Terrek vowed revenge against the United States and Russia.

To accomplish this, Terrek needed safe bases to train, stage, and execute his attacks. His latest purchase was the Citadel, a fortress near the village of Aojin in North Korea. To accomplish his goals, Terrek raised an army of international terrorists. He hired men from all over the world and secretly brought them to North Korea. There, he planned his first bold move in a campaign to bring America to its knees.

General Cho put down the report and reached for a pack of cigarettes. He drew another white stick of tobacco from the pack, put it to his lips, and lit up. Taking a deep drag, Cho leaned back in his chair and stared at the smoke circling the fluorescent light. He raised his right hand to massage his forehead as he tried to analyze his situation and his chances.

Cho knew how hard things were in North Korea. The people of North Korea were barely surviving, particularly after several devastating years of economic collapse and agricultural famine. Every means of making money to help the regime survive these hard times was being used by the government in Pyongyang. Missile technology was exported to Iran, but that wasn't enough to make up the deficit. For seven hundred million U.S. dollars, Terrek had purchased the right to operate a training base on North Korean soil. General Cho was assigned to oversee Terrek's activities. All activity at the secret mountain base was to remain completely covert.

Cho shook his head in disgust. His superiors in Pyongyang were eager to accommodate Terrek—as long as the price was right and the bill was paid in U.S. dollars to the Swiss bank accounts of the great leader, Kim Jong Il, and his inner circle.

Cho took a long drag from his cigarette. The Japanese tobacco burned his throat, but he continued to puff. In North Korea, life held few luxuries. The one pleasure that he enjoyed was his cigarettes.

Terrek is insane, Cho brooded. *Only a handful of North Korean officials have ever met Terrek, and fewer know what I know about this lunatic. Mad or not, I have to give the man credit. Terrek is not only immensely rich, he is a brilliant organizer and possesses a ruthlessness that would make the venerated Kim Il Sung or Joseph Stalin shudder—if those two iron-willed murderers were still alive. Above all, I must never forget that Terrek cannot be trusted.*

Terrek had named the Brotherhood camp the Citadel. The Citadel was an isolated compound in the mountainous northeast corner of North Korea, near the point where North Korea touches China and Russia. The nearest North Korean town was Aojin, and Aojin was really nothing more than a dozen brick houses clustered near a railroad station. In this remote base, Cho was on his own with no security force. He was 545 kilometers away from Pyongyang, the capital of North Korea, and 170 kilometers from the Russian city of Vladivostok. The nearest North Korean garrison, a brigade of the 121st Infantry Division of the 7th Army Corps, was fifteen kilometers away over rough, winding mountain roads north of the port city of Najin. Cho's only link with the garrison near Najin was the AM radio in his office in the headquarters of the Citadel.

Why have my superiors in Pyongyang put me in such a tenuous position? Do they expect me to be sacrificed? For what purpose? Cho fidgeted in his chair, puffed his cigarette, and sifted through the rest of his papers. He realized that his situation was increasingly precarious. Most North Koreans, himself included, agreed with Terrek's crusade to wage war against America, but he also realized that Terrek's agenda did not include North Korea's best interests. Cho had no love for America, but he was worried that no one could control Terrek.

Terrek was doing things that went way beyond the original charter that had been agreed to in Pyongyang. Terrek was a demon who had the power to possess men's souls. In the huge, forty-kilometer-square complex, deep in the northeastern mountains of North Korea, Terrek had put his vast wealth to work to improve the fort's defenses and create a high-technology research laboratory. Cho had no idea what Terrek was working on in that heavily guarded, secret lab. Terrek's people came and went as they pleased, and a small fleet of Russian-made HIP helicopters landed constantly throughout the day.

His superiors in Pyongyang seemed unconcerned about his reports. They were only interested in Terrek's money. In essence, Cho's superiors had given Terrek unlimited freedom to do as he wished but had left Cho holding the bag. What was more worrisome, Terrek's small army of international mercenaries guarded the compound. These men swore allegiance only to Terrek and the Brotherhood.

Cho knew that his superiors in Pyongyang would hold him responsible for anything that went wrong at the Citadel. What was worse was that Lieutenant Colonel Lee, one of the officers that had been sent to train with Terrek's men, had turned his loyalty from the Democratic People's Republic of Korea to Terrek and his sinister Brotherhood. Lee had become Terrek's latest protégé, and he had abandoned his responsibilities to Cho and North Korea. Last week, Lee had taken the ultimate step by swearing an oath of fealty to Terrek's Brotherhood.

Cho was virtually a prisoner in his own compound. He recognized that Terrek was a danger to the Pyongyang regime, even if his superiors did not. Somehow he had to warn his superiors and notify the garrison at Najin.

A loud knock sounded at the door.

"I am busy," General Cho replied angrily. "Do not disturb me!"

The door swung open. Two of Terrek's commandos,

wearing the black uniform of the Brotherhood, stood at the door. Both soldiers held submachine guns slung around their necks. The men sneered at Cho. There was none of the usual disciplined courtesy that soldiers held for generals in the North Korean Army. "Come with us, General. Brother Terrek wants to see you immediately."

Cho put down his papers, stood up, and headed for the door.

1100 hours, in the Yukon Mountains, Canada

Beads of sweat rolled down the climber's brow as he traversed the steep, rocky face of one of the Yukon's tall peaks. He wore heavy brown leather climbing boots, green shorts, and a thick khaki cotton short-sleeved shirt. The belt around his waist held a hammer and a half-dozen metal climbing chocks. A coil of rope and a long, heavy rifle were slung over his right shoulder, Cossack style.

It was a sunny day, unusually warm for November. The sky was as blue as a fine porcelain vase. His short cropped brown hair was wet with perspiration and sprinkled with dirt from the long climb up the sheer cliff. By every indication it was the kind of day that he enjoyed, but for some reason he couldn't shake off the feeling of a dark shadow nearby, posing some ominous threat. He wanted it to go away, but he couldn't shake it.

Concentrating on the task at hand, he blocked the feeling and slowly moved with the skill of a practiced rock climber, working his way up a jagged vee in the mountain. This was something that he had yearned to do for several years. High on a mountain peak in British Columbia, Major Travis Beauregard Barrett was stalking the game he had dreamed of, a big stone sheep—a prized species of bighorn sheep that live in the high altitudes of the Yukon.

It wasn't the climb that filled him with dread, nor the hunt. These things he cherished. In fact, the challenge and the activity eased his mind. As he concentrated on the climb, the fear seemed to subside. For some it was golf, but for Travis Barrett, action was his antidote.

The challenge seemed simple enough. Climb the mountain, reach the summit, and bag a big stone sheep. But of course, nothing is ever simple when hunting a wild animal. Travis had to find a place where he could take a shot at such an angle that the ram would drop in just the right spot. Picking off his prey at long range, only to see the ram fall to the ground hundreds of feet below, was not acceptable. No, he would do this the old-fashioned way. He held a mystical fascination for the hunt and a respect for his quarry. He would hunt the ram and find a way to carry his prize off the mountain, just like his ancestors had done.

As he worked up the cliff, ascending one hand- and toehold at a time, the feeling of dread subsided. He felt his breathing increase as he climbed, and felt the weight of his .50 caliber Hawkins black-powder muzzle-loading rifle and a coil of climbing rope, which were slung over his back. The load was heavy. He had to compensate so that the extra weight would not shift, throw off his center of gravity, and cause him to lose his balance.

It was a long way to the bottom—a very long way. Travis Barrett tried not to look down. The feeling of foreboding returned. He had felt the shadow before, in times of personal stress or loss: once when his grandfather died; again when he was with the Rangers in Somalia; and during his experience in Grozny, Chechnya.

He came to a difficult spot on the cliff that was a sheer flat face of rock with no easy hand- and toeholds. Searching for a way up he spied a slight crack in the wall of stone, a narrow crevice that offered an anchor for the metal chocks he carried in his hip pouch. He looked up and saw a narrow ledge to his left, then spied a goat track that led from the ledge to the top of the mountain.

Almost there, only a little bit farther, he thought, *and I'll be at the top.*

With both feet planted on a narrow lip of rock and his right hand on the last obvious handhold, he carefully placed a metal chock into the crevice. He pulled on the nylon cord attacked to the chock. The anchor held.

He closed his eyes for a moment and remembered the family motto he was taught as a child: "A Barrett never quits."

He looked for his next move, trying not to think what anyone would find if he fell three hundred meters to the ground below. He thought about hammering a piton in the stone but decided against it. He might need them later. With his left hand firmly secure on the nylon cord of the metal chock in the crevice, he reached out with his right.

He found a small rock outcropping with his right hand and grabbed it. He pulled up, and the rock abruptly gave way. His left hand held fast to the wire loop around the metal chock as he lost his footing and his body swung down, off balance, dangling in the air, held only by a metal chock and a thin piece of nylon cord. His heart raced as he reacted, catlike, like a panther climbing a tree. Holding tight with his left hand, he scratched the surface of the cliff with his right boot and found a ledge just big enough to support his weight.

His heart pounded like a hammer in his chest. He heard the thumping in his ears but struggled to fix his concentration on the rock. He continued to press against that small lip of rock with his boot while his left foot searched for a similar surface. As his breathing quickened, he found a ledge and placed his left boot on the tiny edge. In this business, a few millimeters made all the difference.

Slowly, he moved up and pulled himself to the shelf. Carefully, he found another crack in the wall and inserted another metal chock from his hip pouch. He reached the ledge and slithered up over the precipice. Safe on the shelf, he sat with his back to the cold stone mountain, his feet dangling over the ledge.

After a few seconds, he regained his composure and smiled. Gazing out into the distance he surveyed the scene. The view was breathtaking, beautiful and serene. He was high up on the peak, all alone, where the rough gray and black mountains rose up to the heavens, their tops covered in a haze of white, cotton-puff clouds. The mountains seemed to defy him, as if a visible argument for the insignificance of man as compared to the magnificence of nature.

An eagle, flying high above, circled in the clear, crisp air. Travis Barrett watched it circle for a few minutes and fancied that the bird was studying him, as if it were inspecting the human who was trespassing in nature's sacred domain.

He pulled out a crucifix, which was attached to the same chain as the military ID tags around his neck. Travis kissed the crucifix and put the cross and the tags back inside his shirt.

He felt the sudden rush of tranquillity that accompanies a successful brush with mortality. The shadow resided, as he rested on the ledge. He looked down, running his dirty hand through his wet hair.

Through deep brown eyes he took in the sight, sound, smell, and feel of the mountains. He sensed the cold stone against his back and smelled the fresh air that held the mingled scent of dirt and fresh grass. It was as if he was becoming part of the cliff, as if his six-foot-two-inch muscular body was slowly turning to granite and joining in a mysterious union with the mountain, the earth, and his prey.

He closed his eyes. He needed this. Now, all alone, up here on this rugged mountain, he felt content. Once in a while he wished that he could forget it all, the responsibility and the fear, and live a normal life. But, as the TALON Force commander—the tough, legendary Brigadier General Jack Krauss—was fond of reminding him, "Travis Barrett just isn't made that way."

His thoughts raced to a hundred happy times—times with his son Randall and daughter Betty Sue—then flashed back to his unhappy divorce and his guilt and sorrow at not being with his children as they grew up. He thought of his father, a veteran of the Vietnam War and a professional soldier, a hard man who was difficult to talk to. He thought of the man who meant so much to him in his life, a man he could talk to: his godfather. His godfather was a man of great compassion and love of life who was also his father's best friend. He had spent his last two years of high school with his godparents while his father and mother were deployed to Germany on a tour of duty with the Third Armored Division in Frankfurt. Between his father and his godfather, Travis Barrett had learned how to be a man.

Travis felt a slight warming sensation under his right ear. He slowly raised his right hand to feel the miniature cybernetic communications implant that rested right below the skin.

At the same moment, out of the corner of his right eye, Travis saw movement. Slowly he turned his head to the right. There, on the next ledge, perched in magnificent glory, was a big stone ram, the most majestic round horned sheep he had ever seen. The shot of a lifetime waited for him.

Travis sensed that a gentle wind was blowing in his face. The ram had not smelled his scent and stood like a monumental statue, silent and unaware. He quickly calculated the shot. The situation was perfect. The shot would force the ram to fall on the flat area away from the cliff.

Slowly, silently, with rapid precision, he reached back for his Hawkins rifle. Carefully, without the slightest sound, he brought the rifle to his shoulder.

The eagle flying above shrieked out, as if to warn the ram that a human intruder was about to do him harm. The big stone sheep, standing on the ledge, merely gazed down to the valley below, posing as a king surveying his domain from the keep of his castle.

Travis gently clicked back the hammer on the Hawkins rifle, glancing quickly to see that the cap was still secured to the striker. The Hawkins is a heavy rifle and fires a large, fifty caliber bullet, but Travis Barrett held it steady as if it were nothing more than a broomstick.

He took aim at the ram.

Just before his finger pressed to squeeze the trigger, the shrill alarm of the cellular phone attached to his belt rang. The ram immediately heard this unnatural noise and was off in a flash, bounding back to the top of the mountain and out of view.

Travis held his fire, shook his head in disbelief, then closed his eyes. The shot of a lifetime, he thought. The shot of a lifetime!

Travis reset the hammer, then gripped the rifle with his left hand and lowered its metal-tipped butt to the ground. Snatching the phone off his belt with his right hand, he flipped open the cover and pressed the talk button.

"Whoever this is, it had better be damned important," Travis snarled. He stared at the phone. He wanted to toss it over the cliff, but he knew that he was duty bound to keep it with him at all times when he was on pass.

The deep, baritone voice of his second-in-command, Lieutenant Commander Stanislaus Michael Powczuk, United States Navy, sounded in the receiver of his cellular phone.

Right now, however, Travis wished that Stan Powczuk was on top of this mountain with him so that he could kick his ass.

"Sir, Powczuk here," the steady voice responded on the other end of the phone. "Sorry to interrupt your time off, but the force is recalled. All of us. Effective immediately."

"Stan, this had better not be one of your sick jokes," Travis Barrett sneered.

"I never joke with my commanding officer," Powczuk replied, his voice devoid of humor. "I just got the word from Sam Wong. The proverbial shit has hit the fan. General Krauss wants us to assemble ten hundred hours for a briefing. The word is that only one team is going operational."

Major Travis Barrett listened patiently. He knew that Powczuk was just following procedures and that he wouldn't have called unless it was urgent.

"Do you know where they'll send this team?"

"No," Powczuk answered. "I've got Wong working on it. He may have some intel for you when you arrive."

Travis Barrett looked down from the top of the mountain. "It's going to take me a while to get back. I don't know if I will make it in time."

"Don't worry, boss. I've sent a helicopter to pick you up. It should be there . . . well . . . right about now."

Travis Barrett looked to the south and saw the sleek, black outlines of a UH-60 Blackhawk helicopter speeding his way. The helicopter had located him by sensing the specially coded cybernetic implant just below Travis Barrett's left ear.

"Chopper in sight," he answered, amazed at Wong's and Powczuk's ability to react to events almost before they happened. Travis glanced at his watch. He might just make it if he hustled, he thought. "How'd you arrange the chopper?"

"Let's just say that Little Sammy sent the nearest Army air station a top-priority message," Powczuk said with a laugh. "Thank god the little nerd is on our side!"

Travis smiled and waved at the helicopter. If anyone could fake official orders, it was Sam Wong.

The swell of the revving engines engulfed Travis in a swirl of dust. The helicopter hovered overhead and dropped a line to the lone figure on top of the mountain. The wind blew hard around the Green Beret major as he shouted into the phone, "I'm on my way, Stan. With luck, I'll be there by late tonight. Assemble Eagle Team. I want everyone ready at oh-six-hundred tomorrow, full suits and weapons. Everybody fights and nobody quits. You got that?"

"Yes sir," the confident voice of his second-in-command responded. "I've recalled everyone else. You are the last to be notified, as you are out of range of the normal alert response beacons. Good thing you had your cellular with you. Eagle Team will be ready when you arrive."

"Good. I'll see you soon. Barrett out," he said as he closed the cover on his cell phone.

"Damn!" Travis Barrett cursed, shaking his head, as he placed the nylon loop from the helicopter over his head and under his arms. He snapped the cell phone to his belt and made sure that his rifle was securely slung over his shoulder. The powerful winch on the Blackhawk started pulling him up toward the hovering bird.

As he rose into the sky, he looked down and saw a pair of big stone rams bounding off away from the helicopter on the rocky plateau of the mountaintop.

All I needed was one more minute! Sixty seconds! That's all! The shot of a lifetime!

Chapter Five

When the hour of crisis comes, remember that 40 selected men can shake the world.

—Yasotay, Mongol warlord

November 11, 1900 hours, near Aojin in the mountains near the northeast coast of North Korea

A heavy, wet snow fell from the dark sky, covering the world in a blanket of white. Three military five-ton trucks slipped and skidded down the icy road. The convoy looked routine, normal. The trucks contained the garrison's weekly food rations, but these trucks held additional cargo. Inside, under the wet canvas, heavily armed men sat silently, waiting for the right moment to leap out and execute a deadly rendezvous.

The three trucks slowly cleared the first security checkpoint, the unsuspecting guards happy to wave them on rather than leave their dry, warm guard shacks to check the driver's security papers. In the dark, snowy evening, the guards did not notice anything unusual.

A man in a black uniform and a black balaclava sat on a wooden bench near the canvas-draped tailgate of the lead truck. A small oval around his eyes was the only part of his face that was not covered in black. His eyes were narrow and mean, as if constantly searching for targets, and shone with a special fire, an energy that registered the determination and ruthlessness of a fanatic.

The man in black was Lee Chu Bok. He was tall for a North Korean, standing six foot one, and he had the muscled body of an expert gymnast. He lifted the canvas slightly and peeked out. The snow fell in a strong, steady flow.

Lee checked his watch. He had a few minutes left. He steadied his breathing and mentally prepared himself for the challenge. The men next to him sat motionless, waiting for his cue for action. The truck moved on, passing through another checkpoint and entering the inner security perimeter.

Lee was North Korea's latest export—a mercenary terrorist leader for hire. To prepare him for his role, he had been through the most intensive training in the North Korean People's Army. He was an expert in Hopkido, the Korean martial art that was a blend of karate and judo, and his discipline and intensity to this art was legendary. He had graduated first in his class at the Kumsung Military Institute in North Korea, the training ground for special forces leaders. Many of his peers—not friends, for he didn't have any—felt that Lee led a perfect career, that he was destined for greatness. He was a complete loner, with no family. Only his hatred gave him purpose. He bragged that he never allowed personal relationships to dissipate his energy. In training for combat, and in sports, he always won.

He was an effective killer, a man bred from childhood to the discipline of hate and death, the kind of man who made you feel uncomfortable just by his presence. The only person he respected was Yuri Terrek. Lee's duty to the Brotherhood was his only preoccupation, his hatred of Americans his only religion.

As a result of his talents and his loyalty, Terrek had appointed Lee as the commander of the Dragons, a special fighting group in the Brotherhood. The Dragons were an extraordinary band of cutthroats and killers—a terrorist dream team. Recruited from all over the world, Lee's men swore complete loyalty to him. As part of the initiation of every recruit, an oriental dragon was tattooed on the forearm of each member of Lee's group. Lee saw the dragon tattoos as a blood tie—a visible bond of service to the Brotherhood and him. Since Lee had the power of life and death over his men, no one disagreed. Lee used his absolute power swiftly and without remorse. His orders, therefore, were never questioned.

Like Lee, the other terrorists in his group were dressed in completely black uniforms. Around his chest Lee wore

special Kevlar body armor. Like the rest, he was armed
with a special 9 mm Carl Gustav submachine gun with a
short but effective silencer attached to the barrel. To
keep in constant communications with every member of
his team, he wore a communications receiver in his left
ear and had a throat microphone around his neck.

The truck stopped at the predesignated point. Lee
knew that his fifteen men and another truck with fifteen
more men had infiltrated into the heart of the enemy
position. The objective was a command bunker in a se-
cluded mountain retreat, heavily guarded by elite troops.
The heavy snowfall and the special passes helped them
through the toughest security checkpoints. Now it would
be up to Lee and his men to do the rest.

A big-muscled Brazilian named Montoyez sat across
from Lee and peered from the canvas to observe the
target area. Montoyez listened intently to his small earpiece, waiting for the signal to begin their attack.

"Sir," the hard-looking man said. "All the trucks are
inside the compound. Group One is ready. We can pro-
ceed according to plan."

Lee checked his weapon and tightened the silencer on
the end of the barrel of his submachine gun. All the
unit's weapons were untraceable. It agonized him that
everything he used, everything his men used—weapons,
gear, watches—were made in foreign lands. He recognized that his North Korean countrymen couldn't even
make a decent watch. Lee blamed all this and more on
the United States. The Americans were responsible for
North Korea's suffering. They had caused the war in
1950 and they were to blame for North Korea's dire
straits.

Lee knew that things had to change. He wanted to be
a part of that change. He wanted to see this change happen in his lifetime. He wanted to be proud again.

It tormented him more that he led an international
band of mercenaries consisting of Brazilians, Germans,
Russians, Serbs, Chinese, and North Koreans. He would
have preferred to lead a completely North Korean team,
but his country was too poor to enlist and train a unit

such as the Dragon Team and unwilling to act against the hated Americans. Terrek, the leader of the Brotherhood, had provided him with a cause, men, weapons and, most importantly, the money to exact revenge against the hated Yankee imperialists. For Lee, the Brotherhood was a dream come true, a source of pride and purpose.

Lee nodded. "Just as we rehearsed."

Montoyez nodded. They had practiced this mission at least a dozen times. Each time the result was the same: targets serviced, time line met, and mission accomplished. Lee's men never failed.

Lee looked nervously at his Japanese-made watch. He knew that timing was everything. He had to beat the clock to succeed. Somehow he sensed that this time, things were different. "Give the order," Lee commanded.

"Vulture!" Montoyez whispered into his transmitter, repeating the code word *vulture* several times.

The commandos quickly filed out of the truck.

"Silence the guards. No noise," Lee ordered quietly, patting each of his soldiers on the back as they left the truck. "No prisoners."

Like a well-oiled machine, the terrorist team sprang into action in rehearsed unity. They moved forward and took out the guards one at a time, before any of their enemies could sound the alarm. The men in the first truck silently secured the outside of the compound. Snipers ran to the towers where the guards had been and quickly set up to cover the entrance to the command compound. Others moved forward to place command directed antipersonnel mines. Two men set up RPK 7.62 mm machine guns, while another two carried antitank rocket launchers to cover the single approach into the inner security perimeter that surrounded the entrance to the underground complex.

As the rest of the enemy security force was neutralized in rapid succession, Lee attacked the main target with twelve men. The instant his assault team entered the tunnel that led to the underground facility, the lights inside the complex went out. Inside, Lee's men found a labyrinth of dark hallways and pitch-black offices. Using

night vision goggles and infrared flashlights, the lead
commandos knocked down targets as they appeared in
the hallway. Within two minutes, the assault detachment
had silenced sixteen guards without setting off the alarm.

Lee smiled. The drill was going perfectly. He was
proud of his men, even if the guards couldn't shoot back.
Each guard was actually a wooden target—man-shaped
silhouettes made of plywood, representing enemy soldiers. The targets were triggered to fall when hit by a
bullet. Several were placed in mock machine gun positions and guard towers.

Lee and his men were attacking an elaborately constructed live fire range. Terrek had built an exact replica
of the target that Lee's team would someday take down.
Lee didn't know when he and his men would execute the
real mission, but he sensed that it would be very soon.

His men had eleven minutes to get inside, blow a hole
through the steel doors guarding the underground facility, and secure a special room in the center of the complex. Lee looked at the nearest camera. Specially placed
television cameras watched every move of the attack
team. The movie of the attack would be replayed later
in detailed after-action reviews that focused on improving the team's timing and actions.

Lee studied the doors in the pitch black with his night
vision goggles. The screen of his monocular viewer
painted the darkness in shades of green. A target popped
up near the door, and the man behind Lee dropped it
with a well-aimed shot. Lee watched through the green
world as his men shot two more targets standing in front
of the door of the special room. The demolitions team
ran up to the large, eight-foot steel doors and placed two
egg-sized explosives on the door handles. Signals were
exchanged, and the commandos shielded their night vision goggles.

"Issue the code word. We are in and ready to execute
phase four," Lee uttered quietly to his radio operator.

Lee's men knelt in the dark, their backs against the
cold concrete walls to protect themselves from the detonation of the demolition charge. A man carrying a small,

sophisticated radio pack spoke the words into his hand-held transmitter. "Viper! I say again, *Viper.*"

A terrorist next to Lee pressed a button on a pen-sized detonation device in his right hand. A brilliant bright light and the roar of the explosives filled the air. Lee felt the shock wave and heat from the blast as the demolitions charge kicked in the heavy steel doors protecting the command bunker.

"Grenades!" Lee shouted.

One of Lee's men lobbed a concussion grenade into the opening. He sensed the bright light and roar of the grenade, then the shock wave. His men rushed in, firing silenced 9 mm rounds at a cluster of targets inside the building. Lee was the third man into the opening.

In seconds, the room was secure. Bright, emergency lights came on inside the bunker. Lee and his men took off their night vision goggles.

This room was the purpose of the mission. The two men with Lee placed their weapons on a table. One of the men carried a silver metal briefcase. The man placed the briefcase on the table and then, with the help of the other man, quickly donned a biocontagion suit that hung on the wall.

Once the man was suited up, he walked to the glass door that was the entrance to a specially designed vault. He punched in a twenty-three-number combination in the computer lock that was fixed to the wall. The door opened, and a red light began flashing. The man in the biocontagion suit stepped inside, briefcase in hand, then quickly turned and sealed the outer door. The red light stopped flashing. The man in the suit then walked over to an inner door, inside the vault, and punched in another long combination of numbers.

The inner door opened, and the man walked inside. The door to this inner containment area shut automatically behind him. Lee and the other man waited. In less than a minute, the man returned through the inner door carrying the metal briefcase.

A red light flashed and a siren went off as the man inside the containment area activated the decontamination process. The air was sucked out of the outer chamber and flushed with clean air. Simultaneously, a strong ultraviolet light swept across the room from the ceiling to kill any germs that might be left out in the open. After two and a half minutes, the outer door opened and the man stepped out of the room and took off his mask.

"That's it. Our special package is inside."

Lee looked at his watch and grinned. "Excellent. The entire operation took twenty minutes and fifty-seven seconds. We have accomplished the mission in record time. Tomorrow, I will arrange for some particularly attractive whores to join us in celebration."

The two men with Lee smiled, anticipating the celebration. Lee nodded with approval at his men and savored the moment of victory. He walked over and took the briefcase.

An announcement over a loudspeaker resonated like the voice of Orwell's Big Brother over the mock battlefield. "Commander Lee, well done. Report to the debriefing office immediately."

Lee's men rapidly moved out of the underground facility. With the wave of his arm, he signaled his platoon leaders to execute after-mission actions. He shouted a few quick orders and headed out of the underground complex and north up the road. He turned at the bend in the road and entered a fenced area that contained a one-story concrete building.

Two heavily armed guards stood outside the entrance of the building. One nodded to Lee and opened the door. Lee stepped inside and quickly surveyed the room. A single bright light lit the large room. Four deadly looking men in black uniforms—Terrek's bodyguards—stood in the room, their weapons at the ready. Two stood guard near the door. Two stood directly behind Terrek.

Lee carried his Carl Gustav submachine gun slung over his back, barrel down, and held the briefcase in his right hand. He saw Terrek and General Cho sitting in chairs in front of a long, narrow table. General Cho sat to Terrek's left, chain-smoking cigarettes. A pile of extinguished butts littered the ashtray on the table in front of Cho. A wide flat-screen television monitor was fastened to the wall facing the two men. Lee knew that every move that he had made during the exercise had been studied from this control room.

Lee approached Terrek and placed the briefcase on the table. Terrek smiled a quick smile, then nodded to Lee in appreciation of his excellent performance.

Cho slowly puffed on a cigarette, starring at the arrogant young Lee.

Lee returned Cho's stare and his hatred, clearly displaying utter contempt for the small-minded man who outranked him but could never outsoldier him. Lee considered Cho a martinet and a politician, not a warrior like himself. He was sure that Cho would sell his soul for the right price, and he knew that Cho was a spy who had been stealing money from Terrek.

Cho met Lee's gaze, decided that this was the wrong time to oppose Lee, and looked away.

"Commander Lee," Terrek said with a sinister smile, "My sincere congratulations. You have done a superb job during this rehearsal. There is no doubt that you and your men are ready. The Brotherhood, and I, have the greatest confidence in you and your men."

"You are the Brotherhood!" Lee answered, changing his stare from Cho to face Terrek. "I am honored to serve you."

"This is the kind of leader that I need to conduct the next phase of my plan." Terrek turned to General Cho. "Don't you agree?"

Cho took the cigarette out of his lips and merely smiled. "Perhaps. But, of course, I do not know what your plans are. Maybe if you would inform me of your intentions, I could support you more fully."

"My exact plans are secret," Terrek replied. "In the next few days we will strike the Americans and change the balance of power in the world. Lee, do you accept my offer?"

General Cho looked surprised. He stopped puffing on his cigarette, smashed it into the ashtray in front of him, and looked curiously at Terrek, then at Lee. Lee did not answer. He did not need to. The fire in his eyes said yes a hundred times louder than any words.

Cho popped open the cover of his silver cigarette case and selected another cigarette. He closed the cover with the flick of his finger and tapped the cigarette gently against the top, tamping the tobacco. Putting the cigarette between his lips, he lit the tobacco with a lighter.

"In two days I will have a weapon of unbelievable power. Your men leave tomorrow morning. You and the Dragon Team will become the sword of vengeance against the Americans," Terrek announced.

"Yes," Lee replied with fiery emotion. "There is no doubt. Just give me the word, and I will bring victory to the Brotherhood."

"Comrade Terrek, this action must be coordinated with Pyongyang," General Cho offered, taking a puff of his cigarette. Nervously he glanced at the guards next to the exit of the building. "Before you leave the Citadel to conduct any operations, you must coordinate with Pyongyang through me. That is our agreement."

"I have changed your pitiful agreement," Terrek answered coldly. "Did you think that I trust you or your superiors in Pyongyang to keep my secrets?" Terrek paused and studied the general for a moment. "Do you know what a true believer is, General Cho?"

Cho shook his head and looked more displeased than before. He squirmed nervously in his chair and rubbed the hair on the back of his neck.

"A true believer is a man who is ready to make any sacrifice and follow orders without question for a cause. True believers can change the world. I have a hundred such men, General Cho, all men who are loyal to the cause of the Brotherhood. But Lee is my finest disciple."

"I understand your desires for security, Comrade Terrek," Cho answered, startled by the sudden change of tone. "But the Democratic People's Republic of North Korea has security procedures that must be obeyed. I must inform—"

Terrek raised his hand, silencing Cho in mid-sentence. Cho fidgeted in his seat and took another long drag from his cigarette.

"Lee, you and your team will leave at oh-five-hundred tomorrow," Terrek said, addressing Lee. "American intelligence agents track me like a hawk. To cover your special mission, I will make an appearance somewhere else. I trust you, and only you, to lead the force that will secure the purpose of our effort. Together, we will take a series of steps that will break the Americans and bring them to their knees."

Lee smiled. "It will be done!"

General Cho put down his cigarette. "Comrade Terrek, you do not have the authority to make this decision. I will report this immediately—"

"Do you really think that you can stop me?" Terrek jeered. "I don't need your permission."

Cho looked down at the table. Beads of sweat popped on his forehead.

"The problem with you and the weak-willed cowards that rule your pathetic country is that you are afraid to commit yourself totally, without reservation, without looking back. You and your superiors have sat in your miserable 'workers' paradise' for over fifty years like flies on a pile of shit."

Cho made a move to stand up. One of Terrek's guards moved behind Cho and forced him back down.

"I'm not through with you," Terrek said, leaning forward on the table, placing his face inches from Cho's. Terrek grabbed the cigarette from Cho's mouth and threw it on the floor. "Wars are not won by the best men; they are won by the meanest men. At the first sign of weakness you must go for the throat; you must be prepared to commit totally."

Terrek stood up, reached over with his powerful right

arm, and grabbed the short North Korean by the throat. "I cannot allow anyone to know my plans, especially an insignificant worm like you. You have already told your superiors in Pyongyang too much. Secrecy is *life* in my business. It is like plugging holes in the bottom of a boat. If you expect to keep sailing, you cannot tolerate even the smallest leak."

Terrek squeezed Cho's throat, and Cho was powerless to break his hold. Just before Cho's eyes felt like they were about to burst from their sockets, Terrek let go. Cho slumped into his chair, coughing for air.

Terrek straightened his shirt and walked around to the far right side of the table. The two bodyguards that stood behind Terrek moved back against the wall. Terrek nodded to Lee.

Lee quickly punched in the combination to the briefcase and opened the envelope that lay inside. He read the contents of the letter.

Without hesitation, Lee swung his submachine gun from his back. With the sling still on his shoulder, he placed the barrel of the gun against Cho's head and fired. Cho's head exploded, and the lifeless body slumped to the floor.

The echo of the shot rang inside the room. The guards didn't flinch. No one in the room moved except the quivering body of the dead general. Cho's cigarette, still burning as it lay on the white tiled floor, was quietly extinguished by a swelling pool of blood.

The great act is about to begin, Lee thought, as a corrupt smile traversed his lips. *Finally, I have found a leader who has the courage to take destiny in his hands! Our actions will bring the downfall of the United States. The thought warms my soul and will bring meaning to my people's years of sacrifice.*

"We have already struck in Rome." Terrek grinned, admiring the brilliance of the plan he had created. "We will make another loud noise in the West and then we will strike in the East. This will blind the Americans to our true intentions. It is in the East that we will find the weapon that will bring us victory. You will be my best leader, my true right arm, my true believer!"

"For the Brotherhood!" Lee shouted. "Death to America!"

Chapter Six

And behold ye, the mighty one of slaughters, the terror of whom is most great, shall wash himself clean in your blood, and he shall bathe in your gore, and ye shall be destroyed.

—*The Ancient Egyptian Book of the Dead*

**November 12, 11:00 A.M.,
in the Valley of the Kings, Egypt**

"This is so exciting," she whispered, sounding like a schoolgirl flirting with a boyfriend in high school history class.

Jim glanced at his bride of thirty-three years and smiled. He was eight years older than Elizabeth, but age was never an issue for them, as they had been in love with each other since they first met. Though her long blond hair was turning silver, he still saw Elizabeth—Liz—as the most beautiful woman in the world. At fifty-one, Liz still had the allure of sensuality and vitality of a thirty-year-old. She had that look, and the figure, that could still turn heads. He bragged to his friends that Liz could have doubled for Lauren Bacall as the actress appeared in the 1964 movie *Sex and the Single Girl,* and any of his friends who saw that movie heartily agreed.

Jim looked at the thin, plain wedding band on Liz's left hand. He bought that ring for twenty-eight dollars in a pawnshop in Galveston just before they were married. At the time, it was as much ring as he could afford, but to Liz, it seemed worth a fortune. Through all the tough years, she seldom complained and was his rock of support when times were bad. Now that he was retired, they were enjoying life. They looked upon this vacation as a well-deserved second honeymoon.

Technically, the term *second honeymoon* wasn't very accurate. This was really the honeymoon they never had. The intimate weekend they shared together in the Galveston Holiday Inn after their justice-of-the-peace wedding was all they could claim as a honeymoon. The next day, Liz had driven Jim to the airport and he shipped off to Vietnam to join the U.S. Army's 173rd Airborne Brigade. He was twenty-six then and she was only eighteen, but their love lasted through war, separation, and tough times.

Jim knew that his darling Liz had never grumbled about this, but he wanted much more for his wife. After Vietnam, Jim found work driving eighteen wheelers, eventually running his own independent trucking company. For nearly thirty years, he worked the hard life of a trucker, rushing heavy cargoes and consumer goods back and forth across the United States. He knew that he spent too much time on the road and too much time away from his lovely Liz, but that was how he made his living, and somehow she always seemed to understand.

During those busy years, Jim recognized that Liz had accomplished the tougher task of their union, playing the role that was worth more to him than money could reward. Liz had maintained their happy home and for a few years helped to raise and nurture their wonderful godson in addition to their own son. Now, he swore, it was Liz's time. When a large competitor offered to buy his fleet out for a substantial profit, Jim retired. He told Liz that over the years he had saved enough money for the vacation that she had always dreamed of. Yes, it was his chance to make up for lost time, Jim thought. He winked at her and smiled.

She caught his gaze and seemed to read his mind. With a twinkle in her eyes, she brought his strong right hand to her lap and gently squeezed it. The sparkle in Liz's eye was worth more to him than all the gold in all the undiscovered treasures of ancient Egypt. He was a happy man.

For thirty-three years of marriage, while Jim was driving across the country, Liz dreamed of traveling with Jim to exotic places. But such visits were always beyond their budget. The couple had worked hard, sacrificed, and made a life for themselves and their family. Liz worked initially as a seamstress and later for the Red Cross at a local veterans' hospital. Vacations were postponed. There will bills to pay, and raising children was always expensive. Over the years, the closest that Jim and Liz had come to sharing a real vacation together was when Liz would open a travel magazine in their living room after one of her chicken-fried steak dinners. The four of them—Jim, Liz, their son and their godson—would sit in the living room, munching on steak and talking about all the wonderful places that they would visit someday.

Now, with Jim's retirement from driving the big rigs, with their sons graduated from college and following their own careers, it was time for them to have fun. It only took a glance at the latest travel brochures for Liz to set her heart on a two-week tour of the Holy Land and the famous sites of ancient Egypt.

The air-conditioning fought a losing battle as the sun baked the aluminum roof of the Egyptian tour bus that carried the Douglases and thirty-eight other Western travelers. The engine screeched as the bus struggled along the sand-swept asphalt road at thirty miles an hour. The bus driver, a happy old man with a white *ritra* and brown *dish-dash,* the typical headdress and one-piece white gown common to the Egyptian working class, was humming as the bus slowly motored along. The tour guide, a pleasant, fat Egyptian man in his mid-fifties named Nasser Al Habeeb, stood at the front of the bus and held a microphone in his right hand.

Jim grinned. Egypt was turning out to be everything that he had expected—a blending of the best of Hollywood and the Bible.

"You will see, my ladies and gentlemen, that to our right is a glorious and holy place," Habeeb announced with a wide grin. "This is our most famous Valley of the Kings."

Jim's smile grew into a chuckle. Habeeb's happy, round face and dark, bushy mustache cast a comical appearance. He couldn't help himself. *Habeeb is enjoying his job,* he thought, *and he seems determined to give us our money's worth.*

"To our right, my ladies and gentlemen, you will see

the latest excavations of the royal Egyptian burial sites,"
Habeeb continued, determined to run a constant com-
mentary as the bus passed by anything that even hinted
of ancient Egypt. "These ruins contain picture writing,
known as hieroglyphs. These writings tell us about my
ancestors' beliefs in Anu, where the souls of the just
were united with their spiritual and glorified bodies."

There was the usual murmur of ohs and ahs from the
tourists as they glimpsed a ruined, completely deserted
temple to their right. The group was a mixture of young
and old, retired couples and newlyweds. Most were
American, having taken advantage of the latest "See the
Wonders of Ancient Egypt" discount vacation package.
Camera shutters clicked as amateur photojournalists
tried their best to capture the monumental sights on film,
even through the tinted bus windows.

"It all seems so sad," Liz whispered to Jim, as she
lowered her camera. "They were such wonderful
builders . . . such great administrators. But this fascination with death . . . tombs and pyramids."

"Yes, I suppose it is sad," Jim replied, nodding as he
put his right arm around his wife's shoulders. Liz nestled
her head on his shoulder as she gazed at the broken
walls that had once been the walls of a royal dwelling.
"But not unusual. Everyone wonders what lies beyond
the grave. The ancient Egyptians just expressed their cu-
riosity in a different way than we do."

"Why did their empire fall?" Liz asked, as the bus
passed a broken temple.

Jim thought a minute, rolling a vision of the ancient
Egyptian empire around in his mind. He wasn't much of
a historian, but he had read a good book about the ancient Egyptians, Greeks, and Romans in preparation for
their tour. It was a classic tale of survival. Stronger, more
determined cultures had moved in, overcame the ancient
Egyptians, and changed their way of life forever. "Probably for the same reason that most nations fall. Maybe
the ancient Egyptians just ran out of people willing to
stand up and fight for what they believed in. With no

one willing to fight for their way of life, their society forfeited their future."

"You're becoming a philosopher in your old age," Liz let out with a wry face. Then she sighed. "I wonder how our boys are doing?"

Jim smiled again and shook his head. Liz hadn't been away more than ten days, and she was already homesick. "You mustn't worry about them. They're fine and can take care of themselves."

"And, let me remind you, my ladies and gentlemen," Habeeb announced over the loudspeaker, tilting his head up and assuming an air of importance. "My cousin Nassir Al Hassan owns a wonderful shop back in Luxor where you can purchase all of your souvenirs at special prices. The shops that you will see in other places are much too expensive. He has exquisite stone carvings of Ramses, one of the greatest pharaohs, and at cheap cost to you."

Jim smiled. The spirit of free enterprise was alive and well in modern Egypt.

A massive woman named Helga sat in the front seat near Habeeb and fanned herself with a brochure that was printed in Arabic and English. Helga looked up at the tour guide in disbelief and shook her head. She seemed to care as much about the ancient age of Ramses as she cared about Habeeb's cousin; the heat was her major concern. The bus's air-conditioning was on full blast, but the effect that it had on the passengers was insignificant. Several of the tourists opened their windows as a result, making the battle to cool the interior of the bus completely futile. As a result, Helga was sweating profusely and whispering her complaints to her thin, bespectacled husband who sat uncomfortably at her side.

Helga spoke some English, most of which she used to complain about everything she had experienced in Egypt. As soon as the tour bus had left the hotel, Helga appointed herself as the tour safety director, to Habeeb's dismay. She repeatedly gave Habeeb's driver warnings to slow down, or directions to avoid potholes or stray animals in the road. Helga was convinced that all the Egyptian culture needed was organization and discipline.

Then the Egyptians might be able to get the buses running on time, remove the trash from the streets and—most importantly—keep the air-conditioning working.

Jim and Liz met Helga and her husband Karl before the tour group left the hotel in Luxor. Jim admired people with attitude, and he recognized Helga as a personality powered by an attitude with a capital *A*. With shy, withdrawn Karl at her side, the two were a humorous couple, and Liz and Jim had enjoyed swapping stories with Helga.

The smiling, gray-bearded, almost toothless old man driving the bus was oblivious to Helga's suggestions and protests. The old man, who didn't speak any English, let alone Helga's heavily Teutonic accented version of English, merely smiled and softly hummed an ancient tune.

The terrain grew more rugged as the tour bus rolled on into the Valley of the Kings, and the bus seemed to find every pothole in the poorly maintained asphalt road. Ancient mountains of sand and rock, and empty pits where stones had once been quarried, appeared to the left and right. As the bus drove around a tall basalt mountain, Helga shouted a warning to the driver and pointed at a green truck blocking the road.

"Vas is dis in der road?" Helga demanded.

Habeeb looked at the German woman, shrugged, and turned to the front. At the same moment, the old man at the wheel of the bus slammed on the brakes. Habeeb, who had been standing in the front of the bus, lost his balance and jolted forward in an undignified heap against the windshield.

Rifle shots were fired in the air as the bus jerked to a dramatic stop.

A man standing in front of the bus, dressed in black fatigues and wearing a red-checkered *ritra* on his head that covered all but his eyes, aimed a deadly-looking assault rifle directly at the bus driver.

"Jim?" Liz asked, concern painting her face.

Jim shook his head and held onto Elizabeth's hand. "Don't worry. Keep quiet. Everything will be all right."

"Ach, mein Gott!" Helga gasped and then let out an unintelligible prayer in German. "Bandits!"

The rest of the tourists seemed to hold their breath. No one was sure of what was going on in front of the bus.

The man in fatigues banged on the door with the butt of his AK-47 assault rifle, while another man appeared and pointed his rifle at Habeeb. Habeeb screamed at the driver to open the door. The door opened, and the man in black grabbed Habeeb, pulled him out of the bus, and threw the plump tour guide to the dirt.

A dozen armed men suddenly appeared. Like a pack of wolves pouncing on a stray sheep, the bandits surrounded the bus. Each man was similarly armed and dressed—except two. One of these exceptions was a man armed with only a pistol. This man was shouting orders, and Jim guessed that he was the man in charge. The other exception was a man with his rifle slung over his back. This man walked with a video recorder, filming every minute of the action.

Jim got a sinking feeling in his stomach. *Bandits don't film their deeds,* he thought, and he could see that the men with the guns were not Egyptians or even Arabs. These guys were something else. They must have other motives.

The bandit who threw Habeeb to the ground stepped up into the bus. An elderly woman behind Jim and Elizabeth screamed. The bus driver stood up, as if to make a move to help Habeeb, but the man in black fatigues quickly slammed the butt of his Kalashnikov into the old man's face. The gray-haired old man crumpled into the driver's seat.

Jim watched, helpless to do anything. Everything happened very fast. Outside the bus, Habeeb tried to stand up. The man with the pistol kicked him back down with the heel of his heavy military boot. Blood shot out from Habeeb's mouth, and he cringed in a fetal position on the ground, covering his head with his hands. Then, with less ceremony than a person uses to drop refuse into a trash can, the leader of the terrorists fired two shots into the fat tour guide's back.

The leader, a trim man who was a little over six feet tall, kicked Habeeb's lifeless body, turning it over. Habeeb's chest was bathed in red as two large exit wounds gushed blood.

"Everybody . . . out. Out of bus!" the leader shouted in broken English. Then one of the bandits pointed his rifle to the roof and fired off a dozen shots. "Now!"

Amid a sea of screams and cries, the tourists—men, women, and a few children—stood up and moved to the door. Helga, barely able to move between the isles because of her substantial girth, struggled to exit the bus with her husband Karl following behind. The man with the assault rifle standing next to the driver's seat unceremoniously pushed Helga. The big lady reflexively shoved back. The man in black pointed his rifle at her head and laughed. Helga stood perfectly still while Karl, thin and bespectacled, slipped between them, apologized, and carefully ushered his wife off the bus.

In the back of the vehicle, other tourists pitifully clutched their purses and cameras and piled off the bus. Some of the passengers in the back of the bus moved too slowly for the terrorists and were greeted by shouts and threats from the men in black. The man who shot Habeeb pushed them without regard for age or gender as they exited the bus.

Jim and Elizabeth followed Helga and Karl out the door. As Jim walked past the leader, he felt the bandit's eyes following him. Although the leader's *ritra* covered his mouth and nose, Jim could see the man's eyes. They were narrow and mean but displayed a confidence that told Jim that this man was a professional killer with a plan.

Jim dared to return his gaze, meeting the fire in the man's eyes with fire, then moved quickly with Liz past the man and took their place in line.

That was a mistake, Jim thought.

The sun bore down on the passengers as they were unceremoniously formed into a line in front of Habeeb's lifeless body. Pools of thick, reddish brown blood circled in the hot sand beneath him. One lady crossed herself as she saw Habeeb. Once the bus was empty, the scene grew suddenly quiet. At the end of the line, a young, attractive woman in a long yellow sundress held a small baby in her arms. The baby cried, soft whimpering cries, disturbing the silence. A man standing next to her, the baby's father, tried to comfort the mother, who was also on the verge of tears.

All the time, the man in black fatigues with the palm-sized video disc recorder taped the scene, panned the panicked faces of the captives, and zoomed in to capture the traumatic look on the face of the bewildered young mother.

"Don't worry," Jim whispered to his wife, trying to sound brave. He quickly took stock of the situation and searched for a way out. There was none. There were too many men with weapons and no safe place to run. He'd have to bide his time and look for an opportunity. "If they wanted to kill us, we'd be dead already. Stay calm. Do what they say."

Liz, wide-eyed and frantic, looked at her husband. Holding tight to Jim's hand, she turned her head and stared at the bloody body of their poor tour guide.

The leader of the men in black fatigues walked the line and looked at each tourist. He stopped in front of Jim for a second, sizing him up. Jim stood under the merciless sun and looked into the cold eyes of an even more merciless foe. Jim couldn't make out the man's face, as it was covered with the red-checkered *ritra,* but he saw volumes in the man's eyes.

Jim felt a hatred that he hadn't felt since his days as a soldier in Vietnam, when he'd faced a different enemy in a different world. *Damn this son of a bitch,* he thought. *They're not bandits, they're terrorists.*

The man with the pistol stood in front of the line of tourists. The other armed men of his band stood behind him.

"My name is Yuri Terrek," the man with the pistol announced, playing to the camera. "You are all enemies of the Brotherhood and now are our prisoners. You will be punished for your crimes against humanity that

United States and Western powers have waged against the world."

A sixty-year-old Canadian widow standing next to Jim began to pray. Jim had talked with her on the bus and learned that her name was Mary Uley. She had saved for two years to take this trip to the Holy Land and Egypt. Now her lifelong ambition to see these ancient sands had turned into a nightmare.

"I will ask of you each a question, and you will answer me," Terrek announced curtly, as if he were giving commands to a dog. He stood with his left hand on his hip. In his right hand, he cocked the pistol and pointed it skyward. "If you do not answer, you will be shot. If you move, you will be shot."

The tourists stood motionless. The murmur of sobs hung in the air. Terrek walked up to the fat German lady and looked into her terrified eyes. One of Terrek's men laughed.

"Your nationality," Terrek demanded in a voice darker than a morning without a sunrise.

"Deutsche," she replied, the anger in her voice unmistakable, her eyes filled with opposition.

"Maybe I should shoot your husband," Terrek said, placing the cold barrel of his pistol on Karl's nose. "Would you like to see your husband's brains blown all over the sand?"

"Nein . . . bitte," Helga pleaded, dropping her gaze to the man's feet. Terrek laughed, and moved to Karl, still holding the pistol in the man's face.

"Deutsche," Karl answered feebly, staring at the sand. Terrek lowered his pistol and moved on. The next in line was Mary.

"Canadian," the lady sobbed, holding a rosary in her hand.

Terrek took the rosary and threw it on the ground, then crushed it into the sand with his boot. Mary stood frozen in fear. Terrek then moved to Jim. Jim looked at the man, eye to eye, for a second time. He had always hated bullies, and this man was the worst kind. He could see it in the man's eyes, a hatred that would never go away. Jim knew that look. He also knew what was coming next.

"You are American," Terrek demanded. "Your arrogance gives you away. I haven't killed an American for several weeks."

Jim didn't answer. He tried to look blank and not provoke Terrek.

In one quick move, Terrek aimed his pistol at Jim's forehead and pulled the trigger. The sound of the shot echoed in the hills. Jim crumpled to the ground. Blood spattered all over Elizabeth—*Jim's blood!* She screamed and knelt down next to the body of her beloved husband.

Two large helicopters suddenly appeared from the east and landed a few hundred meters away from the terrified tourists. The choppers' blades created a huge wind that blew the desert sand like a storm.

"Let this be an example to you. Obey my orders, and the rest of you not be killed," Terrek shouted above the roar of the engines. "There are thirty-eight . . . thirty-seven . . . people now. Obey me, and all of you will be released in due time."

Time stood still for Elizabeth Douglas. She knelt in the sand, with Jim's head on her lap, as the blood covered her tan pants.

Terrek nodded to a man standing at his side. The man pointed to the men to his right and left, signaling them to move the prisoners onto the helicopters. "Everyone, move to helicopters. Now!" the man shouted.

The terrorists pushed and kicked the thirty-seven tourists toward the helicopters, leaving Jim Douglas, Habeeb, and the bus driver dead at the scene. In shock, and struggling in the sand, the mixed group of nineteen women, fifteen men, and three children complied.

Elizabeth refused to go. She stayed on the ground, holding the body of her dead husband. Sobbing, she looked up at Terrek's cold eyes. "I won't leave him."

Terrek pointed his pistol at her head, ready to drop her on the spot. Helga and Karl, just a few paces away, rushed to Elizabeth's side and pulled her away.

Terrek sneered. "Get the American bitch out of here before I shoot her."

Helga and Karl dragged Elizabeth off to the waiting helicopters.

"I can't leave him here!" she cried, unable to struggle against Helga's firm grip.

"Ve must," Helga said, forcing Elizabeth forward, her voice cracking with emotion as they reached the door of the helicopter, "Ve must."

November 12, 1315 hours, office of the Commander-in-Chief, Special Operations Command, the Pentagon

"Jack, I've called you in here to get you up to speed on the latest intel," the gruff voice announced.

"Yes, sir, I've seen the news," General Krauss said. "All the news stations are playing the tape of the devastation in Rome. My staff briefed me only an hour ago. I've put the TALON Force on alert."

"Good. But what you don't know is that the terrorists also struck in Egypt, killed one American and kidnapped thirty-seven other tourists, most of whom are U.S. citizens," General Samuel "Buck" Freedman, the commander of Special Operations Command (SOCOM), replied.

The lean, rugged-looking, forty-eight-year-old Joint Task Force commander of the newly formed TALON Force shook his head. Krauss's weathered face, hard eyes, and erect carriage looked like they had been copied from a Green Beret recruiting poster. "Does the TALON Force go operational?"

"I know that you weren't scheduled to go operational for another thirty days, but the circumstances may force us to move earlier than expected."

Brigadier General Jack Krauss, United States Army, edged forward in his chair, eager to accept the challenge and ready to prove his new organization in combat. Confidence was written across the Green Beret's face as he prepared to argue his case, but before he could speak, the tough-as-leather Marine four-star general sitting behind the shiny mahogany desk cut him off with a wave of his hand. The Marine General eyed Krauss carefully. He knew Jack's quality. Krauss was the best officer he had ever met, in any service.

Krauss was one of the most decorated combat special operations officers on active duty. He had been in more operations than General Freedman liked to think about. Krauss had a reputation as a bold, brilliant, and utterly ruthless covert warrior. Wounded in his last direct combat action, Krauss had lost his right hand. But Jack Krauss was too good a soldier for the Army to medically retire. Crippled but still combat worthy, Krauss was the general's first choice to place in charge of the TALON Force.

Jack Krauss did not disappoint his mentor. He proved time and again that he was exactly the right man for the job. Krauss moved mountains of obstacles to organize, equip, and train the most advanced special operations force in the world.

"Since the destruction of our civilian airliners over the Pacific Ocean four months ago, we've struggled night and day to put your new force together," the Marine general said, looking at Krauss. "We secured congressional funding, pooled the best minds in industry, and produced some of the most fantastic technologies I've ever heard of. But most of what your teams will use has not been combat tested."

"Sir, it's true that most of our equipment is still in the prototype phase, and there are some bugs that still must be worked out, but we are ready."

"Are you sure about the equipment? Everything depends on whether your special gear works as it was designed to work."

"The terra-byte supercomputers we use have produced equipment that would have been considered magic five years ago," Krauss said with pride. "All the prototypes are computer generated, precision manufactured, and precision tested. We've advanced the teams' situation awareness, survivability, and lethality nearly a hundred-fold.''

Freedman chuckled. "You scare the hell out of me, Jack. You not only know how to soldier, you understand all this high-tech bullshit better than anyone I know. But machines don't fight wars alone," General Freedman answered seriously. "People do, and they use their minds. We forget that sometimes, and I worry that our fascination for precision weapons may get the better of us. I want you to tell me if your *people* are ready.''

General Freedman leaned back in his chair and closed his eyes. Krauss knew that he was warming up to offer one of his sermons.

"I've seen this before," Freedman continued. "We put our trust in our high-tech capabilities and then we underestimate the enemy. That's how those bastards in Lebanon blew up our barracks in Beirut and killed two hundred ninety-nine Marines in the 1980s. That's why the poor, ill-disciplined sons of bitches in Somalia beat us in the streets of Mogadishu. And that's why the Russians lost a brigade in the first *day* of their assault of the city of Grozny in Chechnya.''

"Sir, I've got the best people from all of the services," Krauss said. *"The very best.* As you know, we even have the best civilian specialists on our teams, some of our nation's top experts in microbiology, chemical weapons, and computer technology, among other specialties. Under your special authority, the Congress has appointed these civilians to the grade of temporary captain, and they are integrated into each of our teams. In short, General, our teams have been selected from the *crème de la crème.*''

"Jack, don't speak that French shit to me," Freedman chided.

The two men laughed. In a profession that was often too serious, Freedman enjoyed the close camaraderie and friendship that he shared with Krauss. He was happy to see that Krauss hadn't lost his confidence or his energy, in spite of the nonstop work schedule that the younger Special Forces officer had maintained these past months.

The pace had been grueling, but Krauss knew the international situation was growing more critical every day.

"Jack, I trust your judgment. With the great expense of the TALON Force program, there is a desire to get the teams in the field sooner rather than later. I just need to hear it from you that you have a team ready to deploy today if I get the nod."

"Sir, the TALON Force is a precision instrument of national defense, the ultimate special operations team. They are worth every dime we spend on them. We will be able to do things we could never do before, and we'll do it faster, decisively, and with fewer casualties. My answer is an unequivocal yes."

"Good. I was counting on that. I told the Chairman of the Joint Chiefs of Staff the same thing twenty minutes ago." Freedman popped open a slim, black laptop computer that lay on his desk. He turned the screen around and placed it in front of Krauss.

Krauss grinned, happy at the general's confidence in him. Then his gaze was drawn to the computer screen. The blue screen glowed with the words Top Secret/ TALON Force Only emblazoned across the center in red.

"Computer, start briefing," Freedman ordered.

The lights in the office dimmed at the sound of the general's voice command. The computer hummed for a split second, then a Joint Staff logo popped up on the screen. The logo faded and was replaced by a direct video link to the Joint Intelligence Center. A thin-faced, hard-looking female Air Force colonel appeared on the screen, standing in front of a large digital situation map.

"Good morning, General Krauss. This Briefing is Top Secret, NOFORN, TALON Force Only," the woman announced in a strong, self-assured voice. This meant that the information was not only restricted to those with a top secret security clearance, but that no foreign citizens, no matter how high their security clearance, and only those in the TALON Force chain of command could view the briefing. "The briefing you are about to hear is the latest all-source information concerning the international terrorist group known as the Brotherhood.

"Strategic setting: The United States, the world's only superpower at the dawn of the twenty-first century, is currently under attack by several transnational organizations. Until recently, America's enemies were easy to identify because they were nation-states. Although relations between nation-states are not always peaceful, America has minimized long, bloody ground war campaigns in the past ten years by maintaining a small but powerful conventional military force focused on precision engagement.

"America's nation-state opponents, countries like Iraq, Iran, North Korea, China, Libya, and Syria continue to support large, industrial-age military forces to maintain internal power and secure regional power goals. The joint forces of the United States military—the Army, Navy, Marines, and Air Force—retain qualitative superiority over these opposing forces in terms of precision firepower, information operations, training, equipment, and the ability to strategically deploy anywhere in the world. This combination of capabilities has kept the worst of these rogue states—like North Korea, Libya, and Iraq—in check.

"All of the countries I have just mentioned are at odds with the United States over various issues. These countries—in addition to China and Russia—view the United States as a world hegemon. We have recent intelligence information that indicates that some of these nations are supporting a radical change in the balance of power by financing an international terrorist force that will challenge American interests around the world. In essence, it is a global terrorist campaign aimed against American personnel and interests. The bombings of the U.S. airliners last spring was merely an advertisement of their abilities. They used this to show their capability and to secure financing."

"The Brotherhood," Krauss said. "Yuri Terrek."

"Yes, exactly," the Air Force colonel answered. "The Brotherhood, led by Yuri Terrek, is supported internationally with money, weapons, operatives, and information from these rogue states and by many others whose aims are inimical to ours. The stated goal of the Brotherhood is the defeat of the United States and its allies."

"Do you know where Terrek is?" Krauss asked, almost too eagerly, he thought. "His greatest strength is his anonymity."

"Unfortunately, very little is known about Terrek or his whereabouts. We do know that he is brilliant, ruthless, and willing to use any means of asymmetrical force, primarily terrorism, to accomplish his goals. We know that he was in the United States years ago and was arrested under a different name and identity. He escaped and has been growing his organization ever since. He is not associated with any religion, cult, or country, but is closely associated with international criminal elements and is sympathetic to all who hate America and its allies."

"I am familiar with Terrek's known history," Krauss replied.

"Of course, you know about the operation with the Russians in Ossetia last year."

General Jack Krauss nodded and massaged his prosthetic right hand. "Yes, too familiar. Please continue."

"Yesterday, one hundred twenty-four Americans were killed in the terrorist bombing in Rome. Thirty-two survivors of the blast are critically injured and many of them are not expected to survive. On the same day, one American and two Egyptians were executed by the Brotherhood in Egypt, and twenty-seven Americans and ten Europeans were kidnapped. Their whereabouts are unknown at this time. A videotape of the kidnapping and the execution of the American was sent to the worldwide television services and will appear in tonight's international news broadcasts."

"Any leads?" Krauss asked.

"We think the hostages have been transported to an airfield in Sudan. They may have flown from there to Somalia, but we don't know for sure yet. If they're in the air, they could be anywhere."

"Anything else?" Krauss asked.

"The Brotherhood has issued the following demands. . . ." The computer screen flashed from the J2 briefing room to a video cut. A slim man, with muscular arms, wearing a black T-shirt and black fatigue trousers was sitting in a chair. Shadows covered his face, but Krauss could make out the outline of the figure. The man was obviously bald or had shaved his head. Other than that, Krauss saw only a shadow.

"I am leader of the Brotherhood," the figure proudly announced. The tone of the man's voice was strong, commanding, and haughty.

"Do you think that's Terrek?" General Freedman asked.

Krauss leaned closer to the screen, stared at the figure, and shrugged.

"I present the following demands to the United States of America," Terrek announced in the cold voice of a fanatic. "America must withdraw all its military forces to the borders of the United States and cancel all defense treaties and alliances with all other nations. If the United States does not comply within seven days I will cause a disaster that you will regret for all of time."

There was a pause as a close-up of the dark image of Terrek filled the screen. The cameraman who filmed this segment was obviously looking for a dramatic finish.

"The bombing in Rome and the kidnappings in Egypt are just the beginning," Terrek announced in a cold, deadly voice. "I tell you this because there is absolutely nothing you can do about it. Meet our just demands or face the consequences of your own destruction."

"End of briefing, zero two one two zero, Top Secret, TALON Force." The screen went blank and the lights in the office turned on.

"There is only one way to deal with this fanatic," Krauss said, visibly angered by Terrek's arrogance. "He knows that we can't give in to his demands. He's playing to public opinion, trying to show himself as an equal to the United States."

"You're right, but the pressure is on. The President wants to go on television tomorrow to address the issue.

The public is starting to panic. Tourism is already down from the airline bombings in March. We don't have much time, and Terrek may accelerate his timetable after the President's address, especially if it's a get-tough-on-terrorism speech. We have to find out what Terrek is up to and stop it before it happens."

"Has anyone pinpointed the location where this video was made?" Krauss asked.

"No, but the FBI is working on that," Freedman answered, shaking his head. "This son of a bitch is smart. The videodisks he sent to the news bureaus were not traceable. So far, no clues."

"What do you think Terrek's planning?" Krauss asked.

"Jack, I think he has access or is trying to acquire WMD," Freedman said, using the acronym for weapons of mass destruction—nuclear, biological, or chemical weapons. "If he gets his hands on a WMD, I think he will target an American city."

"Do we know what kind of WMD he's trying to secure?"

"No, but pick your poison. He has the finances to do almost anything."

"The colonel mentioned that the attacks on the airliners were just demonstrations of his capabilities in order to secure financing. What do you think the Rome and Egyptian attacks are aimed at?"

"I'm not sure. These two attacks may just be a cover for the bigger operation."

General Freedman's intercom buzzed. The general pushed the voice button.

"Sir, Lieutenant Commander Hayes with a special report for you," a soft, female voice announced.

"Thanks, Margaret," the general replied. "Please send him in." A U.S. Navy lieutenant commander, an athletic-looking man in his late thirties, walked into the office carrying a briefcase.

"Sir, the latest on Case Red," the Naval officer reported. "This is too sensitive to put out on electronic media. Your eyes and General Krauss's eyes only, sir."

Freedman took the folder, opened it, and leaned back

in his chair, studying the report. After a quick read, Freedman looked up at the Navy lieutenant commander.

"Do we know where the hostages are now?"

"No, sir. Egyptian authorities tracked a dozen cargo aircraft leaving Sudan today, flying in all directions. These orders from the NCA order the CIA, Delta Force, and all available SEAL Teams to move as many assets as required to Egypt and Rome to investigate the attacks, find the terrorists, and take them down."

Freedman passed the report of the terrorist kidnapping of U.S. tourists in Egypt to Krauss. "What about this other report?" Freedman said, holding up a piece of paper that was titled "Brotherhood Activities in the Russian Far East."

"The main effort is the Mediterranean. The CIA thinks that those radioelectronic intercepts about a Brotherhood plan in the Russian Far East are a deception. They think that the most likely target is more tourists or possibly one of our overseas embassies," Hayes answered. "These orders direct you to send one TALON Force team to check out the Russian lead, just in case.

Freedman read the report and whistled. "The President authorized this?"

"Affirmative, General," Hayes answered. "His signature and authorization code are on the next page. He said that this mission was custom made for the TALON Force."

Freedman nodded and handed the folder to Krauss. Krauss studied the report and handed it back to Hayes. "Thank you, Hayes," Freedman answered. "It looks like we'll be plenty busy for the next few days."

"Yes, sir," Hayes replied, saluted, and left the office. Krauss sat forward in his seat.

"This looks like a hell of a gamble," Krauss said. "I understand that time is of the essence, but the intel sucks."

"Welcome to the world of covert operations," Freedman chided. "Jack, those are the orders. The Russians must never know your team is there. We learned our lesson in Ossetia last year."

"Tell me about it."

Freedman nodded.

"What about backup on this mission?" Krauss asked.

Freedman shook his head. "The USS *Constellation* will be in the Sea of Japan and will provide TFV-22 Ospreys for team pickup. Other than cruise missiles, your team will be on their own. There will be no ground force backup. We need a minimum of fireworks on this mission—at least nothing that can be traced to the U.S."

"I understand," Krauss replied. "I have already notified my best team."

"And Jack, if anything goes wrong, we can't let the Russians capture TALON Force technology. Is that clear?"

"Perfectly."

"Good," Freedman nodded. "Not only is the entire TALON Force program on the line, but a lot of American lives. I don't want to think about what Terrek would do with a nuke."

"Yes sir," Krauss answered, massaging his right hand. "I'm eager to get Terrek, too. We'll stop him."

"That's what I expected. Now, get the hell out of here and get to work!" Freedman bellowed, reaching over to shake Krauss's hand. "And wish your troopers good luck."

Krauss offered his left hand. "In the TALON Force, everybody fights, nobody quits, and everybody comes home."

"*Semper fi,*" the Marine general replied.

Chapter Seven

Fight the enemy with the weapons he lacks.
                                    —Suvorov

"Listen up, people," Sergeant Major George Buford bellowed. The man walked a few steps to the left of the formation of soldiers, prowling like a panther eyeing his prey. The lines of his weathered face were as sharp as a saber, and although he was not a young man, he exuded power and energy. He was hard-eyed and serious. It didn't matter that most of the troopers standing in front of him outranked him. Here, he was in charge.

Seven teams of tough, elite soldiers in black synthetic armor and brilliant, high-tech battle ensembles stood at rigid attention as a strong, cold wind swept over that desolate, open field. The TALON Force troopers were lined up in one boxlike formation, each rank with seven soldiers each. In the east, the sky turned to light gray as the darkness retreated like a coward running from a fight.

"At ease," Sergeant Major Buford announced. The soldiers relaxed their stance. All eyes were fixed on the sergeant major.

"When you all volunteered for the TALON Force, we told you that it would be dangerous. Now we are about to go operational and send in our first team." Buford paused, catching the eyes of his soldiers with the penetrating, serious gaze of a veteran. "You are the best we have, the best I've ever seen. Physically and mentally, any one team will outmatch any opponent on the planet.

But war is not about fair fights. One soldier is nothing . . .
nothing. Teams win in war; everything else is nonsense.
You all must be more than the sum of the parts. By now,
if you don't know that this Rambo shit is nothing but
Hollywood crap, you haven't learned a thing."

The wind rustled through the scrub bushes that dotted
the landscape as Buford continued.

"This is your final chance to quit. There is no dishonor
in quitting. No one will say a thing if you decide to drop
out now. One team is going operational today; more will
follow in the weeks ahead. All of you are good, but only
one team can be sent on this mission."

Major Travis Barrett's eyes followed Sergeant Major
Buford as he walked in front of the formation, delivering
his morning sermon. The invitation to quit, like the previous invitations that were made every day for the past
150 days, was met by a cold silence. Travis knew the
mettle of his teammates and the rest of the winnowed-
down volunteers who made up the TALON Force. Although the TALON Force had not yet seen action, he
knew that these people were the best special operations
operatives on earth.

More importantly, as the leader of the Eagle Team,
Travis Barrett was sure that his team could take anything
that any enemy could throw at them and come up asking
for more. Without a doubt, his team was the baddest,
toughest, and smartest in the business, and he didn't
doubt for a second that Sergeant Major Buford felt the
same way.

Of course, what made the TALON Force different
from every other special operations outfit was the technology that each member wore, carried, or had embedded in their body. In order to provide the TALON Force
with the latest prototype gear, no expense was spared.
The national laboratories at Sandia and Oak Ridge produced some revolutionary equipment that made the
TALON Force the most deadly special operations team
ever organized.

Sergeant Major Buford stopped in front of Eagle

Team, breaking Travis Barrett's train of thought. "Do you think Eagle Team is ready for combat, Major Barrett?"

Travis Barrett looked to his left and gazed at the eager faces of his teammates. The four men and two women that he glanced at mirrored the confidence and pride that he felt in his heart. The team was a collection of experts that had been hammered into finely honed steel in the last five months of intense, grueling training.

"Send us, Sergeant Major," Travis Barrett replied. "We're ready."

Sergeant Major Buford nodded. "Well, you've got it. General Krauss selected Eagle Team for this mission. You and your team will receive your instructions via your BSD while you're on your way to the objective. This is a critical mission and top secret. You have been authorized global hot pursuit of this target by the National Command Authority.

"Any questions?"

"No, Sergeant Major," Travis replied.

Travis Barrett realized the importance of the mission. Things must be pretty bad for the NCA to grant unlimited hot pursuit. Politicians were never happy to relinquish control.

Then Sergeant Major Buford did something that hadn't been seen at the training camp since the day everyone had arrived: He snapped to attention and saluted Major Barrett.

Travis Barrett proudly returned the salute.

Sergeant Major Buford started to walk away, then suddenly stopped and turned. "And Major Barrett, sir, we want you all back alive. You got that?"

"I read you loud and clear, Sergeant Major," Travis Barrett answered. He executed a crisp about-face and looked at the faces of his team members. "Eagle Team, report to the airfield!"

November 13, 1600 hours,
the mountains of northeast North Korea

Elizabeth Douglas didn't know where she was anymore. Her world had been torn apart and turned upside down. After the hostages had been forced into the helicopters in Egypt, the terrorists had placed canvas bags over their heads and shuttled them from one aircraft to another. Elizabeth and her fellow hostages had lost all sense of time, but she guessed that they had flown for almost twenty-one hours in four different aircraft.

Now they were on the ground again. The terrorists took the bags off their heads and herded them into trucks. The weather in this new location was very cold, and the hostages had found some relief in a pile of old wool blankets and moth-eaten coats that were stashed in the back of each truck.

Elizabeth looked across the narrow divide between the two benches in the back of the dirty truck. A young couple with an eight-month-old baby sat opposite her. The couple was exhausted and dejected. Their baby girl was crying and had been crying for hours. The baby was hungry and had taken the last ounce of formula they had hours ago. To make matters worse, no one had been given any water for almost four hours. There was nothing they could do for the little girl to stop her crying.

Elizabeth then looked at the body that lay in between the two rows of seats, and closed her eyes.

The baby's cries filled the truck.

The temperature, she guessed, was around forty degrees Fahrenheit. She pulled an old blanket over her shoulders as the column of trucks drove along a winding mountain road. Few of the people on the truck had carried clothing that would protect them in this environment. She wondered how her life could change so dramatically, so unexpectedly, in such a short time. Two days ago she was enjoying her second honeymoon in the arms of her loving husband. Now she was a widow, with no time to mourn, and she was watching more people die.

She shivered and tried to make some sense of it all. She half-expected to wake up from this terrible nightmare and find herself at home, in bed, with her wonderful husband still alive.

But she knew that this was real, that this nightmare would not end, and she felt certain that her own death was near.

Twelve scared, dirty tourists sat in the back of the dark green truck, each one quiet in their own thoughts. The rest of the prisoners were in other trucks, moving one behind the other across a nameless, winding road.

Already, the ordeal was taking its toll on the prisoners. One-third of the people who had been captured were elderly. Some of the younger couples, like the one opposite Elizabeth, had children. Elizabeth had seen three children in the group, some as young as the baby opposite her and others as old as twelve. The trip had been particularly devastating on the old and the children.

One older woman—Elizabeth did not know her name—had died right before her eyes. The lady must have suffered a heart attack as the truck bounced across the rough, rocky road. Several of the people on the truck tried to help the old lady, but there was nothing that they could do for her. The old woman grabbed her heart and, in a weak voice, cried out for help. Then, in a slow twitch of agony, her complexion grew pale, her breathing became erratic, and she died.

In the truck, Elizabeth was seated closest to the driver's cab on the left side. When the old lady collapsed, Elizabeth yelled and banged on the back wall of the truck's cab. But the driver ignored her pleas. The truck did not stop, and no one came to help. And so the old woman died. Two of the men in the truck placed her in the space between the two opposing benches and covered her face with a jacket.

The truck groaned as it bounced along the difficult road, slowly climbing steep hills, then precariously descending. At times, Elizabeth thought she would be crushed against the side of the cab as the vehicle plunged down the slope. Several people in the truck seemed to have given up hope. When the old woman died, a few people cried, and the rest turned away. Elizabeth felt that it would only be a matter of time before they would all meet the same fate.

As if to make up for the lack of mourning for the old lady, the baby wailed even louder. The mother, consumed with worry, rocked the little girl and tried to comfort her.

Suddenly, the truck stopped and the passengers jerked forward on the hard wooden bench. Men shouted in harsh, gruff voices from outside the truck.

"Everyone out!"

Elizabeth's nerves grew taut, almost to the breaking point, then snapped back. She expected the worst but realized that she had to do what she could to keep hope alive among her fellow prisoners. The canvas flap at the rear of the truck was thrown open, and a group of tough-looking men with weapons stood outside, gawking at them.

The gate at the back of the truck came down with a heavy clang. "Out, I said. Everyone get out!"

The scared, tired people scrambled off the truck as best they could. No one had any belongings. The terrorists had stripped them of their bags, cameras, watches, jewelry, wallets, and purses long ago. They wore only the clothes and shoes that they had when they were captured and a ragged jacket or coat that was provided to each prisoner when they landed in this cold climate.

The couple with the baby moved carefully to the rear of the truck. As the mother held the child in her arms, the father jumped down and reached up for the baby. A guard pushed him against the rear of the truck, and he fell sideways to the ground.

"Bastard!" the husband screamed. He turned around to confront the guard who had pushed him.

A big man in the black fatigue jacket pointed his short-barreled HK 9 mm carbine in the man's face. "Just give me excuse, you puny piece of shit, and I kill you, your pretty bitch, and your baby."

The father of the little girl leaned against the truck,

frozen with fear, as the terrorist placed the barrel of the gun firmly against the young man's forehead. Beads of sweat rolled down the young man's face.

His wife stood in horror in the truck, watching her husband and the man with the gun, her crying baby girl cradled in her arms. Elizabeth moved over to the mother's side and put her arm around the younger woman to steady her.

"Move there!" the terrorist in the black fatigue jacket ordered, pointing to where the rest of the prisoners were gathering. The man motioned with his weapon. "Women move to left. Men go to right."

Voices mumbled in the group. The guards moved into the group, like sheep dogs among the flock. Reluctantly, the men were separated from their women. A young woman in the group cried out "No!" as she was forced to leave her husband, but she moved all the same.

The father of the little girl moved toward the group of men, casting a forlorn look back at his terrified wife and baby.

Elizabeth took the baby girl as the mother climbed down. Once the mother was on the ground, Elizabeth handed her the baby. The guard who had threatened the father reached out and grabbed the young woman by the chin, inspecting her face.

"I see you again, dearie," he jeered. The young mother stood petrified as the man held her chin. The baby whined.

Elizabeth looked back into the truck and saw the old lady with the jacket over her face lying all alone. She sought an opportunity to draw the man's attention away from the younger woman. "There's a dead woman in the truck."

The man in the black jacket let go of the young woman's chin and looked inside the truck. After a quick glance, he turned around, eyeing Elizabeth. "So what? Move over with rest of them."

Elizabeth climbed down from the truck and moved toward the group of women. She searched her surroundings for clues to determine where they were. She looked up at a gray, overcast sky. She was in the middle of a courtyard of a huge compound. The compound was wedged in between large, barren mountains. Inside the compound she could see several armored vehicles and at least a hundred armed men. A twenty-foot stone wall surrounded the stronghold. The wall appeared to be at least five feet thick. On top of the walls, at each of the four corners of the fort, steel gun turrets bristled with menacing armament. She could see machine guns and what she guessed were missile launchers positioned along the walls.

My God, she thought. *These people are at war with us. This is an army.*

Men in black fatigues carrying guns seemed to appear from every angle. Several of the women and most of the children began to cry. The three mothers in the group tried their best to comfort their children as the prisoners were huddled together in a circle.

Elizabeth was on the outer edge of the female group with Helga. She felt weak and all alone.

Everything got very quiet, except for the crying children. Terrek, the man who had killed her husband, walked up between the circles of men and women. Terrek had the same evil look, the exact same sinister smile as he did in Egypt. He walked with an air of confidence that was fueled by pure arrogance and hate.

Elizabeth stared at him. Suddenly she felt a real reason to live. She wanted to survive to see Terrek get what he deserved.

"Whether you live or die depends on your willingness to cooperate," Terrek said in his Eastern-European-accented English. "You are prisoners of the Brotherhood. Let this be perfectly clear. I will not hesitate to shoot anyone who does not obey my commands instantly."

Elizabeth continued to glare at the man. *If I were a man, I would rip out your goddamned throat*, she thought. *Hell, I may do it anyway.* But she knew that she wouldn't get two steps toward Terrek before one of his goons would drop her in her tracks with a bullet to the head.

"You will be here for about a week," Terrek continued. "If you cooperate, I will free you unharmed. Is that clear?"

The people didn't answer. A few nodded their heads. Some suddenly looked relieved, happy to cling to any scrap of hope that was offered. Others just stared at the ground and shivered in the cold air.

"What about the dead woman on the truck?" Elizabeth shouted. She was suddenly surprised at the force of her own voice, surprised that she had spoken up at all.

Terrek looked at Elizabeth, sizing her up. In spite of the blood on her clothes, Elizabeth had the appearance and strong-willed character that made her alluring to men.

"What is that? A woman of courage?" Terrek held his eyes on her for a few seconds.

Elizabeth felt violated by his gaze. Her hatred of Terrek burned even brighter. She looked away, unwilling to stare at the man who had murdered her husband and might now murder so many more.

"That was unfortunate. We need every one of you," Terrek answered, then looked at one of his officers. "Move them into the Citadel and place them into the holding pens. Anyone who doesn't wish to follow these instructions can join that old lady lying in the truck."

The big man in the black jacket nodded and shouted orders to his men. In a few seconds, the hostages moved obediently toward the big metal doors of the massive square building that Terrek had called the Citadel. With a loud groan of metal on metal, the fifteen-foot blast-proof doors opened as the hostages approached. The men and their guards entered first, followed by the women and children and more guards.

Elizabeth moved with the women and children down a well-lit hallway. The inside of the Citadel was a maze of corridors filled with offices and busy people, but at least it was warmer inside than in the courtyard. As she walked down the hallway, she read the words to a sign that was printed in English and Korean. The sign had an arrow and the word: Laboratory.

The men were forced down a corridor to the left. The women were herded to the right, then down a stairway toward a set of cells. As she trudged along with the rest of the women prisoners, Elizabeth Douglas doubted that she would ever see the outside world again.

Chapter Eight

The blood red blossom of war with a heart of fire.
                                        —Alfred Tennyson

November 14, 1828 hours,
high over the Pacific Ocean, south of Kamchatka

Major Travis Barrett sat in the command drop capsule of the specially designed X-37 rocket plane that was hurtling through the upper atmosphere faster than he wanted to think about. During the past hour, he and his team had reviewed the latest intelligence update concerning Terrek and the Brotherhood. After viewing the briefing, he was convinced that there wasn't a meaner group of thugs and psychos on the planet right now than Terrek's Brotherhood.

The latest intelligence reports indicated that Terrek's men were headed for a secret weapons research plant near Vladivostok. The Rybacky Weapons Research Complex was supposed to be heavily guarded by the Russian security forces, but no one knew what the Russians were guarding there. As a result, Eagle Team would deploy to Rybacky and check it out.

The trick was for Eagle Team to infiltrate Russian territory, enter a heavily guarded weapons research facility, stop Terrek's men from taking whatever it was they were trying to take, and not let the Russians know that U.S. forces were on Russian soil. Piece of cake.

Travis Barrett only hoped that his team arrived before Terrek's men did. Time, he knew, was one thing that was working against them. In this race, the Brotherhood held the initiative and had a big head start.

A quick scan of his situation map depicted the precise location of Russian military forces in the area. If the

Russians were expecting a terrorist attack, the major mused, the deployment of their forces surely didn't show it. A few small Russian military camps, situated near the Rybacky Complex, were conducting normal garrison operations. An infantry unit, the 177th Motorized Rifle Battalion (MRB), was the nearest ground force and was located ten miles east of the Rybacky plant. Russian air forces were just as scattered and on standard alert status. Su-25 Ground Attack Bombers and MIG-29 Air Superiority Fighters were also positioned in routine peacetime locations at airfields in the Vladivostok region. *Lyotnaya Polye Sorok Tree,* or Military Airfield 43, was the nearest transport aircraft base, and it contained only three military aircraft.

Russia. There was never another country like Russia. *God, how I hate Russia,* he reflected. He remembered his last time in Russia, during that terrible, hellish night in Grozny. The cold, fear and confusion swept over him again like a bad dream.

Back in 1994, when he was a young, eager Green Beret captain, he was assigned as a secret military observer from the United States Army to the Russian military. In those heady days that rang with the promise of democracy for Russia, the Russians wanted to improve military-to-military contacts with the United States. But the hardliners in the Russian military didn't like Americans, so Captain Barrett's mission was kept a secret to everyone but the most informed Russian and American officials. His mission was to observe the Russians as they conducted a brief peacekeeping mission in a minor province called Chechnya. The Russians wanted to show the Americans that their military was still capable of instilling fear in the local ruffians of the dismantled Soviet empire.

The only problem was that someone had forgotten to tell the Chechen ruffians that the Russians should be feared. A century of hatred of all things Russian had filled the Chechen people with the determination to resist. The Chechens harbored no illusions about the real purpose of the Russian peacekeeping forces. Most

Chechens believed that the 40,000 Russian soldiers advancing on their country were coming to grind the Chechen people into dust.

To provide for a ringside seat for their American observer, Travis Barrett was assigned to a twelve-man Russian special forces team, *Spetsialnoye Nazhachenuiye,* or Spetznaz team, led by a Captain Krayevski.

The Russian Spetznaz were not happy about hosting an American officer, but they had their orders, and they obeyed. Someone at the highest levels, probably Defense Minister Grachev himself, had ordered the Spetznaz to keep an eye on the American but to allow him to observe everything that went on. Grachev bragged that this whole episode with the Chechens would be over in a week, that a single paratroop battalion was all that was needed to put these gangsters in their place. Grachev expected that the American captain would witness a triumphal Russian victory and report the prowess of the new Russian Army back to the Pentagon.

The Spetznaz were Russia's equivalent of Green Berets. Travis's Spetznaz team moved in two BTR wheeled armored personnel carriers with six men in each BTR. It was obvious to Travis that he was as welcome as an IRS investigator at an accountant's convention.

Nevertheless, he did his best to get to know his Russians. In a few days, speaking in excellent Russian and giving away several boxes of American cigarettes, he managed to make a few friends. Travis didn't smoke—being a good Texan he liked a chew every now and again—but every Russian he met did smoke, and there was no better way to break the ice than to offer his Russian friends a Marlboro.

In the meantime, the advance into Chechnya slowed to a crawl. Grachev's plan looked great on paper, but what looks good on paper often fails to measure up in action. The friction of war quickly twisted the Russian peacekeeping effort into anything but a triumphal road march. Instead of being welcomed as liberators, as the Russian generals had told their troops to expect, Chechen women and children blocked the roads and stalled the Russian tank columns. Chechen snipers shot out the tires of the armored vehicles and then picked off the drivers. The muddy roads to Grozny, Chechnya's capital, were soon clogged with stalled tanks and stuck BTRs. It took the Russians fifteen days to travel less than 120 kilometers, but they finally made it to Grozny.

On New Year's Eve, Travis's Spetznaz team was attached to the *Maikop* Rifle Brigade for the movement into Grozny. One look at the hastily assembled assault force, and he could sense a disaster in the making. He began to wonder whether he had been sent as an exchange officer because he was the most qualified or the most expendable. The Spetznaz troopers grew sullen as the operation soured, and they made him feel as welcome as a whore in church.

As a professional soldier, Travis Berrett was not impressed with the Spetznaz. In fact, he felt damn sorry for them. He quickly realized that the term *elite* was applied loosely to these guys. They were definitely loyal to their unit, but loyalty couldn't make up for their lack of training. The level of expertise of each individual soldier was not what it should be in an elite special operations unit. Most of this, he knew, was not the fault of the Spetznaz soldiers. The Russian Army was in deep financial and organizational trouble, and every unit was feeling the pinch. Most importantly, it was very hard to keep good men in this kind of business when they hadn't been paid for six months.

The *Maikop* Brigade was much worse off than the Spetznaz troopers. Limited training, no spare parts, bad food, terrible leaders, and sagging morale didn't exactly set the perfect conditions for the start of a major military operation. The brigade had been hastily filled with new recruits. Some were not even issued ammunition for the advance into the city for fear that they might shoot friendly civilians. Riding in their heavily armed BMP infantry fighting vehicles, BTR armored personnel carriers, and reinforced with a battalion of tanks, the mechanized rifle brigade made its way into the center of Grozny.

Travis Barrett remembered the long, cold ride down

the eerie deserted streets of Grozny. The Russian brigade advanced along *Mayakovskiy* Street without encountering any organized resistance, and then moved directly to the presidential palace. For a while, it seemed that the tanks had scared the Chechens away and that the show of force would work.

The Spetznaz team stood in the open top of their BTR armored car. The BTR was equipped with a 14.5 mm machine gun, but was thinly armored. Travis stood with the others directly across from Captain Vladimir Krayevski, the commander of the Spetznaz team.

Travis scanned the buildings lining both sides of the road that led to the presidential palace in Grozny, an old Soviet administration building that had become the seat of power of the separatists. As the Russian armored column entered the open square in front of the presidential palace, he felt a strange sensation. He had learned to pay attention to this feeling in the Gulf War and in Somalia, and it had saved his life. Now, the short hairs on the back of his neck were standing up, and he was worried. What he knew about the Chechens told him that they would not give up their capital without a fight.

The long column of Russian armored vehicles churned down the street, one following the other. This was too easy. He looked at Krayevski. The Russian captain silently eyed Travis Barrett as if they were both fighters who would meet soon in a boxing match.

Travis couldn't shake off his dark mood. He spat a stream of tobacco juice. "This doesn't look right," he said in Russian.

Sergeant Sokolov laughed, one of Travis's cigarettes hanging from his lips. "The Chechens are bandits and cowards. They wouldn't dare fight the Soviet Army."

Travis shook his head. Yeah, Spetznaz guys always said Soviet Army, not *Russian* Army. For most of them, the Berlin Wall had never fallen and the glories of the Soviet Union were something that would return.

Captain Krayevski chuckled along with Sokolov and scolded the American. "If you're afraid, Captain Barrett, we can drop you off at the next corner. I've never liked spies anyway."

Travis Barrett shook his head, but he chambered a round in his Barretta 9 mm pistol, his one link with the U.S. Army. *"Nyet,"* he replied, shooting a cold glare at Krayevski for the insult. He was in it this far; he'd go the extra mile to see how these Russian cowboys operated.

Bad decision.

Travis's icy reply, followed by the chambering of a round in his pistol, seemed to unnerve Krayevski. "Stay alert. Lock and load," the Russian captain ordered. The Spetznaz team replied instantly, a model of military efficiency. Bolts were cocked, and each rifle chambered a round. Every gun turned out. Every man scanned the windows and alleys.

The column stopped right in front of the presidential palace. Vehicles moved forward and halted in an accordion effect, bunching up next to each other. Then there was nothing. No orders. No commands. Travis listened to the sound of tank engines idling in the cold, December air. They waited.

The rest of the column stretched at various intervals between the presidential palace to the jump-off point, a string of armored vehicles reaching nearly ten kilometers long. Many of the Russian conscripts were sleeping, exhausted after days of hard driving and hurry-up-and-wait operations. Security was nonexistent. Only the Spetznaz crew in the BTR armored personnel carrier with Travis Barrett seemed to be taking the operation seriously.

Travis's sixth sense began to work overtime. He knew, just as sure as the inevitability of death and taxes, that there was going to be a fight.

Fifteen minutes later, his premonition came true. The quiet night was abruptly interrupted when the lead tank was rocked by a terrific explosion. Almost at the same moment, tanks and infantry carriers at the rear of the column erupted in flames as Chechens appeared from every window, every alley, and blasted the invaders with rocket propelled grenades.

The sky suddenly filled with the green tracers of machine gun bullets. The bullets smashed against the sides of armored vehicles and ricocheted off into the night. Two vehicles in front of Travis's BTR, the ramp of a BMP infantry fighting vehicle dropped to the ground. The Russian infantry stumbled out of their armored personnel carriers right into the fire. Before the men in the front row could take a step forward, bullets slapped into them. Body parts were torn away and blood sprayed inside the cramped metal crew compartment. Men crumpled to the ground and screamed. Those behind tried to pull away from the open ramp, but the bullets found them, clanged against the metal sides of the infantry carrier, and splattered guts and brains against the cold steel.

More explosions echoed in the plaza. The Chechens were shouting now, a surging, primeval shout . . . the shout of victory. Travis Barrett hated that sound. He had heard it before in Somalia. He felt that horrible feeling, the churning in his stomach that accompanies the fear you feel in battle.

All around them, men were falling and tanks and armored cars were erupting into flames. By sheer luck, the Chechens had not hit Barrett's BTR. Captain Krayevski fired his AK-74, spraying wildly at Chechens scurrying in and out of the shadows. Krayevski's gunner fixed the armored car's 14.5 mm machine gun. It hammered away at the Chechens and seemed to be the only gun firing at the enemy. Barrett felt a sick, sinking feeling in his stomach as he realized that only a few of the other Russians were firing their weapons. Most were running away in panic.

The ground shook as a tank exploded nearby. Travis saw the tank's turret lying upside down near its tracks. The hull was burning like a torch. A Russian, bathed in fire, ran a death race between the armored vehicles until he was shot dead by Chechen snipers. Chechen fighters rushed between the charred vehicles, gunning down Russian soldiers who were running away. A Chechen threw a Molotov cocktail into one BTR and the young, confused Russian boys inside burned like matchsticks.

Sergeant Sokolov spun back inside the BTR, his face

shot away by a Chechen assault rifle. Blood and pieces of Sokolov's brains splattered inside the BTR. Travis took Sokolov's place and aimed his pistol. A Chechen stood twenty meters away, ready to launch a rocket propelled grenade at the BTR. Two shots from the American's 9 mm pistol dropped the Chechen to the ground, and the grenade smashed harmlessly against the wall of a nearby building.

"That is how to kill Chechens." Captain Krayevski nodded at Travis, then screamed to the BTR driver, "Move out! Go south. Head toward the railway station."

The night air was thick with tracer bullets, whizzing metal, and explosions. The scattered bodies of Russian soldiers—many burned and disfigured beyond recognition—lay everywhere. The Spetznaz BTR ran over the dead and dying in a frenzied dash to break away. All around, armored vehicles were exploding.

In the pandemonium, some Russians abandoned their vehicles and fled on foot. There was a crazy game of hide and seek, with Russian soldiers hiding in apartments, bunkers, and even toilets, and the Chechens hunting them with swords, knives, and pistols. Travis heard on the radio that the commander of the 81st was killed and more than half its men killed or wounded. Only a few Russians escaped the slaughter.

The memory of that night remained a horrible, painful nightmare. Somehow, Travis and his Spetznaz crew fought their way to the railroad station. At first they raced through alleys in their BTR, then, reaching a dead end, they abandoned the vehicle and ran through buildings to the train station. They shot at everything that moved or stood in their way with the desperation of trapped animals. Finally, they found a dank, dripping cellar near the station. Here they hid from death, low on ammunition and hope, for over eighteen tense hours, as Chechen hunting parties searched for Russians to kill.

Late the next day, two Russian airborne battalions from the 106th and 76th Airborne Divisions broke through the Chechen defenses and seized the Grozny-Tovarnaya railroad station. Travis never thought he would be so happy to see Russian Airborne troops. He, Captain Krayevski, and two Spetznaz soldiers were rescued along with six other survivors of the 131st Brigade and 81st MRR.

Travis later found out that the *Maikop* 131st Brigade lost 20 out of 26 tanks, 102 of 120 infantry fighting vehicles, and all six *Tungas* self-propelled antiaircraft vehicles. Only ten men and one officer—Captain Krayevski—survived. For security reasons, Travis Barrett was not listed with the survivors. Quickly whisked away from the fighting, four days later he was safely back in the U.S., happy to be alive. His short tour with the Russian Army officially ended as the bloody Russian debacle in Grozny and the bloody war in Chechnya dragged on until the Russians, on the verge of defeat, withdrew in 1996.

"Major Barrett," Sam Wong yelled over the sound of the aircraft's engines. "It's almost time. We'll be at our exit point in fifteen minutes."

Travis Barrett nodded, relieved to be back in the present.

Sarah Greene sat next to him, strapped into her drop capsule. This was her first jump from the X-37. Travis Barrett gave her a thumbs up, and she smiled a tight-lipped grin and nodded. He could smell the tension in the air and turned to speak to her.

"I hate these drop capsules," Sarah said. "I'd like to find the guys who designed these damn things and make them take a ride in them, and let them see what it's like to fall through the upper atmosphere in a ceramic egg."

"Remember, the TALON psychiatrist said we may feel trapped when we're inside them, almost claustrophobic, but there ain't no other way to exit the Air Force's newest and fastest top-secret aircraft," Travis explained. "Without the drop capsules, the rapid deceleration we experience upon exiting the rocket plane would tear us to pieces."

"I'm really beginning to enjoy these jumps," Stan Powczuk said over the comm net, as if mocking Travis's words to Sarah. "It's better than sex."

Travis turned to Powczuk and shook his head in disgust.

"You must really suck at it, then," Jenny Olsen chided.

"Hell, I'll take sex any day," Jack DuBois answered. "Any offers?"

"Jack, watch your language. What would your mama say?" Jenny joked.

"Hey, let's leave my mama out of this," Jack replied.

"Major, next time we have a mission, I volunteer to fly commercial and act as the advance party," Olsen offered.

"No way, Olsen. You're too eager. In TALON Force, everybody drops." Travis smiled and pulled his seat harness straps snug.

The engine noise changed as the aircraft started to decelerate for the jump.

"Major Barrett," Sarah said, "Jenny has a point. Why do we have to fly in this damn thing?"

Hunter Blake saw his opening and answered as if he were briefing an audience of visiting congressmen. "Ladies and gentlemen, this is the fastest means of delivery on earth. The X-37 Reusable Advanced Hypersonic Rocket Plane can rapidly deliver a TALON Force team anywhere on the planet in only a few hours. The X-37 rocket plane carries seven fully equipped TALON Force troopers—like us—and ejects them in specially designed drop capsules. The drop capsules, fondly called eggshells by those of us who use them, protect the jumper from the shock of exiting the aircraft at high speed and altitude."

"Oh, please, tell me more, O aged one," Sarah kidded.

"Aged? Who's aged?" Blake continued, "As I was saying, the X-37—the only American aircraft that yours truly has never piloted—is approximately seventy-five feet long, has a twenty-eight-foot wingspan and is twelve feet tall from the bottom of the fuselage to the top of the tail. Two Fastrac rocket engines power the X-37. The rocket plane is carried piggyback style to high altitude by an L-1011 carrier aircraft before the rocket engines are ignited and the rocket plane separates from the L-1011. The X-37 can achieve altitudes of up to 250,000 feet—or 50 miles up—and speeds up to Mach 8, or eight times faster than the speed of sound. Following the exit of the eggshells, the X-37 accelerates to Mach 8, achieves low earth orbit, and returns to a designated runway where it lands horizontally, like an airplane."

"Bravo! And you didn't even take a breath!" Jenny Olsen joked. "But, I don't care what you say, Hunter, I still don't enjoy falling to earth in an egg. Why can't we just HALO in?"

"HALO requires that we exit from an aircraft inside or close to enemy airspace," Travis Barrett answered. "That's okay if we're going up against an unsophisticated enemy. But against the Russians or Chinese, we need a stealthier method."

"But pretty boy here didn't describe the best part," Powczuk interjected, taking over Hunter Blake's monologue. "Right before arriving at the target area, the X-37 slows down to a speed that will permit the ejection of the specially designed ceramic drop capsules—kinda like now. The troopers are shot out of the rear of the aircraft like a hen squeezing out an egg. The eggs fly through the atmosphere, guided to their target by computerized fins. The shells are treated with a special chemical that is activated once the drop capsules are ejected from the aircraft. At a designated altitude, the chemically treated shell breaks apart into pieces too small to be recognizable. The jumper, strapped into a specially designed parachute, then free-falls to the target area and opens his or her parachute at low altitude."

"The perfect covert entry. The X-37 flies too high to be detected by radar, and the drop capsules are too stealthy to be picked up as we enter normal airspace. What could be simpler?" Jenny added. She looked over at Sam Wong who was just short of green from airsickness. "So, Sam, how's it going?"

Sam sat frozen in his egg and didn't answer. Travis looked at Wong, then sensed the steady vibration of the Fastrac engines as they decelerated to execute the drop. In a few minutes it would all begin.

"Five minutes and counting," a loud female voice gen-

tly echoed in the receiver embedded right below his right ear. Each member of Eagle Team received the message.

Travis Barrett looked at Powczuk, Blake, and DuBois. They were professionals; steady and experienced. Powczuk gave Travis a quick, confident nod. Jenny Olsen, who seemed to have nerves of steel, smiled as if she was on an amusement park ride. Captain Sarah Greene shot another nervous smile at Barrett, trying to hide her apprehensions about jumping, but Barrett knew she was a steady type, the kind of person you could count on in a pinch. She would calm down once they were on the ground.

Sam Wong, on the other hand, looked like he was about to puke. "Sam, are you going to be all right?"

Sam looked to his left at the major, his face a mask of classic motion sickness and nausea. Sam spent most of his life living in virtual reality connected with the most intelligent supercomputer in the United States. Reality was always a shock to Sam.

"Hang in there, Sammy! Just a little bit longer," Jack offered.

Travis quickly accessed his team's medical vital signs. Sam Wong's heart was racing with anxiety. The Eagle Team commander watched as biosensors in Wong's smart suite registered his nausea and automatically injected Sam with just the right amount of Dramamine to help him get through the jump.

"One minute to jump," the voice of the unseen pilot announced over their comm net.

"Prepare for drop," Travis ordered calmly, as if conducting a parade ground drill.

Each trooper tugged at a handle, which locked down their protective eggshell covering. A flight technician moved from eggshell to eggshell, checking the connections. He arrived at Travis's capsule last.

"They are all set, ready for the jump, sir," he announced. "Good luck."

Travis nodded. The technician pulled down the cover and sealed the major's capsule. Travis was now cut off from the outside world as the eggshell covered his head, forming the top of the sphere. Each of the drop capsules was configured with special gravity-rack suspension belts that counteracted the high acceleration and deceleration forces encountered when dropping to the earth's surface. The G-racks allowed each trooper to survive forces up to thirty times the force of Earth's gravity.

Travis Barrett took a deep breath, then contacted the pilot over his comm net. "Pilot. Eagle Team, ready for drop."

"Let's kick some butt!" Powczuk's steady voice announced.

"And everybody comes home," DuBois added.

Travis nodded, then added a silent amen. He knew the deal. *Attitude* was important to the TALON Force. You had to have attitude in his business. You had to believe in each other to throw yourself through the atmosphere in a drop capsule, enter a hostile country with six teammates, and fight against impossible odds.

Travis checked each trooper's vital signs again. Eagle Team was ready—even Sam. Travis Barrett knew that members of the team understood they might be wounded, and they might die, but they would do it facing the enemy, fighting as they went, and with the knowledge that their fellow troopers wouldn't let them down. In the TALON Force it was important—very important—that nobody was left behind. Everybody drops! Everybody fights! Dead or alive, everybody comes home.

Travis Barrett said a silent prayer, the one he always prayed before a mission: "Give us the courage to fight and win, and the faith to die rather than quit."

A green light flashed across his battle sensor screen. His stomach jumped into his throat as the capsule was launched out of the X-37. The egg buffeted and bounced as it skipped through the thin air, hurtling toward the ground.

Travis concentrated on his tactical display, trying to keep his mind busy. The BSD eyepiece created the illusion of a three-dimensional grid in front of his eyes. A three-dimensional map at the bottom depicted the terrain below the team. Seven blue dots, falling from the sky, like embers from a Fourth of July fireworks display, depicted Eagle Team's descent.

He felt the capsule warm as he hurtled through the upper atmosphere. Then, in his receiver, he heard several of the team members reciting familiar words. An electric feeling shot up his spine, and his heart swelled with pride. In a few seconds, everyone in the team, even Sam Wong, had joined in. As his capsule shook and began to break up at the designated altitude, he found himself shouting the words that his team members were all chanting in unison.

"Lord, give me what no one asks for—not wealth, nor success, nor even health. People ask you so often for all that. You cannot have any left. Give me insecurity and disquietude; I want turmoil and brawl. And if you should give them to me, once and for all, let me be sure to have them always, for I will not always have the courage to ask for them. Then, most of all, give me victory!"

2015 hours, at the remote Rybacky Weapons Research Complex, northwest of Vladivostok, Russia

The snow fell gently in the cold Russian night. Private Ivan Ivanovich Kazak stood outside his small wooden guard shack, stamping his feet in the early morning hours. It had not been a good day. In fact, Ivan could not remember a good day since he was conscripted in the Russian army nearly thirteen months ago. Every day was a trial of survival. His unit, the 135th Security Battalion, Vladivostok Military District, was filled with misfits, malcontents, and complainers. His duty was a far cry from the heroic tales that his grandfather had told about the Great Patriotic War against the Fascists.

Let's face it, Ivan thought. *Life in the Russian Army is shit.*

In the old days of the great Red Army, there was discipline, pride, and sacrifice for the cause. That army had absorbed the terrifying might of Hitler's Wehrmacht from 1941 to 1943, blunting the German blitzkrieg at Stalingrad, pushing the invader back throughout Mother Russia and marching on, inexorably, to take Berlin. Today, the Russian army was a sad shadow of that once-proud force. Underpaid, poorly led, and badly trained, the modern Russian Army spent most of its time just trying to hold itself together. Today's Russian soldiers went for months without pay, good food, or training. Ivan lived on a diet of cabbage soup or potatoes, only there were usually no potatoes. As a consequence of not being paid, he and his mates were ordered to go to Vladivostok on weekends and beg for money. If they did not return with at least ten rubles each, the older soldiers in his unit would beat them.

Such was the deplorable state of the Russian Army. When he wasn't pulling guard duty or working in the battalion's vegetable garden, he was out on the streets of Vladivostok, trying to earn a few extra kopecks for his unit and himself to survive the harsh winter that was sure to come.

Ivan Ivanovich stood outside his guard shack stamping his feet, trying to keep from freezing. Winter had come early to the Vladivostok region, and the dark green greatcoat that he wore was barely warm enough to keep out the winter chill.

Things were so bad in the 135th Security Battalion that Ivan sometimes thought about deserting. Several of his fellow soldiers, friends who had gone to school with him in his hometown of Volgograd, talked about the same thing. In spite of the talk, he didn't believe that any one of them would actually desert. Their two-year enlistment was more than halfway over. Why should they risk ruining the rest of their lives? How could he face his grandfather who had fought at Stalingrad? With only eleven months left to go, he felt that he could make it, even if this meant selling a few odds and ends from the government equipment stores in order to make ends meet.

The wind picked up, swirling in the cold night. Standing his post was lonely duty. His mission was to observe a snowy one-track road that led into the Top Secret research facility and deny access to anyone who did not have the proper security clearance. Ivan did not know what was in the compound; he only knew that it was secret. In fact, the compound was so secret that it was not even listed on maps, and the soldiers were forbidden to mention where they worked or what they did.

Security, however, was extremely lax for such a sensitive facility. The electric fence that surrounded the compound had been turned off for lack of electricity. The guard dogs that were supposed to be patrolling the perimeter outside the fence had been let loose, or, as some of Ivan's friends joked, had found their way into the battalion's soup pots.

The 135th Security Battalion consisted of seventeen officers and three hundred riflemen on paper, but this was on paper only. In reality, the battalion had six officers and could muster no more than two hundred men on a good day. Most of the officers were drunk by four in the afternoon, as alcoholism was rampant in the Russian Army. The demands of these shortcomings caused everyone to pull extra duty. It became a hardship merely to accomplish even the simplest tasks. The special regulations pertaining to his guard post demanded, for instance, four armed guards changed every four hours. Instead, he guarded the post alone, and would be relieved after six long, cold hours.

To impress intruders with the seriousness of the security at the facility, Ivan carried an AK-74 assault rifle with thirty rounds of 5.54 mm ammunition in the banana shaped magazine. The 74 had replaced the simple but lethal AK-47 rifle over twenty years earlier. His orders were not to let anyone in without the proper red security pass. If anyone attempted to get into his gate without the red security pass, he was to use whatever force was necessary to stop them. Sometimes he wondered what he would do if thirty-one intruders tried to enter without authority.

He had stopped guessing what was inside the compound several months ago. All Ivan knew was that the gate opened every morning at 0800 for a bus full of civilian technicians, and opened again at 1600 to let them out. He never talked to any of the technicians and they seldom acknowledged that he even existed.

Tonight was different. Tonight the technicians had stayed and were working through the night. Ivan didn't know why.

The telephone line that ran from his shack to the central guard post was checked every two hours. Today, the telephone was working, which made Ivan happy. This was a very good thing. He knew that tonight his friend Oleg was on duty in the command center. He planned to call Oleg and remind him to bring him a cup of hot soup. Oleg was a good lad and an old friend from Volgograd. He hoped that there would be potatoes in the soup tonight.

In the meantime, Ivan stood his post, stamping his feet, and waited for his duty to end.

The snow fell lightly in tiny, wet flakes. The ground was covered in about a foot of snow, and Ivan thought of the snowy afternoons after school when he and his friends would sled down a steep slope near the Volga River. If the sledder wasn't careful, he might crash into the river dike that paralleled the cold, deep Volga. Luckily, Ivan had never crashed into the wall, but he had seen some of his less fortunate friends smack into it, tumble off their sled, and fall in the snow to the laughter and jeers of their comrades.

Those were happy times, Ivan thought, and he felt the old pangs of homesickness that were the eternal curse of the soldier.

Ivan reached up and took off his warm fur cap. With his rifle slung barrel down over his right shoulder, he brushed the snow off his cap and placed the hat back on his head. Bored from the monotony of guard duty, he decided to go inside and try the telephone. Maybe he could convince Oleg to bring him some potato and cabbage soup just a little earlier than usual. Ivan opened the door, stepped inside the small guard shack, and reached for the telephone.

He didn't see the three vehicles coming up the road,

without their headlights on, moving quietly toward his guard shack. As Ivan talked to Oleg on the telephone, he didn't see the two men come up to his guard post and silently open the door. As Ivan put the phone back on the receiver, he turned around to find two men in black uniforms and ski masks pointing pistols at his head. Each man wore night vision goggles and an earpiece microphone setup for internal group communications.

One of the men spoke in clear Russian. "Call the central guard desk to open the gates, and I'll let you live."

Ivan nodded. He felt the AK-74 slung over the shoulder. He knew the rifle was locked and loaded, the safety on. He knew this was the moment of truth, the moment where he would have to choose his life or his friends. He thought about the stories that his grandfather had told him about the great Red Army, about the heroes of Stalingrad, Kursk, and Berlin. He remembered the medals that were proudly displayed on his grandfather's wall. He remembered his friend Oleg, and he realized that he could not betray his friends.

Ivan turned toward the phone, then quickly reached for his assault rifle. It was the last thing that he ever did. The two men dropped the young Russian guard with two brutally devastating shots to the head.

"We are in," Lee said into his microphone. Lee nodded to Ratchek, his second-in-command. "Commence the attack."

"Vulture!" Ratchek whispered into his transmitter, repeating the code word several times.

The black uniformed commandos quickly filed out of the trucks.

"Silence the guards. No noise," Lee ordered quietly. "No prisoners."

Just as they had rehearsed, snipers ran to the four guard towers and quickly shot the guards with silenced weapons. Other soldiers moved forward to place command-directed antipersonnel mines at the approaches to the compound, in the case of a Russian counterattack. Several squads set up RPK 7.62 mm machine guns to cover the approaches along the road that led to the entrance to the complex. Other men took out the guards one at a time, before the Russians could sound the alarm.

Dark figures ran to their positions near the entrance that led to the underground facility. Within record time, and the entire Russian security force on the surface had been killed. No alarm had been sounded.

Lee grinned. In the green-tinted, eerie glow of his night vision goggles, Lee surveyed the compound. The thing he wanted, the prize he would secure, was underground.

The thick steel doors at the entrance to the underground facility were shut tight. Lee ordered two men carrying satchels to open the doors. The men ran to the doors, attached explosive charges at critical places, and sounded the warning.

"Demolitions in six seconds," one of the men sounded over the voice net.

All the terrorists near the doors dropped down and waited for the blast. A sharp, loud explosion flashed, blasting the doors open. Without hesitation, Lee's men charged into the smoke-filled entrance, firing as they advanced. They met a wounded Russian officer who was stumbling toward the door. The lead terrorist cut him down with a short burst from his submachine gun, then continued the assault down the dark hallway. Emergency lights flickered in the hallway and a Klaxon sounded a screaming alarm. More stunned Russian soldiers appeared in the smoke-filled hallway and were immediately shot by the attackers.

Within minutes after blasting through the doors, the terrorists reached the inner security perimeter. At this point, an alert Russian soldier manning a machine gun in a bulletproof glass pillbox fired into the advancing terrorists. The first three terrorists were sliced in half by the Russian's fire. Within seconds, however, the terrorists behind the bodies of their comrades launched 40 mm grenades at the pillbox. The grenades ripped through the bulletproof glass and plastered the Russian soldier's guts against the far wall of the bunker.

"Commander Lee," Ratchek said, touching his hand to his earpiece, "our helicopters have landed on the surface of the compound. Everything is on schedule."

"Excellent. Assault team with me to the laboratory," Lee ordered into his throat microphone.

More terrorists raced forward on Lee's order. Another set of locked steel doors blocked their approach. A second demolition team moved up to the doors and placed a small explosive charge on the doors' lock mechanism. Again there was a flash and explosion as the doors were blown inward. Within seconds of the blast, Lee's men were racing through the doorway. They were now inside, in the center of the most deadly germ warfare research facility in the world.

A Russian colonel, with a telephone transmitter in one hand and an AK-74 in the other, fired and killed the first terrorist to come through the door. The second black-clad figure fired and placed half a dozen holes in the officer's chest. The Russian colonel jerked against the wall and crumpled to the ground.

The black-clad figure rushed inside and knocked the telephone off the wall with the metal stock of his submachine gun. More of Lee's men entered. A dozen startled civilian technicians inside the room hid behind desks and filing cabinets. Lee's men quickly dragged them from their hideouts, tied the technicians' hands behind their backs with plastic zip cord, gagged them with tape, and placed hoods over their heads. The prisoners were quickly huddled into a group and led out of the compound to the helicopters.

Lee walked into the room, filled with the arrogance of a man who has trained at a difficult task for months and has now accomplished it. He walked over to the Russian officer who had just been hit and turned his bloody body over with the toe of his boot.

The Russian colonel was still alive, but just barely.

Lee placed his boot on the man's neck and watched the life drain from the man's eyes. In a few seconds, the Russian was dead.

"What a pathetic excuse for a soldier," Lee announced. With a quick jerk of his right arm, he signaled for the two men behind him to move forward. Ratchek stood to Lee's side with his submachine gun at the ready.

The men moved forward and placed their weapons on a table near an inner entrance that was labeled Restricted—Biohazard Level 6 in Cyrillic.

One of the terrorists carried a briefcase, slung across his back with a web strap. He placed the briefcase on the table and quickly donned a biocontagion suit hanging on the wall. The other man helped the first zip up the suit, then assisted the man in putting on an air mask and rubber gloves. The second man hooked up the air mask to a foot-long air canister at the back of the suit.

Covered from head to toe in this airtight outfit, the man picked up the silver, metal briefcase in his left hand and walked up to the door. Carefully, he punched in a twenty-three-number combination.

The door opened, and a red light flashed. The lab, which dealt in the deadliest biotoxins on the planet, was designed to make sure that these lethal experiments did not get out by mistake. Lee knew that the entrance to that room contained one of the most deadly viruses known to man. He could see that the far inner door was still tightly sealed.

The man in the biocontagion suit stepped inside. The outside door closed, and the red light stopped flashing. Through a window in the outer door, Lee could see the man turn and lock the outer door. The man in the suit then walked over to an inner door. He punched in another combination, but this time, nothing happened.

Lee glared at the man inside the containment area. It was clear that the man inside was nervous and obviously having problems with the combination. Lee pointed his finger at the man as if to say, "Try again."

The man in the suit punched in the combination a second time. His bulky gloves made the process difficult, and he took care this time to press each number precisely. Finally, after the last number of the combination was entered, the inner door opened.

The man looked back at Lee. Lee nodded, stern-faced.

The man walked into the biohazard containment area, and the door automatically shut behind him. Lee could not see through this door, as it had no window, only the words in Cyrillic in bright red letters: Extremely Hazardous. Biological Warfare Samples. No Unauthorized Entrance.

The time ticked by. The door did not open.

"Maybe he's dead," Ratchek suggested. Ratchek's huge forearms, each decorated with an ornate oriental Dragon tattoo, grasped his Carl Gustav submachine gun and pointed toward the door. "Maybe the bug got him?"

Lee shot a deadly glance at Ratchek. "I pay you to kill, not think."

The big, muscular man dropped his eyes and stood in the room in silence, waiting, as the sound of the Klaxon screamed in the hallway. After a few agonizing minutes the inner door opened.

A red light flashed and a siren went off inside the room as the man in the containment chamber activated the decontamination procedures. The air rushed past him, and a strong burst of infrared light swept the chamber.

After a few minutes, the outer door opened.

"Did you find it?" Lee demanded.

The man in the white biocontagion suit nodded, then took off his protective hood and smiled. "Yes. Specimen 175, N1-2, is in the sealed container inside the briefcase. The combination on the briefcase is activated. Only you will be able to open it."

Lee nodded. "I want this lab destroyed as soon as we leave. Plan your explosives to release as many contagions as possible that are left inside."

"A change in plans, sir?" the man said as he unzipped the protective biocontagion suit. "An explosion like that could form a cloud of biological and chemical agents that will wipe out half of Vladivostok. Are you sure that you want to do that?"

Lee took a step toward the man and grabbed him by the throat, pinning him against the door of the chamber.

"Normally, I'd kill you for not obeying my orders instantly."

The startled man struggled to breathe. His face turned purple. "Sir . . . the . . . briefcase."

Lee looked at the briefcase in the man's left hand and slowly let go of the man's neck. He took the briefcase from the man. "Obey my orders. I am leaving immediately. You will stay here with Ratchek and destroy this facility. I want an ecological disaster, Russian style. Is that clear?"

The terrorist in the white suit fell to his knees and nodded.

"All Dragons," Lee ordered over his communications system. "Our mission is nearly accomplished. I want our dead and wounded collected and brought with us. Ratchek will stay behind with Detachment B to complete the facility's destruction. The only thing I want to leave behind are dead Russians and a dying city."

The big man with thick arms covered with dragon tattoos, a shaved scalp, and a scar that ran down the left side of his face nodded. "I understand and obey," Ratchek replied, bowing his head slightly. "Detachment B has twenty men still effective. They will be more than enough. When we're finished, the job I did in Rome will look like a picnic."

"I expect nothing less," Lee replied coldly and left the room with the briefcase in his hand.

Chapter Nine

Tell them of us and say, for their tomorrow, we gave our today.

—The Kohima Epitaph

November 14, 2056 hours, above Rybacky, Russia

It is a basic military maxim that no battle plan ever survives contact with the enemy. In the first fifteen minutes of the drop at Rybacky, Travis knew that this martial adage was true.

While the major was falling through the atmosphere, he accessed his Battle Sensor Device on his helmet to scan the area of operations. Although it was dark, the thermal view of the Rybacky Complex that Travis saw in his BSD showed that the compound was filled with thick black smoke. Evidently, TALON Force had arrived too late. His scan showed that Terrek's men were already on the ground and had overpowered the Russian security detachment. Overhead imaging satellites also reported the departure of three helicopters. Two more helicopters were parked inside the inner defensive perimeter of the Rybacky Complex, their engines running, ready for takeoff. Travis's Battle Sensor Helmet registered ten enemy soldiers on the ground guarding the outer perimeter gate. The rest of the terrorists must have been inside the complex, since they did not register on his screen.

The altimeter in his helmet ticked off the seconds before his parachute would open and announced them in his cybernetic implant in a calm, feminine voice. "Twenty seconds."

"DuBois, this is Barrett," the major radioed over the Eagle Team comm net.

"DuBois here. I see two choppers. Do you want me to stop them?"

"You must be reading my mind," Travis answered. His eye scanned the satellite image of the camp. In a couple of seconds he modified the plan and sent a sketch of the changes to the Eagle Team. "You and Wong use your HERF guns to stop the choppers from leaving. Greene, you and Blake are with me. Powczuk and Olsen, block the front gate."

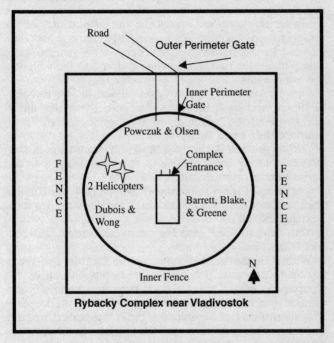

Road
Outer Perimeter Gate
Inner Perimeter Gate
Powczuk & Olsen
Complex Entrance
F E N C E
2 Helicopters
Dubois & Wong
Barrett, Blake, & Greene
F E N C E
N
Inner Fence
Rybacky Complex near Vladivostok

Without a word, each team member acknowledged Travis Barrett's orders via their computer link in their Battle Sensor Helmet. Their response was similar to sending an Internet reply, only in this case, they scrolled down the commands on their BSD retina screen by flicking their eye to the upper left portion of the battle sensor device.

"Six seconds," the gentle, feminine computer voice warned.

Quietly, accurately, the parachutes opened at low altitude. Barrett felt the reassuring tug of his parachute as it opened and caught the wind. As soon as they got close to the ground, the stealth camouflage system engaged. In a few seconds, the ghost troopers of Eagle Team, invisible to the naked eye, landed within a hundred meters of the inner defensive wire of the Rybacky Weapons Research Complex.

Six terrorists rushed out of the tunnel entrance of the underground facility. The terrorists looked up and gawked at the parachutes that carried no paratroopers. The parachutes fluttered to the ground and then blew in the wind against the inner perimeter fence.

One by one, the Eagle Team landed in the Rybacky Complex and took up their positions. In stealth mode, the Brotherhood rifleman on the surface of the compound didn't see a thing.

"What the hell is that?" a large, black-uniformed thug asked, pointing to a parachute that was tangled in the perimeter razor wire. "Should we fire?"

"At what? Empty parachutes? Maybe they are Russian paratroopers that chickened out!" the terrorist standing next to him joked.

"Hold your fire," another man answered. "I'll contact Ratchek."

Within earshot of this conversation, DuBois and Wong lay on the ground, a pair of chameleons unseen by the scurrying enemy. They activated their wristband RF generators and aimed them at the two HIP-17 helicopters. The silent burst of high-energy radio frequency fried the unprotected electronics in the HIPs. Suddenly, the whirling rotors of both helicopters sputtered and slowed. After a few more seconds, the engines staggered to a noisy, gear-crunching stop.

A terrorist wearing a black beret and carrying a hand-held radio, night vision goggles, and an automatic rifle rushed up to the helicopter nearest to the research complex entrance and shouted obscenities at the pilot. The pilot argued back, ripping the headset from his ears and flipped an obscene gesture to the man on the ground.

The pilot then rushed outside the cockpit, opened his helicopter's engine access panel, and surveyed the damage.

Travis smiled. The bad guys couldn't figure out why their helicopters had mysteriously stopped. It didn't matter. Those birds weren't going anywhere.

"Barrett, this is DuBois. Choppers nullified. I can see six dead Russian soldiers on the ground near the choppers. A dozen tangos are running around the choppers, trying to figure out what happened to their ride home. There's six more in the outer defense perimeter. Some of them have antitank weapons. Do you want me to take them down?"

"No, hold your fire," Travis replied, acknowledging Jack's use of the code word *tangos* to mean terrorists. "I'd rather get out of here without a fight if I can help it. Leave the tangos to the Russians."

Barrett and Greene walked past the confused enemy soldiers without being noticed. Barrett watched as he made footprints in the snow. They seemed to appear from nowhere, as the members of Eagle Team blended in perfectly with their background. He hadn't thought about that before, but luckily, there were so many footprints already on the ground that an extra set probably wouldn't be noticed in the dark. He would have to bring this up to General Krauss when they returned.

"Wong, call the nearest Russian command base," Travis whispered into his comm net. "I'm going to give you a message in Russian. You'll record it and broadcast it. I'll tell them that I'm the radio operator at Rybacky and that we are under attack by about fifty terrorists with automatic weapons, antitank rockets, and helicopters, and to get the cavalry here fast."

"Wilco," Wong replied. "I've been monitoring their net. They've already dispatched an armored security company here."

"Good. I'll make sure they have directions, I wouldn't want them getting lost," Travis said. "Stand by for message. Here goes." Travis spoke the message in flawless Russian, then walked toward the entrance, unseen by the tangos rushing around on the surface of the complex. The camouflage system was working perfectly. He moved next to the entrance, his XM-29 Individual Combat Rifle slung over his back and a special .45 caliber pistol with a laser aiming module (LAM) and a sound and flash suppressor attached to the barrel, in his right hand. Greene followed right behind him.

"Barrett, this is Powczuk. A Russian tank and three BMPs are moving up the road. There may be more vehicles behind them. It looks like somebody already sounded the alarm and the cavalry's on the way—Russian cavalry."

"Roger," Travis replied, nothing that Blake and Wong were in position near the front perimeter gate. "Don't shoot the Russians. If a fight starts, stay in stealth camouflage mode; don't show yourselves. If we have to, we'll help the Russians take down the tangos. Let's not forget that we are here uninvited by either party."

Each member of Eagle Team acknowledged their commander's instructions. "Wong, get me an FM radio link to the Russian tank commander coming up the road," Travis Barrett ordered. "Make it look like I'm calling from inside the facility."

"I'm on it," Sam replied.

Travis and Sarah swiftly moved to within twenty feet of the entrance. As he walked forward, the major saw a man with a radio and a submachine gun blocking the entrance.

"God damn it," the terrorist at the entrance screamed into a hand-held radio transmitter. "It's spooky. We've counted seven parachutes fall into the perimeter, but there's nothing in the chutes. I've never seen anything like it. Now, both helicopters have malfunctioned and both engines are out. It's fucking weird."

"Get a grip and knock off the superstitious bullshit," a strong, harsh voice sounded in the radio receiver. "Go to alternate transport. Use the trucks we came in on. I'll have the explosives ready to blow this facility sky high in five more minutes."

"You're connected," Sam announced to Travis over the comm net.

"This is Major Petrovna, inside the Rybacky facility," Travis said in Russian over the Russian FM radio frequency. "The compound has been attacked by terrorists from an organization called the Brotherhood. All personnel on the surface are enemy. They are heavily armed and have antitank weapons. You must attack immediately and secure the underground facility."

"Sir, this is Captain Strasavitch," the Russian replied. "We are attacking now. Reinforcements and air support are on the way. Hold out as long as you can. We are coming to rescue you."

Travis grinned and turned off his FM radio connection with Captain Strasavitch. He moved toward the entrance to the underground facility. He knew that his camouflage and the darkness made him difficult, but not impossible, to see.

A man at the entrance looked twice at him, as if he was seeing the outlines of a ghost. The man suddenly jutted his jaw forward, as if he couldn't believe his eyes. Then, in a move of panic, he raised his submachine gun toward Travis. The major shot him in the head with two rapid-fire, well-aimed, silenced shots. The man jerked backward from the shots, smashed into the wall of the entrance, and slid to the sidewalk.

Travis rushed through the entrance and into the hallway with Sarah and Hunter following close behind. At the same time, the sound of gunfire broke near the gate to the outer perimeter. The Russian armored column was engaging the terrorists that blocked their way into the complex.

"Major, the Russians are catching hell from these guys," Powczuk announced over the comms system. "They've already taken casualties. The lead tank hit an antitank mine and is burning like a Roman candle."

"Okay, let's even the odds. We can't have the cavalry getting ambushed, now, can we? Take out the tangos, but keep your distance. I don't want any of our people hurt. This isn't our fight. Let the cavalry be heroes."

"Didn't know you cared so much!" Powczuk answered.

"Blake, stay at the entrance to the underground facility and guard the door. No one comes in or out."

"Consider it done," Blake replied.

Travis didn't have time to respond. He turned the corner in the narrow hallway with Sarah following close behind.

The wail of an alarm sounded in the corridor. A door opened in the hallway twenty paces down the hall, and two men ran toward Barrett. Both carried submachine guns and both seemed oblivious to Barrett and Greene's presence. Travis instinctively lowered to one knee and shot the two men in swift succession. He moved on quickly, stepping over the dead men, and heading farther down the corridor.

Travis reached an opening in the hallway that was guarded by a mounted machine gun security position. The pillbox was made of reinforced concrete with a large bulletproof glass viewing area. Travis turned his head and looked through the glass. Two large holes had penetrated it. Inside the position, he could see the bloody pieces of a Russian soldier splattered on the far wall.

"Duck!" Greene announced over the comms device.

The major acted without hesitation, dropping to the floor, pointing his pistol forward. He heard the bullets zing overhead as Greene fired her pistol at the men running toward them. Sarah fired three shots—and then there were three dead terrorists.

"Not bad shooting for a microbiologist, eh?" Sarah Greene whispered into her communication system.

"I owe you one," Travis Barrett replied, then he rushed down the hallway, through a set of large steel doors that had been ripped open by explosives, and turned left in the direction that the three terrorists had come from.

To his left of the hallway was a door. The door was open. The sign above the door read in Russian: Virological Center. Restricted—Biohazard Level 4. Authorized Personnel Only.

Travis told Sarah to halt. He heard a voice inside the room.

"Damn it!" Ratchek screamed. "I don't give a shit how many fucking Russians there are. Kill them all and get those trucks ready to roll!"

Travis whispered to Greene, and they walked swiftly past the opening. He took a quick glance into the room, then placed his back to the wall to the side of the door. Greene was at the other side of the entrance, her back to the wall, pistol raised.

"I thought I saw something at the door," a different voice announced.

"Set that damn timer on the explosives, or I'll throw your big ass through the fucking door," Ratchek yelled.

"There," the other man replied. "That should do it."

Travis whispered over his comms set. "There's two inside. On the count of three, you shoot left and kill the guy working on the explosives; I'll shoot right and get us a prisoner."

"Ready," Greene replied.

"And Sarah, don't hit the explosives."

"No sweat," Sarah said. "If I do, you'll be the first to know."

"Okay, here we go. One . . . two . . . three!"

Travis and Sarah turned, faced the door, and pointed their guns at the terrorists. The major fired and hit Ratchek in the right shoulder. The big man spun around and hit the wall, dropping his weapon. At the same time, the other man looked up from his chair at the shimmer in the doorway. Sarah Greene put a well-aimed shot into the man's forehead. The man jerked backward, his blood and brains splashing the white walls. The bomb, armed and its timing device indicating ten minutes until detonation, sat ominously on the table.

Ratchek was on the floor, his submachine gun within arm's reach. He tried to grab his weapon with his left hand. Travis knelt down next to him and poked Ratchek's wound with the end of the silencer of his .45 automatic. The big man howled in pain.

"Stealth off," Travis said, turning off his camouflage

suit. As he materialized in front of Ratchek, he could see the big man's eyes grow wide with disbelief.

"I'm going to ask you a question, and I want a straight answer," Travis demanded. "What did you take out of this containment room?"

Ratchek grimaced in pain and shook his head. Sarah suddenly materialized, opened up a medical pack in the cargo pocket of her ensemble, and gave the man a shot from a small silver hypodermic. She then placed an auto-bandage on his shoulder—a self-sealing quick fix smart bandage that stopped hemorrhages. Ratchek's wound ceased bleeding.

"That will stabilize him and the shot should make him talk," Greene announced.

"What was your mission?" Travis asked.

Ratchek shook his head again, but his expression turned blank.

"Major Barrett, this bomb is armed," Sarah announced, looking at the device on top of the table.

Travis reached into a pouch on his belt and took out a small, matchboxlike device. He squeezed both ends together and placed it on top of the device. In a few seconds, the small radio-frequency disc did its job, and the LCD clock on the explosive device froze at 0923, nine minutes and twenty-three seconds until detonation.

"That will hold it," Travis said. He turned toward Ratchek. The drug had taken effect. A temporary calm masked Ratchek's face, in spite of the small pool of blood that covered the floor. Travis knelt down and gripped the man's chin, forcing him to gain consciousness. "Now, before I turn you over to the Russians, who are you and what is your mission?"

"My name is Ratchek. I am second-in-command of the Dragons of the Brotherhood."

"What did you take from here?"

"We took a vial . . . a vial from the inner biohazard chamber," Ratchek answered, then dropped out of consciousness.

Travis shook Ratchek's head. "Who has the vial?"

"Commander Lee has the vial. He left fifteen minutes ago."

"Where is he going?"

"Dragon Base," Ratchek answered. Then his body twitched and he lost consciousness again.

Sarah knelt down and checked his pulse. "He'll live, but you won't get anything more from him."

Travis noticed a global positioning satellite receiver attached to Ratchek's belt. He pulled it off the wounded man's belt and quickly scrolled through the data, then stuffed the GPS in his pocket.

"Sir, we've taken down most of the tangos," the voice of Stan Powczuk sounded over the comms system. "The Russian troops are stalled beyond the outer gate. It looks like they are waiting for reinforcements before they move forward. After the heavy losses they've taken, they're not acting too brave, so I don't think they'll be in the inner compound for about fifteen minutes. We've blown a hole in the south perimeter fence. We can exfiltrate on your order."

"Roger, Stan. Move to rendezvous point Charlie." The major flicked down the three-dimensional map of the Rybacky area. He designated the Charlie rendezvous point with a flick of his eye. Next he checked his team's status and was pleased to see all his troopers were safe and systems were green. He fired off a report to General Freedman and received confirmation of pickup. "Hold your position until we get out to the surface of the compound, then move to rendezvous point Charlie. An Osprey will meet us there in one hour."

The team acknowledged Travis's orders. The Osprey, or TFV-22, was designed for long-range covert penetration missions. It combined the capabilities of a helicopter and an airplane and was excellent for operating under the cover of darkness. The TFV-22's Pave Lows and Pave Hawks radar systems allow the TFV-22 to find holes in an enemy's radar coverage, slip through, and go to the objective over the path least likely to attract attention. Refueling was possible in blackout conditions at breathtakingly low altitudes. With their array of extra

fuel tanks, Forward Looking Infrared Radar (FLIR) turrets, infrared countermeasures, antennas, and other gad-
getry, the TFV-22 Osprey provided the TALON Force
with a tremendous infiltration and exfiltration capability.
The Osprey topped out at 300 knots and even incorpo-
rated advanced stealth features, such as infrared suppres-
sors on the exhausts and passive radar jammers.
Combining the speed of a turboprop with the attributes
of a helicopter, the TFV-22 could take seven Talon Force
Troopers 700 miles in, 700 miles out, and drop them off,
all in the hours of darkness.

"What about him?" Sarah asked, pointing at Ratchek.

"Leave him for the Russians," he replied. "What do
you suppose is in the vial?"

"Only one way to find out," Sarah answered, and before Travis could say anything, she opened the outer
door of the containment area and walked inside. The
door quickly shut and sealed behind her.

"No!" Travis yelled, his concern clearly resonating in
his voice. "Sarah, damn it! I need a fully functioning
biological warfare expert, not a casualty!"

Greene turned around, looked through the protective
glass door, and smiled. "No need to shout into your
comm net, Major. My suit is designed to act as a biopro-
tection garment."

Travis watched silently as Sarah pulled down the face
shield over her Battle Sensor Helmet. She activated a
button on her belt that started the flow of oxygen for
her containment suit. The flashing light of the biocontain-
ment hazard room came on and the Klaxon screamed
its warning.

"The inner door is locked," Sarah announced. "It's a
digital combination lock. Sam, scan this lock and give me
a combination."

"Give me a good thermal close-up of the touch pad,"
Wong replied over the comm net. "Okay, I've got a good
picture. I'll measure the heat of the electrical charge
given off by each button that was pushed. Stand by, this
will take a few minutes."

The sound of the fighting up above mixed with the

wailing of the Klaxon. Travis waited patiently as he watched Sarah Greene inside the biohazard containment chamber.

"Got it. The combination is displayed now on your BSD," Wong's voice announced over the comm net.

Sarah punched in the combination, opened the inner door, and stepped inside.

Travis fidgeted outside trying to wait patiently. He lowered his Battle Sensor Device over his left eye and accessed Sarah's view monitor. On his BSD, he watched what she saw. Her suit contained only fifteen minutes of oxygen.

After three nervous minutes, she opened the inner door and punched in the combination and started the air evacuation pump. A siren wailed as overpressure was applied to the connecting room. After a few moments, the siren stopped, and Greene walked outside, sealing the outer door behind her.

"I saw the chamber, but you're the expert. What did they take?" Travis asked.

Sarah slid her helmet shield open, a look of shock and fear clearly written on her pretty face. "We're in trouble—big trouble."

Chapter Ten

Plans are a basis for a change.
—A saying in the Israeli Army

Captain Sergei Lysenko sat in front of his radio-electronic intercept console, pressing the earphones to his ears and watching his screen go crazy. His station, Radio-Electronic Combat Node 75 of the Vladivostok Regional Command, was equipped with the latest Japanese-made electronic surveillance and jamming devices in the Russian Army.

The Array, as those who served it knew it, was the newest weapon in the Russian information warfare arsenal and comprised one of the most sophisticated electronic warfare networks in the world. The Array used a combination of ground-based and satellite-based jammers. Lysenko had trained for two years to operate this important eavesdropping and jamming station in the Far East, and he was one of the best operators in the business. In spite of everything that he had learned in training, however, he had never seen anything quite like this.

Normally, his job was rather boring. He could eavesdrop on telephone conversations, radio broadcasts, high-frequency telemetry—almost anything that had an electromagnetic signature. But the latest intercepts had him baffled.

The station was on red alert. Someone had attacked the Rybacky Weapons Research Complex, a top-secret research plant only fifteen kilometers away from his station. Twenty minutes ago, the entire Vladivostok Defense Region had jumped to Condition One—the code word for war. Su-25 Ground Attack Bombers were en route to support the troops. A motorized rifle battalion, reinforced with tanks, was on its way to retake the compound. MIG-29 Air Superiority Fighters were scrambled from airfields in the Vladivostok region, racing across Russian air space looking for intruders.

To make matters more tense, his equipment registered a high-frequency digital burst transmission source that was definitely not of Russian origin.

"*Polkovnik* Yarov, you must see this. I think that I have discovered an alpha-level intercept. I am detecting a high level of sophisticated communication transmissions in sector four."

Colonel Yarov walked over to Captain Lysenko's computer station, his hands clasped behind his back. As a veteran colonel of many years, Yarov was a master of masking his feelings in front of his men. He particularly didn't want to look alarmed in front of Lysenko, whom Yarov knew to be one of the brightest and most talented officers in his small, 353-man radio-electronic combat brigade.

As the senior officer on duty, Yarov also knew that before he could do anything, he would have to notify General Babichov. This was easier said than done. On any normal day, Babichov was difficult to reach. He was a notorious ladies' man, and Babichov had found that the women in Vladivostok were very obliging. It was Saturday night and, given the general's habits, he would be impossible to find.

"Report, Captain Lysenko," Yarov demanded in his most official, authoritative voice. "What is the problem?"

"*Tovarich* Commander," Lysenko replied, using the old Soviet-style greeting still cherished by the officers of the new Russian Army. Lysenko pointed to his computer screen. The screen was divided into four sections, with each section measuring a different electronic indicator. Each box contained a series of squiggly lines that raced across a corresponding graph that depicted wavelength and power output. The top two boxes showed an amplitude of only one fifth of the box. These boxes represented normal Russian Army FM radio communications. "I am intercepting our troop's radio communications in the top boxes, blocks one and two, of my screen. These are our troops at Rybacky. They are in heavy contact with the terrorists, and our forces are taking casualties."

Colonel Yarov looked nervous. He didn't like this. He was the senior officer in charge of radio-electronic combat, and no one else was on duty in a six-hundred-kilometer radius. As a senior colonel, he knew that he would be held responsible if the action at Rybacky failed due to a failure of radio-electronic combat assets. "What are they saying?"

"They are fighting their way into the Rybacky Weapons Research Complex. A force of saboteurs of unknown identity is fighting against them on the surface of the complex. The saboteurs have two helicopters that have been destroyed inside the inner defense perimeter."

Yarov took a deep breath. *Terrorists with helicopters? This is much worse than I imagined,* he thought, trying to keep his face composed to hide his concern. "What about the other two boxes?"

"They are what worries me, *Tovarich* Commander," Lysenko replied. "The third box is normal FM radio communications from an unauthorized source using an unscheduled, low-band frequency. I believe that this is the signature of some kind of internal communication system from the terrorist force fighting our men at Rybacky."

"And the fourth box?"

"Unknown. The bandwidth is extremely large and mostly digital burst," Lysenko said. "These transmissions are very sophisticated, digitally compressed messages that are operating on a hopping frequency sequence. I cannot decipher them."

Colonel Yarov stroked his chin as he looked pensively at the fourth box.

"But I believe that I can lock onto them with our new equipment and jam them, at least temporarily," Lysenko announced. "We will have to use our satellite jammers to maintain this."

Yarov took three steps to his desk. He grabbed the red telephone handset on his desk. "Get me General

Babichov." Yarov continued to wait on the line as the seconds passed by.

"*Polkovnik* Yarov, the fourth box . . . this alternating frequency . . . this is the type of communications that the Americans use. I have pinpointed the master frequency, but may not be able to track it for long unless I lock on it now. We could have an invading American force by Rybacky. I must act now if we are to jam them."

Yarov waited with the red phone glued to his ear. As he had feared, no one knew where Babichov was. The responsibility rested on his shoulders.

Yarov had spent a career avoiding such responsibilities. Now he was trapped. If these transmissions were from an American force attacking the sensitive research center at Rybacky, and he did not act, he could face a court martial or worse. The presence of the helicopters confirmed in his mind that these terrorists must have international support.

He visualized himself in front of General Babichov, being placed under arrest for not acting to support the defense at Rybacky. He saw the court martial and the sentencing. He didn't want to think about the next scene.

Yarov put the red telephone transmitter down in its receiver. His radio-electronic combat unit was the most sophisticated and best equipped in the Russian Army. If he did not act, after the great investment his country had made in his regiment's capabilities, Babichov would be right to court martial him, he thought.

"On my authority, jam this frequency, follow it as best you can, and continue to jam it until I order you to stand down."

"*Tak tochna!*" Lysenko replied enthusiastically, answering with the Russian Army's affirmation to authority: I obey!

2135 hours, Rybacky Weapons Research Complex

Sarah Greene was still numb with the revelation of what she had learned. The vial taken from inside the biohazard chamber had contained the substance N1-2. Travis Barrett put his hand on her shoulder. "Let's go."

Suddenly, a loud explosion sounded above them on the surface. Dust fell from the ceiling, and the emergency lights flickered.

"Barrett, all hell is breaking loose up here," Stan Powczuk announced over the comm net. "Russian aircraft are dropping bombs on the compound, and I'm not sure what they're aiming at. In the dark, those idiots are likely to hurt someone. You better get out of there!"

"Roger, Stan, we're on our way," the major answered. "Blake, you'd better pull out. We'll meet you at the rendezvous point."

"Wilco," Blake responded. "Moving now."

Travis scanned his BSD and saw that his fellow TALONs were also heading toward the rendezvous point. Then, without warning, his holographic reporting screen went blank.

"What the fuck?" Travis's BSD registered the following warning: "Satellite transmission jammed."

"Major," Sarah yelled to draw Travis's attention. "We need to get out of here. Pronto. If the biohazard chamber becomes compromised, we could risk infecting the team with God knows what."

Travis nodded, and the two of them ran into the hallway, leaving Ratchek unconscious on the floor. The explosions up above grew louder, and the emergency lighting inside the hallway flickered again, then went out. Travis and Sarah deployed their BSD monocular and switched to night vision. A small infrared light on the side of their helmets illuminated the area as they scurried up the ascending hallway to the entrance.

Just as they reached the top of the hallway, a large blast detonated on the surface, directly above them. As the ground shook and pieces of ceiling fell, Travis and Sarah were slammed to the floor.

The dust cleared, and the major found himself on his back, looking up at the dimly lit ceiling near the door.

"You okay?" Sarah asked as she stood over him, offering a hand.

Travis took her hand and struggled to stand. He shook off the fog from his mind and quickly checked out his battle ensemble. The communications were still jammed, but all other systems registered in the green. "Yeah, let's activate camouflage and get out of this death trap."

Sarah nodded and activated her camouflage. In seconds, they bolted outside, slipped through the melee taking place on the surface of the complex between the Russians and a few Brotherhood diehards, and ran south. Jack was waiting for them at the southern breach in the compound's perimeter. To the north, several Russian T-72 tanks fired high explosive shells at the compound entrance.

"What the fuck they doing?" Jack asked.

"Typical Russian tactics," Travis answered. "They'll flatten the place, then come in to pick up the pieces."

"Don't they know what's inside?" Sarah questioned.

"Probably not," Travis said. "They only know that some renegades have taken over their compound. The senior officers should know what's inside. Hopefully, they'll take charge before they have a biological warfare disaster on their hands."

"Sir? Russian tank headed our way," DuBois interjected. "I really feel sorry for them and all that shit, but we'd better get our asses in gear if we expect to make the rendezvous point in time for pickup."

Travis nodded and looked up at the dark, snow-filled sky. The weather had turned cold, and snow was falling fast in big, wet flakes. *The chances for pickup are decreasing dramatically,* he thought.

DuBois had already cut a hole in the fence. The three of them went through the breach and took off at a sprint to the south, still cloaked in their stealth camouflage as the battle for Rybacky reached a crescendo of explosions.

2210 hours, temporary TALON Force Command Center, at a secret location in the mountains of Colorado

Brigadier General Jack Krauss paced back and forth in the TALON Force Command Center. He was angry that the permanent command facility, which was being constructed in a subterranean section of the Pentagon, was not yet completed. In the meantime, the TALON Force Command Center was moved into a spare facility near the Cheyenne Mountain NORAD compound.

From the command center, Krauss had followed the action, blow by blow, getting a constant video feed from the TALON Force troopers as they executed their assigned mission at Rybacky.

So far, the raid had been a disaster, but not because of Eagle Team. The intelligence that had sent them to the Rybacky Complex in the first place had been faulty. Eagle Team was expected to stop the terrorists before they entered the compound. Now it appeared that the Eagle Team had only caught the rear guard.

"General, we're analyzing the video feed from Captain Greene before we lost contact," a silver-haired Green Beret colonel announced. "We still don't know what the Brotherhood's men took from the bioweapons vault."

"I'll bet you Greene knows," Krauss replied. "She was about to tell us when we lost communications. Tell me, Colonel Dunlop, I thought that our communications were unjammable. How is this possible?"

Colonel Dunlop hesitated, contemplating his answer. A civilian in blue slacks, a white shirt and a tie looked up from his chair behind the colonel. "Sir, the TALON Force equipment is prototype stuff. Their communications are supposed to be unjammable. The Russians must be using something new that we don't know about."

"Hell, sir, we were there to help them out, anyway," the colonel added. "We didn't plan on active Russian interference."

"That was our first mistake." Krauss shot the pair a cold stare. "We are in their country. The damn Russians don't know that we're there to help them. They probably think we attacked their lab."

The colonel gave a reluctant nod.

Freedman looked up at the big, flat view screen that filled the wall of the operations room. A video clip of Travis Barrett taking cover outside the biohazard containment chamber was frozen at the bottom left of the view screen. All six of the other TALON Force video views were frozen in their own small box at the bottom of the screen. The rest of the screen showed a map of the Vladivostok region and depicted computer icons of known Russian troop and aircraft locations.

Krauss looked back at the colonel and the civilian standing next to him. Colonel Dunlop was the TALON Force mission operations officer. He was one of the most talented special forces planners that Krauss knew. Jerry Rossner was the TALON Force technical team leader and had his hand in every piece of equipment that the TALON Force used. Together, Dunlop and Rossner led a dedicated group of thirty people who worked the highly sophisticated mission control operations center that supported TALON Force missions.

"What about retrieval?" Krauss asked. "We have to get Barrett and his people out of there. Abort the mission. Let's pull them out."

The colonel's jaw tightened. "We can't. We've had to pull the TFV-22s back to the USS *America*. The Russians are barrage jamming all the frequencies and their units are on high alert. The weather has gone to shit, and visibility is less than ten meters. We can't risk them at pickup point Charlie with the Russians alerted and their MIG-29s in the air. Especially not without communications with the Eagle Team. It's too dangerous. Barrett will have to execute the alternate exfiltration plan."

"That's just great," Krauss said, shaking his head. "First mission, and we're in a crisis in less than two hours."

"Sir, I'm working on countering the Russian jamming," a young Air Force major replied. "I've got my tech team on it right now."

"I don't care what it takes," Krauss growled. "Reestablish communications, and let's get our people out of there."

"Sir, I just got this in a few minutes ago." Colonel Dunlop handed Freedman a piece of paper.

"Jesus Christ," Krauss said. "Does he know?"

"No, sir."

"What about Mrs. Douglas?"

"We have no information of her whereabouts or any of the other Americans or Europeans."

"As soon as you find out, you notify me," Krauss ordered. "I will tell him myself. No one else. That's my job."

2250 hours, in Russian air space
heading toward the North Korean border

Three MI-17 HIP Helicopters flew in tight formation through the dark, wet night. The lead helicopter banked to the west, flying into North Korean airspace.

Lee hated flying in helicopters. He frowned as the earphones of the helicopter's radio-intercom system pressed hard against his head. He hated the cramped, dark, noisy compartment of the HIP-17. Hell, he hated helicopters in general.

For Lee had a terrible secret, one that he dared not show. Lee, a master of the martial art hopkido, a trained professional killer, was prone to airsickness.

He struggled to breathe. The HIP flew low to the ground, clearing the mountains and heading toward Terrek's mountainous, remote base in the northeastern portion of North Korea.

Lee looked out into the blackness of the rainy night. The members of the Brotherhood who flew with him were the best in his team. Three other ships, flying in formation around him, carried other members of his elite Dragon team. In his lap, he held the silver briefcase and thought about the power that this small source of death would bring to the Brotherhood.

The HIP's big 1,900-horsepower engine surged as the blades swirled in the wet night. The helicopter quickly moved across the blacked-out countryside, crossing the Russian–North Korean border, heading west to Dragon Base.

By now, Lee had learned that Ratchek and his men would not be joining them. This was too bad, he mused, as Ratchek had proved a capable leader and a ruthless killer. Such men were hard to find. Still, he hoped that Ratchek and his men had not been taken alive. After all, operatives were expendable and, for the right price, could be replaced with a new crop of men ready to demonstrate their loyalty to the Brotherhood.

But how did the Russians react so quickly? How could his intelligence about their capabilities have been so wrong? It had taken considerable energy to make sure that General Babichov was out of the picture and that the alarm would not be sounded. The speed with which the Russians had reacted to his raid was unusual. Could someone have tipped them off?

Still, this was of little consequence. He thought about the brilliant audacity of Terrek's plan. If all went well, the world would wake up in a few weeks to a new world power. A new order would rise in the world, and the hated Americans would know and fear the Brotherhood.

"Commander Lee, we are in radio range of the base," the pilot announced over the helicopter intercom system.

"Good. Put me through to Terrek."

"Immediately," the pilot replied. "You are connected."

"Do you have the package?" Terrek demanded.

"Affirmative. Vial N1-2 is in my possession," Lee replied. "We had some problems leaving. It seems that the Russians were expecting us. They attacked us right after I left with the first contingent."

"This is most disturbing," Terrek answered. "How did the Russians discover our attack so quickly? Could we have underestimated them?"

"Unknown," Lee answered.

"We will accelerate our schedule," Terrek ordered. "I have the test subjects here, waiting to be introduced to your precious cargo. As soon as you arrive we will begin Phase 2."

"I live to execute your orders," Lee said. "Long live the Brotherhood!"

"Yes . . . just get the vial here in one piece. Terrek out."

The helicopter banked steeply to the left as the bird flew around a massive mountain range. Beads of perspiration formed on Lee's forehead. He held his stomach and tried to think about anything else but the cramped confines of the helicopter.

"Commander Lee," the helicopter pilot said in Russian-accented English, "we will be landing in Dragon Base in ten minutes."

"Excellent," Lee replied curtly over the intercom. He shook his head, hating the helicopter and hating to have to command his team in English. Terrek had recruited men from all over the world to join the Brotherhood. To Lee's everlasting disgust, the common operating language of the Brotherhood was English. Terrek believed that his men must know the language of the enemy to fight them effectively.

Someday soon, Lee thought, *I will form an all North Korean team. A team with such discipline and ruthlessness that even Terrek will be in awe of its capabilities.*

Lee lowered his head and took in steady gulps of air. He felt flushed and lightheaded. The walls of the HIP seemed to be closing in on him. He struggled to hold on just a little longer and fought off the urge to puke.

2306 hours, several miles southwest of the Rybacky Weapons Research Complex

Snowflakes filled the sky. You didn't need a degree in meteorology to know that a major snowstorm was under way. Major Travis Barrett looked up at the heavens and knew that only the best pilots would be able to fly in these conditions. The chances of retrieval were beginning to narrow to a very low possibility.

Major Barrett and Sarah Greene were the last to arrive at pickup point Charlie. Normally, the team would operate widely dispersed, connected by the TALON Force version of a tactical internet, with the added feature of video and voice communications. Now, much to their dismay, with communications jammed and a bad snowstorm hitting their little portion of the world, they were on their own.

Pickup point Charlie was a narrow draw in the mountains three kilometers southeast of the Rybacky Weapons Research Complex. When Travis arrived, he saw that Blake and Olsen had already commandeered a Russian truck.

"Where did you dig that up?" Travis said, pointing to the truck.

"I found it along the road just a few miles back," Blake responded with a grin. "The guy driving it didn't need it as much as we do."

Travis raised his left eyebrow.

"Don't worry," Jenny interjected. "We know the rules of engagement. We didn't kill him."

"So what did you do?" Sarah asked.

"I turned off my camouflage and waved him down," Blake smiled. "Olsen opened the door and materialized right next to him. He must have thought we were aliens from Mars or something. He stumbled out of the truck in panic and took off running."

"That's great," Sam Wong offered. "Here we are, stuck in the middle of Russian territory, surrounded by troops that think we are invaders, with no backup, no retrieval birds, and you guys get your jollies by scaring civilians."

Travis Barrett raised his hand to silence the banter. "Status report."

The team went into their well-trained drill, a backup procedure should they lose their networked information stream, with each member reporting in turn.

"Powczuk, all systems internal green. One XM-29. Ten 20 mm rounds, two hundred 5.56 mm rounds. One silenced .45 caliber pistol, forty-nine rounds. Three command detonated micromines. Three Bugs. One knife. One water pouch, and one emergency field ration."

"Blake. All systems internal green. One XM-29. Six

20 mm rounds, one hundred and twelve 5.56 mm rounds. One silenced .45 caliber pistol, twenty-eight rounds. One command detonated micromine. One Dragonfly UAV. One knife. One water pouch with one emergency field ration."

"DuBois, green. One XM-29. Five 20 mm rounds, two hundred and twelve 5.56 mm rounds. One .45 caliber pistol, twenty-eight rounds. Four command detonated micromines. One Dragonfly UAV and one Bug. Three knives. Two water pouches with one emergency field ration."

"Jack, Hunter, post security while I talk this over with the team," Travis Barrett ordered.

Jack and Hunter nodded, moved off fifty meters north and south respectively, charged their XM-29 rifles, and took up prone positions to guard the approaches to the ravine.

"Greene. Systems green. Ha, ha. One 9 mm pistol, thirty-two rounds. One Nonlethal Generator (NLG). One surgical kit. Two water pouches with one emergency field ration."

"Olsen. Green. One 9 mm pistol, twenty-eight rounds. Four command detonated micromines. One Hummingbird UAV. One knife. Two water pouches with one emergency field ration."

"Wong. Systems green. One 9 mm pistol, thirty-eight rounds. One special communications pack. One Hummingbird UAV. One knife. One water pouch and one emergency field ration."

"Barrett. Internal systems green. One XM-29. Ten 20 mm rounds, one hundred 5.56 mm rounds. One silenced .45 caliber pistol, twenty-one rounds. One command detonated micromine. One Dragonfly UAV. One knife. One water pouch with one emergency field ration."

"Captain Wong, why have we lost comms with TALON Force Headquarters?" Travis Barrett asked.

Sam answered, "I lost the link at 2200 hours. We can talk to each other, depict position-location information, and send internet messages and graphics internally, but I can't reach anyone outside of the Eagle Team. I have maps of the area of operations downloaded in my comms pack."

"But why have we lost satellite communications with TALON headquarters?" Travis asked again.

"It looks like we're being jammed with some kind of new high-frequency Russian jammer. The last transmission I received was that our pickup by special V-22 retrieval birds has been called off."

"Great," Stan said as he moved next to the rest of the group. "A billion dollars worth of technology, and we're operating as a lone squad in the wrong country with no support." Powczuk abruptly realized that he should have kept his mouth shut. He turned to Barrett. "What are your orders?"

Travis Barrett pulled down the menu in his BSD screen that depicted a three-dimensional map of the region. He quickly highlighted the location that he found on Ratchek's global positioning receiver. The grid coordinates depicted a location just over the border in North Korea. "We still have our mission. It's just that our plan needs to change. We're heading to North Korea."

"Where?" Sam asked, his jaw dropping. "You're kidding."

"No, I'm dead serious," Travis Barrett said.

"I was afraid you were going to say that," Jen said. "Why?"

"We arrived too late to stop the Brotherhood from stealing what they wanted from the Russians," Sarah Greene interjected.

"And what was that?" Stan Powczuk asked.

"Viral pathogen N1-2," Greene replied. "Our Russian friends were developing some pretty nasty biological warfare agents in the Rybacky facility. Viral pathogen N1-2 is a genetically engineered Ebola virus spliced to a smallpox germ agent."

"How nasty is nasty?" Olsen asked.

"Let me put it this way," Greene answered. "The terrorist armed with a chemical or radiological agent could kill hundreds, possibly thousands of people. By contrast, a terrorist armed with this strain of Ebola-smallpox can kill tens of thousands in days and cause a nationwide epidemic in weeks. This biological agent rivals a thermonuclear weapon and could produce several million casualties in a single incident."

"But don't they need an aerosol spray or something to deploy it?" Stan asked.

"Not in this case," Greene said. "Nearly all microorganisms die quickly when exposed to sunlight. They are adversely affected by high temperatures and succumb easily to desiccation. Simply put, they are fragile. This is not the case for this strain of Ebola-spliced smallpox. It is a hardy organism, the Arnold Schwarzenegger of killer germs. If it doesn't kill its victims outright, N1-2 was designed to incubate in a living person, multiplying the amount of pathogen a thousandfold in the infected body. After an incubation period of several days the disease becomes airborne. Each infected person or body that has brought N1-2 to full incubation will generate thousands of spores. Once these spores become airborne and are ingested in the lungs, the process begins again, expanding the area of contamination exponentially."

"What about vaccinations?" Wong questioned.

"We don't have one for this strain. Even if we developed one today, it would be impossible to produce enough vaccine in time for the entire U.S. population. As far as I know, we have only a few days at most to stop these guys, or we'll lose track of the germ, and there's no telling how they will use it."

"Now tell me the good news," DuBois said.

"There is no good news," Greene answered. "If this virus is let loose in a city it could kill everyone in a very short time. But it is genetically designed to mutate after a fixed period into a nonlethal form."

"Making it an ideal weapon," Powczuk interjected. "Kill all the people and leave the area safe to occupy later."

"Exactly," Greene replied.

"Okay. So they've got one helluva nasty bug. Why North Korea?" Stan asked.

"I took the GPS receiver from one of the terrorist

leaders. He stored the coordinates of his base camp in the receiver and labeled the coordinates Dragon Base. All we have to do is get to the ten-digit grid I've depicted on your battle maps."

"Pretty sloppy operational security, if you ask me," Stan said, studying the map depicted on his BSD screen for a second. He flipped the monocle up and looked straight at Travis. "But sometimes the good guys get lucky."

Travis nodded. "Time is short. If they get this out of their base, there is no telling where this germ will show up."

"You know that we're on our own on this," Stan added. "Our alternate plan, in case of communications failure, is to head to a coastal rally point, seventeen kilometers southwest of Vladivostok, for fastboat retrieval."

Travis nodded. "TALON Force operations require bold, imaginative, and audacious action. They picked us for this mission, Stan, because we are smart enough to know when to disobey orders."

Powczuk nodded. "So what's the plan, boss?"

"Sixteen klicks from here is a Russian airfield, *Lyotnaya Polye Sorok Tree*," Travis Barrett said in perfect Russian. "We need an airplane. The Intel reports that I picked up prior to losing comms with TALON Force headquarters indicated that there were three aircraft on that airfield. From that airfield, Military Airfield Forty-three, it's only eighty miles to the Brotherhood's base in North Korea. The seven of us, in one small plane, can do this."

"Those who discern when to use many or few troops are victorious," Jack DuBois added with a grin, quoting his favorite author, Sun Tzu, the ancient Chinese philosopher of the art of war.

Sam Wong looked sideways and shook his head. "So, let me see if I have this right." The team gathered around Travis, waiting for Sam to recap the mission. "All we have to do is fight our way onto a Russian airfield, steal a plane that can carry all of us, fly through a snowstorm, evade Russian fighters from shooting us down, cross into North Korea without being killed by North Korean air defense, infiltrate a heavily armed enemy base camp, find the virus, and destroy it. All seven of us."

"Yes, Sam," Travis said with a grin as he put his arm on the smaller man's shoulder. "Exactly."

"I was afraid of that." Sam smiled. "Sometimes I hate it when I'm right."

"One more thing," Olsen added.

"What? There's more?" Sam yelped.

Travis nodded. "We have to get back home."

November 15, 0020 hours, Cell Block One, the Citadel, near Aojin, North Korea

Elizabeth Douglas held the baby girl in her arms while the young mother slept with her head in Liz's lap. It was difficult to tell, but Liz figured that it was somewhere past midnight. Everyone except Beverly, a nineteen-year-old college freshman from New Jersey, was sleeping. Helga, who had become Liz's best friend in the past two days, was snoring loudly in the bed to her left.

The cell that they shared was cold and had few comforts, just three metal-framed beds placed along three walls. Liz was in the center bed, facing the metal bars that opened to a narrow hallway. The beds were uncomfortable, with thin mattresses and only a couple of old wool blankets for warmth. Two steel buckets and old Korean newspapers were all they were allowed for bathroom facilities.

Still, she thought, it was better than lying on the cold, cement floor.

Tonight was their third night in captivity and their second night in the mountain fortress. The temperature was cool, and most of her cellmates were catching colds. At least Helga was healthy, if her loud snores were any indication.

The uncertainty made the evening seem colder than the fifty-degree temperature of the cellblock. No one had seen the men from their group since they were separated. The women were held six or seven to a cell. Liz had learned from the guards that they were somewhere in North Korea. Many of the workers in the compound were Asian, and Liz assumed that these people were Korean.

The food was horrible. Twice a day they were given a large bowl of rice and a bucket of fish soup for the entire cell. The six women in her cell were Helga from Germany; Rachel and her baby girl Sonia, who were both American; an elderly Canadian named Mary; Beverly, the pretty, young American; and Liz.

So far, some of the older women were taking captivity better than the younger ones. Rachel was consumed by fear for her husband and her baby. Beverly was in a state of constant depression. When she wasn't sleeping, she was sobbing. She refused to eat the food that the guards provided.

As meager and tasteless as their rations were, Liz knew that their chances for survival depended on their ability to stay as strong and healthy as possible. This was particularly important to Rachel, who was trying to breast-feed her daughter Sonia.

Liz felt determined to survive and knew in her heart that this is what her husband would have demanded of her. She remembered him saying often that Douglases never quit. Liz, therefore, volunteered to take on the leadership of their small group. Her strong personality made her a natural for the job that no one else wanted. She tried her best to keep everyone's spirits up by telling stories, singing lullabies to the baby, and finding simple ways to pass the time.

The most distressing thing was that Liz did not know why they were being treated like this. What did these people expect to gain from holding this small group of Americans and Europeans in jail? Except for the guards who brought the food every day, no one had come to tell them what was happening.

"Do you think that they will kill us?" Beverly lamented as Liz rocked little Sonia in her arms.

"Well, they sure have gone to a lot of trouble, if that's all they wanted to do," Liz answered. "No, if they were going to kill us, why the long trip from Egypt to Korea?"

"I can't stand the waiting!" Beverly said in a shattered voice, her dirty blond hair falling across her pretty face. "I want to go home!"

Liz gently let Sonia's head slip down to the mattress as Liz edged closer to Beverly. "Is that how you want them to see you? Do you want them to know that you are afraid and ready to give up?"

"I don't care what they think," she said in tears. "I'm not supposed to be here. I didn't do anything wrong."

"Nobody did anything wrong, honey," Liz said in a soothing tone. She placed Sonia in Beverly's arms, then put her arm around the younger woman. "Little Sonia here sure doesn't deserve this. She needs you and me to take care of her."

Beverly's eyes rested on the little baby girl. Sonia fidgeted slightly and rubbed her tiny fist across her face.

"We need to stay strong," the older woman suggested. "We're Americans. Somebody will try to get us out of here. It's only a matter of time."

"Do you really think so?" Beverly asked, hoping beyond hope.

"Yes, I do. We have to hold on."

"I hope that you're right." Beverly smiled and scooted closer to the older woman. "Mrs. Douglas, do you mind if I ask you a personal question?"

"No, honey, go ahead."

"How did you get those nerves of steel?"

Liz laughed. "They're not steel, kiddo, they're rubber. The trick is not to stretch them too much."

November 15, 0120 hours, _Lyotnaya Polye Sorok Tree_ (Airfield 43) near Vladivostok

The completely black Russian sky was filled with snowflakes. Close to the airfield, Eagle Team dismounted from their borrowed Russian truck and moved in a dispersed V formation to the west. Sam traveled near the rear of the formation, followed by Jen Olsen. The snow fell in heavy, wet flakes. Sam could feel the bitter, icy wind cut through his suit as he trudged through the ankle-deep snow. As the cold began to set in, his suit made a quick adjustment to raise the temperature and compensate.

Sam felt a rush of adrenaline surge through his body. He realized that his suit had just sensed his weariness and hunger. His brilliant biochips automatically injected a precision dose of bioengineered antifatigue drugs into his system. Using these state-of-the-art stimulants, a TALON Force trooper could operate for five to six days without food or rest. The crunch period usually came on the sixth day, when the human body would no longer react to the stimulants without serious physical breakdown. On the sixth day of stimulants, the average person just shut down and he or she went into a deep sleep.

So far, Sam had never experienced conditions over two days on stimulants, but the plan had already gone awry. He worried that he might get a chance to test the maximum stimulant limit in the days ahead.

The TALON Force troopers moved silently, each member separated by 30 meters, covering the ground quickly in spite of the difficult terrain. The snowstorm picked up, and Sam realized that it would be difficult to see without the use of their excellent thermal viewer in the BSD monocular.

Sam suddenly felt uneasy. He tried to shake it off. After all, when the seven samurai were outnumbered by ten to one, they didn't despair, Sam Wong argued with himself. *Major Barrett will lead us out of this, just like Kanbei.*

Sam smiled as he thought about his heroes and, at the same time, witnessed the precision movement of the Eagle Team through the fir trees. Sam knew that the ease with which the TALON Force maneuvered was not just the result of their technology that allowed them to see in the storm. It was more a factor of discipline that molded them into an efficient team. He understood that the discipline and training that Travis enforced as the team leader was paying off. The after-battle status report was a case in point. After every engagement, as soon as the team could assemble in a safe place, Barrett expected a full inventory of systems and weapons. Much of the critical information was displayed automatically on Barrett's BSD screen, but the major, like Wong's mythical hero Kanbei, demanded that each member of the Eagle Team report in person his or her status, to reinforce battle discipline.

Wong's breathing grew heavy as Eagle Team trudged up a wooded slope just east of the airfield. They automatically closed up the formation as they climbed the rise, moving carefully through the snowstorm like a pack of wolves on the prowl. Their stealth camouflage was turned off to conserve power. Sam had learned that conserving power was more critical than saving ammunition.

Several weeks ago, during a training exercise in the wilds of Montana, Sam had learned the value of husbanding his suit's electrical power. Members of Eagle Team kept repeating, "Remember Wong's Last Stand," as if it were the Alamo.

But that was in training. This was real, and the bad guys were playing for keeps. Sam wondered if their teamwork would keep them alive. *I don't intend to be a posthumous hero,* he thought.

"Take cover," the major's voice whispered in the communications earphones of every member of the Eagle Team. "The airfield is two hundred meters due east. Blake, DuBois—check it out. Everyone else remain here. Form a perimeter defense."

Eagle Team complied without hesitation, moving silently and quickly. Each member checked his or her position on the virtual map that was projected in their BSD screen. The technology of the virtual map was a powerful tool. Sam Wong scanned his eyepiece and instantly knew exactly where he was, where every other team member was located, and where all the weapons in the team were pointed. In a combat situation, this picture was worth a thousand words.

Hunter and Jack moved forward to the fence that surrounded the Russian airfield. The air was thick with snow. The two TALON Force troopers crawled up to a barbed wire fence and quickly cut their way through the circular razor wire with wire cutters that were attached to the barrels of their XM-29 rifles. Free of the fence, Jack DuBois and Hunter Blake crawled on their bellies through the deep snow.

"There she is," Hunter said. He pointed to a pair of wings and a tail covered in snow. A Soviet hammer and sickle adorned the tail. "That's the one."

"You're kidding me, man," Jack replied. "That's a bi-plane! How the hell is that piece of junk going to get us all the way to North Korea?"

Hunter scanned the small Russian airfield. The runway was only long enough for short takeoff and landing planes. A couple of old, Tupolev cargo planes were parked at the far, southern side of the runway, next to a large hangar. A complex of buildings stood next to the hangar. One of the buildings had smoke coming from a metal pipe. Two trucks were parked next to the building. There were no guards to be seen.

"That's not a piece of junk," Hunter said with glee. "That's an AN-2, an Antonov Colt." Hunter dropped the BSD screen over his left eye and studied the biplane parked all alone on the icy runway. "That baby is a lot sturdier than she looks. I haven't had a chance to pilot anything like that for years. This will be fun."

Jack stared at the single-engine aircraft. Images of World War I dogfights danced in his head as he studied the plane that Hunter was so eager to steal. "Pardon me if I don't share your enthusiasm, flyboy, but how the fuck are we supposed to get that Russian Sopwith Camel into the air?"

"You leave that to me, jarhead," Blake responded. "There ain't nothing with wings that I can't fly. That baby will hold twelve people and can land on a dime.

It's the perfect bird for what we need. Besides, look around. Not much else to choose from."

"Okay, hotshot, you're right on that one. I'm game. But what about fuel? How do we know it's topped off?"

"You know, Jack, you're a lot smarter than you look. That's a hell of a question. I'll tell you what. I'll get the bird ready to fly, and you find me some gas."

"Well, as Sun Tzu said, 'Borrow another's hand to kill.' "

"What's that supposed to mean?" Blake said, with a wide grin.

"The best way to kill the enemy is to use a borrowed knife."

"Dude, you scare me sometimes."

"Confusion to the enemy," DuBois smiled and patted Hunter on the shoulder.

Travis crawled up behind them, followed by the rest of Eagle Team. "Report."

"Major, that aircraft is our ticket out. I'm going to get her ready to fly while Jack borrows some fuel."

Travis scanned the AN-2 Colt with his thermal viewer. "Think it will fly?"

"Yes, sir. It's a sturdy aircraft, custom made for puddle jumping," Blake answered. "This one looks to be of mid-1960s vintage." He pointed to the two other aircraft parked on the snow-covered tarmac. "We certainly can't take one of those Tupolevs. They're too big and slow, and we'd never find a place to land them. With the Colt, I can fly low enough to avoid enemy radar."

"But how do you know that it can fly?"

"I scanned it with my thermal sights," Blake answered. "It's still warm around the engine cowling. It's been running today, that's for sure."

"Looks like we don't have any other choice." Travis searched the airfield. The place was as deserted as a whorehouse after a police raid. He nodded to Blake, then activated his communications. "DuBois, you and Wong get the fuel. Blake—Powczuk and Greene will help you with the aircraft. Olsen and I will provide security. Activate stealth camouflage."

One by one, the members of Eagle Team acknowledged the order and turned their TALON Force ensembles to stealth mode. Powczuk and Greene moved with Blake toward the aircraft. Travis Barrett faced the hangars and aimed his XM-29 rifle at the door of the building with the metal stovepipe. Olsen aimed her pistol to the north. DuBois and Wong headed toward the fuel truck.

Travis Barrett watched the ghostly infrared figures of DuBois and Wong through his BSD screen. After a few moments, they crossed the airfield and reached the fuel truck. Wong went for the cab as DuBois stood by the door of the building that had the smoke rising from the stovepipe.

Wong opened the cab door and moved into the driver's seat. He searched for the keys, came up empty, then started to hot-wire the ignition system. DuBois stood watch near the door of the building, prepared to take on anyone who might rush out and attempt to stop them.

Sam fiddled with the ignition wires. They sparked, and the starter screeched, but the truck engine was cold and wouldn't turn over. Sam tried again, and the sound of the protesting starter echoed across the snow-filled night air.

"Come on Sammy, we don't have all day," Jack chided into his comm net.

"This ain't a Detroit diesel," Wong replied into his comm net. "The Russkies don't make them like they used to."

"Hell, they never did," DuBois added. "Shit, I stole better wheels than this when I was a kid."

The engine suddenly coughed and came to life. Wong stomped down on the gas pedal and gunned the engine.

The door to the shack opened. A shirtless Russian soldier, wearing no shoes, stood in the door with a rifle in his hands peering into the snowy night air. He couldn't see past the strange shimmer that was standing in front of him. Before he understood what was happening, DuBois knocked him out with one quick strike. The Russian crumpled to the ground. Jack reached in and shut the door, then took off running.

Wong backed up the truck and turned just as Jack

jumped up on the running board on the passenger's side. Holding onto the mirror, Jack looked back at the door to the building as the truck pulled away. The door was still closed.

Sam raced the truck across the snow-covered tarmac, sliding to a stop just inches away from the two-winged aircraft. Blake was in the pilot seat, a wide grin on his face as he scrolled down the preflight checklist for the AN-2 Colt in his BSD. Stan Powczuk, his camouflage turned off, pulled down on the propeller. Jen and Sarah stood to the side and brushed the snow from the wings and fuselage.

"There's half a tank of gas already in her," Blake announced through his comms receiver to DuBois. "We need more. Fill her up!"

"Where?" DuBois asked.

"Bottom right wing."

Travis saw the door to the shack open. Two men with AK-74 rifles peeked out. Travis blasted off a short burst of fire from his rifle and hammered the concrete just above the door. The Russians dove for cover and shut the door. "Hurry up. We'll have company here in a few minutes."

DuBois jumped off the running board of the truck and examined the fuel pump. He quickly ran over to the plane, unscrewed the gas cap, and placed the hose in the aircraft fuel tank. He then ran back to the rear of the truck and pushed levers until the fuel pump started. Soon, aviation fuel was flowing into the biplane. At the same time, Travis kept his eyes glued to the door of the guard building. The door opened again, and he blasted off another stream of lead at the top of the door. The rounds smashed into the concrete above the door once more, stitching a straight line of holes across the top of the entrance.

This time the Russians returned fire. Green tracers zinged through the night air, sailing harmlessly above the aircraft.

"How much longer, Hunter?" Travis asked. "The

guards are getting feisty. I would hate for them to improve their aim."

"Two minutes," Blake answered. The engine of the aircraft sputtered, barked, then surged to life.

"Tanks full!" DuBois shouted over his intercom.

Travis flicked the selector switch on his XM-29 and fired a 20 mm tear gas grenade at the top of the door. The round hit the archway and smashed into the concrete, sending dust and chips splattering to the floor.

The Russians stopped firing, apparently having taken enough for the sake of duty. Travis watched as the Russians climbed out a side window, gagging and coughing, and ran to a nearby hangar.

"Everyone get on," Travis ordered. Sam entered first, followed by Sarah, Stan, and Jack. "Okay, Jen, hop aboard."

The engine roared as Olsen stepped on board. The major fired one more 20 mm tear gas grenade at the hangar—just to keep the guards at bay—then ran for the door of the aircraft. The AN-2 Colt picked up speed as Travis ran forward and Jack and Stan pulled him on board.

Within seconds, the AN-2 Colt was airborne, flying through the snow-filled sky to the southwest toward North Korea.

Chapter Eleven

There is many a boy here today who looks on war as all glory, but, boys it is all hell.
—General William Tecumseh Sherman

November 15, 0300 hours, the Citadel near Aojin, North Korea

It was early . . . or late, depending on your point of view . . . but Lee knew that Terrek was the kind of man who never seemed to sleep.

Lee walked up to the computerized eye retina scanner and placed his eye in the viewer. The scanner verified Lee's identity, and the massive steel blast doors opened like the jaws of a huge trap. Four tall guards stood in the opening, their assault rifles at the ready as the muscular Lee entered. The guards—two Caucasian, one Black, and one Asian—wore the all-black uniform and body armor of Terrek's personal security contingent. Terrek was an equal-opportunity terrorist employer.

Lee was tall for a North Korean, but these guards were all six foot five and towered over him. Their cold, steely eyes followed Lee as he moved. It was clear that these men trusted no one but their master, Yuri Terrek.

Without as much as a nod, Lee walked past the four big men and entered the room that was deep inside the Citadel, the inner sanctum of Terrek's control center. Terrek sat in a massive black chair in the center of the room. To Lee, the chair looked more like a modern throne made of black-painted steel and leather than a control console. But Lee knew better than to think that the chair was merely ceremonial. From that chair, Terrek could control the defenses of the Citadel and the automatic guns that lay at each of the four corners of the fortress.

The room was busy with activity, even at this early hour. Several staff officers hovered around their computers as other men attended to their tasks of monitoring Terrek's communications. A huge flat-view television screen covered the wall in front of Terrek. The screen was divided into smaller sections, each one showing a separate television news broadcast from various cities around the world. The bottom row of boxes contained the views of the approaches to the Citadel and the surrounding defensive zones.

"Any word from our North Korean friends?" Terrek asked.

"They worry that they have not heard from General Cho. I told them that he is sick and will not be able to talk to them for some time. They offered to send a replacement, but I told them that that was not needed; that I would be their liaison."

"Did they accept your answer?"

"In North Korea, no one trusts anyone, but I ended the conversation with the promise that they would receive twice the usual payment."

"Good. That should hold them off for a while. What news do you have of Ratchek?"

"According to the latest reports from our Russian contacts in the Vladivostok Military Region, he was wounded in the Russian attack and captured," Lee answered. "At least three more of our men were captured by the Russians."

"Unacceptable!" Terrek said, pounding his fist against the arm of his chair. "My plans depend on secrecy. The Russians will make them talk."

"Our Russian contacts also report that a skirmish took place at one of the Russian airfields near Rybacky and that a military aircraft was stolen."

Terrek shot Lee a stern glance. "What? Did some of our men escape?"

"Not likely," Lee replied. "I am still not sure what happened. The Russians should not have been a problem for our men."

"Then who attacked the Russian air base?"

Lee didn't answer.

"I want no more excuses." Terrek glared. "We have come too far to be disrupted by a lack of attention to detail. I expected you to destroy the plant and trip a disaster that would focus the entire world on Vladivostok and the illegal Russian experiments. I expected a biological Chernobyl. Instead, I have a third of my team killed or captured, and the world is focused on finding us!"

Lee stood silent. He knew better than to argue with Terrek.

"We must plug this leak," Terrek demanded. "What if the Russians make Ratchek talk?"

Lee looked straight at Terrek. "Our Russian contacts will take care of Ratchek. As far as the others go, I have already arranged for them to be killed trying to escape."

Terrek shook his head. He knew that his days in the Citadel were numbered. His men were good, but the Russians had a history of being experts at making prisoners talk. It would only be a matter of hours, or a few days at most, before they pieced together what had happened. And the Russians would want their viral agent back. Viral pathogen N1-2 had cost them a small fortune to develop. Terrek knew that with the right bioengineering, N1-2 could become the perfect weapon—the Russians had designed it to eradicate the upper level of a society or kill selective groups and cause social chaos. But if his tests proved successful, it would be more powerful than that, and more powerful than nuclear weapons. If his experiments succeeded, and he had every reason to believe that they would, N1-2 would breed itself. A small amount could consume a city in a few days and a country in a few weeks. He needed time to complete his plans and with the missteps that had occurred so far he felt that time was running out. The North Koreans would not be able to maintain his secrecy for much longer once the Russians started to put on the pressure.

Terrek punched a button on the arm of his chair. The small boxes that depicted the major television news broadcasts from around the world disappeared, and the scene changed to a laboratory. Eight men in white lab coats—the Russian research scientists kidnapped from the Rybacky Complex—sat behind a table facing Terrek. Behind the scientists stood several of Terrek's black uniformed guards.

"Gentlemen, time is running short. I want answers."

One of Terrek's men translated the order into Russian.

The Russians were tired and dirty. They had not slept more than four hours in the past two days. Terrek's men had kept them working almost nonstop since their capture. A thin, bald man in his mid-fifties, whose head looked oversized for his puny body, stood up and looked at the camera. "What . . . what you have asked us to do . . . is impossible. We . . . we need more time. This will take three more days . . . possibly a week."

"What is the problem?" Terrek said bitterly. "Professor Kashkin, my patience is running out."

"The beauty of N1-2 was its rapid rate of growth in human hosts and the airborne transmission of the spores that grow in the infected living victims. The rate of growth predicted in my studies at Rybacky were accelerated to a factor of 100,000."

"That's why I stole N1-2, doctor. A small sample will spread across a wide area like a wildfire and then it burns itself out after a specific time period."

"Yes, but those predictions were never tested," Kashkin said. "N1-2 was designed with our problems in Chechnya in mind. Once unleashed, N1-2 would kill everyone within the country and then mutate into a benign form in less than seventy-two hours."

"Quit wasting my time, Kashkin," Terrek snapped. "Imagine what I will be able to do once you establish the right parameters for N1-2. You know what I want. Make it happen."

"To expand N1-2 to kill on a larger radius takes time. We have not been able to extend the genetic triggers to stop the seventy-two-hour mutation into a benign form. The victims are dying before the pathogen incubates to the level necessary for airborne transmission of the spores. We have not been able to make the pathogen self-replicate at the rate that I predicted in my earlier study."

"Do you need more equipment? Do you need more subjects?"

"No," Kashkin answered painfully. "Several of the American men have already died in experimentation, and we have not been able to achieve the desired replication rate. It's possible . . . there may be a different effect on the rate with infected women . . . we are running computer simulations now but we need more time to test."

Terrek stared at the old man. Kashkin looked pale and weak. But he suddenly stood up straight and gathered his strength. "I won't continue to subject these people to these inhuman experiments."

The room grew silent. Kashkin sat down, drained of the fleeting surge of courage that had momentarily pulsed through his body.

Terrek sat quietly, considering the information. "Professor Kashkin. This is your black business, so don't give me any of that crap about humanity. You didn't invent N1-2 to improve the health and longevity of your fellow man. You Russian bastards would have used it against the people of the Caucasus if you thought you could get away with it. Now it's your turn to show me that you can do what your study said you can do. I just want to direct your brilliant efforts to a worthy cause."

"Sir, I cannot do the impossible," Kashkin offered.

"Oh, but you can. You just need more motivation. You are the world's expert in biological warfare pathogens. Your top secret paper on N1-2 is the reason that you are here. You described in your study that you could develop N1-2 to remain contagious for any time period— a programmable period pathogen weapon. It's really a brilliant idea. With N1-2, a few ounces are all you need. Using the projections in your study, and with the dose of pathogen that I intend to unleash, N1-2 can consume the entire United States in only three weeks. But at the end of three weeks, after killing every human being in the United States, N1-2 burns itself out and becomes benign."

The old man shook his head. "You might kill all the

people in a large city, but I'll need more time, possibly weeks, to attain the rate of replication necessary to develop N1-2 into a virus that could consume the entire United States in only three weeks. Under ideal conditions, with the equipment in my lab, I might have been able to—"

"Enough!" Terrek screamed. "Who is the least valuable member of your team?"

"I don't understand," Kashkin said feebly.

"Guards. Shoot the Russian who sits to the far left of Professor Kashkin."

One of Terrek's men jerked the man seated to the far left of Kashkin to his feet and threw him against the wall. With one hand on the man's shoulder, forcing the terrified scientist against the cold concrete, the guard placed the barrel of his rifle at the small of the horrified Russian's neck.

"Nyet. Nyet. Kashkin. Pomogee!" the scientist pleaded.

The guard fired one round into the man's head. His skull ripped apart, splattering brains and blood all over the wall. The guard let go of the man's shoulder, and he crumpled to the ground like a broken doll.

"Use the women. Use whatever you need," Terrek demanded. "You have twenty-four hours. Kashkin, I've read the secret study that you filed last month. In that report you bragged that you could have N1-2 operational in hours, not weeks. It cost me a fortune to buy that report, and I am a man who always makes money on his investments."

Kashkin, who looked utterly defeated, merely nodded.

"I intend to use N1-2 to change the world," Terrek growled. "I may only get one chance at introducing this weapon into the United States. I cannot afford half measures. If you do not have N1-2 working in twenty-four hours, I will shoot all of you, one at a time."

0330 hours, at the temporary TALON Force Command Center at a secret location in the mountains of Colorado

"Yes, sir. I understand the President's instructions." Brigadier General Jack Krauss put down the telephone receiver.

There comes a moment in every crisis where events can go either way. If you had the courage to make bold decisions, you won. If you hesitated, you lost. This was one of those times.

General Krauss stood with his hands on his hips looking up the latest update on the flat-screen electronic situation map. In the soft, dim light of the TALON Force Command Center, the long row of ribbons on the left breast of his Army green uniform glowed from the reflection of the big screen as if they were phosphorescent. The growth of stubble on his chin and the fatigue in his eyes could not be seen in the eerie gleam of the computer screens.

Absentmindedly, he held his prosthetic right hand in his left, massaging the plastic, almost lifelike limb as if it were real skin. He was worried. His troopers were engaging the enemy, and he was helpless to support them. *The most high-tech force on the planet, and I can't talk to any of them,* Krauss fumed.

The room sloped down toward the huge, flat-screen projection, as in a large movie theater. Two rows of computer terminals and workstations were located just below him, close to the screen. Special operations command C^4I (Command, Control, Communications, Computers, and Intelligence) specialists from all four services manned the computers.

From this command center deep inside the mountains of Colorado, General Krauss could observe TALON Force operations anywhere in the world—that is, until they had lost communications with the Eagle Team.

The last known location of the Eagle Team was depicted on the computer-generated map. A small triangular icon depicted each member of the team. The icons were clustered just to the northwest of Vladivostok.

Krauss looked away from the screen to the chief of staff of the TALON Force Command Center who was busy on the telephone. "Colonel Dunlop, do we have any idea if the Russians know we are there?"

"No, sir," Dunlop replied, cupping his hand over the phone's transmitter. "I'm on the line with the NSA right now. They are monitoring forty-six regional Russian military channels. The Vladivostok Military Region Command Center has reported that the fighting is over at the Rybacky compound and that the facility is secure. They have killed sixteen terrorists and captured four, but there is no indication that they know anything about our people."

The tall Special Forces general nodded and placed his hands behind his back and paced a few steps. "Get me more information, Colonel. We have to know what to do next. Is the Cobra Team ready?"

Colonel Dunlop nodded, acknowledging that a second TALON Force team had been alerted and was moving to the deployment airfield. "Our second X-37 is fueled and awaiting the arrival of the Cobra Team at Groom Lake."

Krauss managed a quick smile. Groom Lake, sometimes known as Area 51, was the secret military facility about ninety miles north of Las Vegas that was home base for the X-37 rocket plane. If only the UFO nuts and alien enthusiasts saw the X-37 rocket plane and the high-tech gear that had been developed for the TALON Force they might just think that it came from beyond the solar system.

But Krauss didn't have time to daydream. He had real problems that involved the life and death of his troopers and the fate of the citizens of the country he had sworn to protect. He worried about the real-world problem of a Russia still armed with 25,000 nuclear weapons, and how they would react to an invasion of their sovereign territory. He worried that if the Russians captured the Eagle Team, there would be an embarrassing international incident.

He wasn't the only one who was worried. He had already received three phone calls from the Secretary of Defense and now the President. The President was particularly unnerved by the loss of communications with the Eagle Team. The Commander-in-Chief had authorized the use of the TALON Force on Russian territory based solely on the belief that they could slip in, accomplish their mission, and slip out without being detected. It had taken a strong argument by the Chairman of the Joint Chiefs of Staff to convince the civilian decision makers that the TALON Force's combination of ultrasophisticated technology and superb training could accomplish the mission without the Russians even knowing it. The information that had tipped the balance was an intelligence report from the CIA that predicted that the Brotherhood had a very good chance of stealing the most lethal biological warfare germs in the world from the Russians and that they were intent on using it on an American city.

Now that TALON headquarters had lost contact with the Eagle team, everyone was concerned that the quick in-and-out preemptive strike against the terrorists would turn into an embarrassing incident that bordered on an act of war against Russia.

Hell, Krauss thought, *they were running around in circles with their hair on fire. I had better get moving to play the role of the fireman or, once the news that U.S. forces were captured or killed in Russia gets out, there won't be a TALON Force.*

"General, I think we may have figured out what happened to our comms," young Jerry Rossner reported. "The Russians are using new technology, something we've heard rumors about but have never seen before. We believe that they discovered the TALON Force frequency, their jammers locked on to that HF signal, and they are blocking them with some kind of homing wave."

"Mr. Rossner, the President will shut us down if we don't get communications back up with the Eagle Team. The people at the State Department are edgy as a herd of deer at an NRA convention. They want to start talking to the Russians about this operation. I need results, not explanations, and I need them fast."

"Yes, sir. I think I have a solution. All we have to do is to reverse the polarity of our signal and boost it back at the Russians. We have more satellites up than they do, and ours are more powerful. If my guess is right, we can fry their systems and free up our communications with the Eagle Team. We can then hop to another frequency, and with any luck, our communications will be clear."

Krauss looked at the young civilian technician. *Times are changing,* Krauss thought. *The geek-to-warrior ratio is rising dramatically.*

Confidence gleamed in Rossner's eyes. "We can do it, sir. They'll never know what hit them."

Krauss nodded. "Let's do it. How long will it take?"

Mr. Rossner looked over his right shoulder to two Army captains sitting at the computer console listening to this conversation with General Krauss. One of the captains shrugged and said, "Ten minutes?"

Krauss looked at the screen and studied the seven little white triangles that represented the Eagle Team. The icons were clustered northwest of Vladivostok near the Rybacky complex. He knew that those locations were eighteen hours old. He looked to the south and noted the location of the nearest aircraft carrier, the USS *Constellation,* steaming just to the southeast of North Korea at 132 Longitude and 44 Latitude, in the Sea of Japan. He knew that the TFV-22 Super Ospreys, the aircraft that were to be used to extract the Eagle Team, were standing by on her flight deck.

He checked the elapsed running time that scrolled across the bottom of the big screen. The longer the Eagle Team remained out of contact, the greater the chances that they would be killed or captured. He didn't want to think what would happen if the Russians got hold of TALON Force technology.

Krauss looked at the telephone that linked TALON Force headquarters in the mountains of Colorado with the White House. Information warfare operations may not cause casualties, but they are still acts of war. But if he called and asked for permission, it might take another three to four hours before the decision makers made up their minds.

In the meantime, the clock was ticking, and he couldn't help his troopers without communications.

"Mr. Rossner, is there any way that we can make the disabling of the Russian systems look like an accident?"

Rossner lowered his head and rubbed his hand across his face. After a few seconds he looked up at Krauss with a wide grin on his face. "Well, sir, the Russians are using two satellites as part of the network for this new jamming system. We know which satellites, and we can determine their frequencies. If we could refocus their satellites onto their own ground sources, we could make it look as if a burst of feedback from their own systems caused the malfunction."

"We could send a few messages out in the clear from Japan and nearby ships at sea warning them of our own satellite problems due to electromagnetic interference," Colonel Dunlop added. "The Russians may think that their jamming caused these malfunctions. That might reinforce the deception."

General Krauss knew that it was now or never. His team, the success of the mission, and many other lives hung in the balance. Krauss looked to his left and shot a glance at the chief of staff, Colonel Dunlop.

"We must act now sir, or we will lose the data link on their system," Rossner added.

Dunlop looked at the general and nodded. "Sounds like a plan to me."

"Okay," Krauss answered. "On my authority, make it happen."

0400 hours, thirty kilometers east of Aojin, North Korea

The stars shone brilliantly in a clear sky dominated by a bright full moon. The storm had passed, and the ground was covered in bright, white snow.

Hunter Blake checked his instruments, then scanned the horizon. Mountains. Nothing but mountains, more mountains, and bigger mountains. He worried that there wasn't a flat patch of ground in the entire godforsaken country. Abruptly, he reacted to the outline of a mountain, straight ahead, much too close for comfort. He pulled up on the stick, the engine sputtered, coughed, and gagged, then surged back to life. The AN-2 Colt climbed, struggling against gravity, barely clearing the top of the craggy peak.

"Hey Hunter, I could have reached out the window and taken a soil sample on that last hill," Jen Olsen said over the comm net. "What's the matter? Don't you believe in altitude?"

Blake, who was too busy to answer, checked his analog dials. "I think that we'll have just enough fuel to make it." He looked at Major Barrett, who was sitting in the right-hand seat, acting as copilot. "At least I hope so."

"I thought you said that we'd have no problem making it in this thing," Travis Barrett said. "What's the problem?"

"The fuel consumption on this baby is a bit worse than I first thought," Blake answered. "It looks like this engine is in bad need of an overhaul. Don't worry, one way or the other, we're almost there."

"Just make sure that *there* is near those coordinates, not the side of some godforsaken pile of rock," Travis said. "Wong, what's the status on our comms?"

"The jamming is pretty sophisticated, Major. They found our frequency and put a precision block on it, kind of like a carrier code that followed our frequency no matter how many times we hopped. They even used satellites to block our straight-up comms."

"Just give me the bottom line, Wong. When will I have communications with TALON Force headquarters?"

"I'm working on it, Major. I should have it in the next fifteen minutes."

Travis reviewed his location on the three-dimensional map in his BSD screen. The team was ten minutes out from the grid coordinates of the Citadel. "Put us down on this stretch of highway, six kilometers north of the target area. I make it to be three minutes out."

"Roger," Blake replied. "I just hope that that road is as straight as it looks on the map."

The aircraft banked slowly to the north and Hunter

searched the ground for signs of the road. Landing an AN-2 Colt on a road made for automobiles was hard enough, but making the landing at night, using night vision goggles, was a task that only a few pilots in the world could even hope to accomplish. Blake felt his hands grip the steering wheel tightly as perspiration streamed down from the brim of his helmet. He knew the seriousness of the situation. He would only have one chance to do this right, and he hoped that the forces of gravity wouldn't work against him and send his ancient aircraft nose first into the ground.

"Brace yourselves," Blake reported into his comm net. "I see the road up ahead, and it looks fairly level. We'll land in sixty seconds."

"What are our chances?" Travis asked.

"One hundred percent that we'll be on the ground in fifty-five seconds," Blake replied without taking his view off the road ahead. "I'll tell you the rest later."

The AN-2 Colt had four seats in the front—one for the pilot and copilot and two behind—then three seats on two opposing rows along the fuselage. Jen Olsen sat in the backseat along the right side of the fuselage. Jack DuBois sat to her right, checking the action on his XM-29 rifle. She tightened her seat belt and looked across the belly of the plane at Sam on the other side. Sam had placed his communications pack in front of Jenny on the floor of the plane. He was busy pressing the digital buttons on the top of the comm pack, trying to work through the jamming. Suddenly, his head jerked up, and Jenny saw a broad smile fill his face.

"Major Barrett, I rerouted our comms and accessed a secure computer system at the NSA. I can't send video or voice, but I can send a brief coded internet message."

"Good job," Travis said into his comm net. "Send them our location, that all systems are green, and the grid coordinates of the Brotherhood base camp."

"Wilco," Wong replied. "I'll work—"

"Okay, boys and girls," Blake interrupted. "This is it. We're going down. Hold on!"

The aircraft plunged through the black sky as the

moonlight shimmered off the snow-covered road that lay dead ahead. Jenny Olsen felt her stomach roll. She closed her eyes and leaned forward into the crash position with her prodigious chest on her knees. At the same time, Jack DuBois leaned over and put his left arm around her. Jenny felt the power of Jack's muscular arm and was comforted by the touch of a teammate.

We are one team, like a close-knit family, she thought. *Let's hope it doesn't all end here in the mountains of North Korea.*

The aircraft bounced violently as the wheels hit the hard, snowy road. The engine of the AN-2 Colt roared as the aircraft shifted off one wheel, then went back to the other. After an anxious moment, the craft settled onto both wheels and Blake struggled to keep the Colt on the road. Seconds later, the aircraft rolled to a stop, sliding into a steep bank of snow. Blake cut the engine.

There was a long silence, then a collective sigh of relief.

Jenny, a look of grateful deliverance on her face, turned her head toward the pilot. "Blake, if you weren't prettier than me, I'd kiss you."

"What?" Blake responded in mock horror. He pulled off his helmet and took in a deep breath. "Hell, babe, they don't make them any better than Hunter Blake. There isn't a thing with wings I can't fly or a girl that I can't charm."

Jenny smiled, happy to be alive and totally content to let Blake have the last word.

A twitch of amusement played on Travis's lips. *Well, I've cheated death one more time,* he thought to himself, shaking his head in disbelief. "Okay, Eagle Team, let's get cracking. We have some tangos to surprise."

0430 hours, at the Radio-Electronic Combat Node 75 of the Vladivostok Regional Command, near Vladivostok, Russia

Captain Lysenko sat at his computer terminal, sending encoded commands to the Array, the high-power combination of ground-based and satellite jammers. He was exhausted, along with the rest of the crew of his radio-electronic combat station. It had been a long night, and they were under orders to stay at their posts until the mission was over. At the rate things were going, that might be a very long time.

The Array was still jamming the high-frequency net that was discovered during the attack on the Rybacky Complex. Since the attack on Rybacky, the entire Vladivostok region had continued on full alert.

From the moment that Colonel Yarov made the decision to jam the intruder frequency and satellite transmissions, the Array had operated flawlessly. Yarov was particularly pleased that the new system had surpassed all expectations in its first trial by fire. Whoever was trying to use those frequencies, Yarov boasted, would eat static until Colonel Yarov turned the jammers off.

Lysenko moved the track ball mouse of his computer to issue new instructions to the satellite. The cursor did not move. Suddenly, the coordinates of the satellite area of coverage changed. Lysenko frowned. *Our satellites are not responding as I have programmed,* he thought.

Lysenko tried again. Nothing happened. He rubbed his tired eyes. Someone else had control of his satellites. Suddenly, the screen of his terminal flickered.

"What the . . . !" The computer console abruptly burst into a shower of sparks. Captain Sergei Lysenko threw off the headset and fell backward in his chair. The lights in the building went off, and all of the computer screens at Radio-Electronic Combat Node 75 of the Vladivostok Regional Command went blank.

Lysenko was flat on his back, dazed, lying on the cold, concrete floor of the station. He shook his head, then rubbed his face with his hands. "What the hell is going on?"

The emergency lights kicked on, then failed. One of the technicians in the dark room moved toward the sparking server and tripped over Lysenko.

"Ugh!" Lysenko screamed as the man's knees fell on his chest. "Get off me, you clumsy buffoon!"

"Captain Lysenko, forgive me," the man answered as he groped to avoid stepping on his captain. The emergency lights suddenly flickered, then remained on, flooding the station room with bright, battery-powered light.

The man who had stepped on Lysenko moved to the side and stared at the computer terminals as the internal wiring popped and sizzled. Lysenko looked up at the main server, a closet-sized computer purchased at great expense from the Japanese. The server smoldered and crackled as black smoke wafted to the ceiling. Another soldier behind Lysenko in the crowded computer room grabbed the fire extinguisher off its wall bracket and frantically sprayed the server to extinguish the tiny fires that glowed inside the box.

Lysenko was suddenly covered in a cloud. He couldn't breathe; he panicked, then realized that the idiot with the fire extinguisher had shot a full blast of powder in his direction, covering him in white dust. The captain gagged, rolled over to one side, and staggered up, seeking air.

Colonel Yarov rushed into the station, looking like the owner of a new sports car that had just been vandalized by teenagers. Yarov seemed to be looking for the vandals. The room smelled of burning electrical insulation. The open door behind the colonel let a gust of fresh air into the room.

"Lysenko!" Yarov demanded. "What in God's name is happening?"

"*Tovarich* commander," Lysenko answered as he staggered up, his immaculate uniform disheveled and doused with white powder from the fire extinguisher. "Station seventy-five . . . is out of service, but God had nothing to do with it."

Colonel Yarov was stunned, angry, incredulous, annoyed, and perplexed—all at the same time. How could this happen to him? What would happen to him? His project, which was one of the few bright spots in an otherwise bleak Russian Army, was fizzling in front of him. His typically tight-lipped mouth was wide open, and his normally calm, patrician face seemed frozen in shock.

His brilliant career, the years of struggle and sacrifice, now flashed before his eyes, and he saw himself standing before his boorish, unfeeling superior, General Babichov, trying to explain the unexplainable. He stared at Lysenko, unable to speak, as the station's server burst into another shower of sparks.

Chapter Twelve

. . . attaining one hundred victories in one hundred battles is not the pinnacle of excellence.
Subjugating the enemy's army without fighting is the true pinnacle of excellence.

—Sun Tzu, *The Art of War*

November 15, 0630 hours, near Aojin, North Korea

"Sir, I have contact with TALON Force headquarters, loud and clear, on full-spectrum bandwidth," Sam Wong announced over the comm net.

"Major Barrett, what the hell are you and Eagle Team doing in North Korea?" General Krauss demanded. "The NSC is shitting pickles. Do you want to start a war?"

Travis dropped his BSD monocle. The image of General Krauss appeared before his eyes.

"No, sir. I hope to prevent one." Travis's left eye activated the scroll command in his BSD screen and highlighted an update file of the last twenty-eight hours. Blinking, Travis clicked on the Send command. "You have the update now, sir," Travis said coolly. "I had hot pursuit authority. We lost communications, and I acted on my orders."

There was a pause on the other end of the comm link. Krauss was quickly searching the update for critical information. "Stand by," the general answered.

Eagle Team was on the move, climbing the eastern slope of Hill 350, southwest of the village of Aojin. The five men and two women troopers struggled up the slope in the dark, one step at a time. The terrorists' base was only a few kilometers away. The early-morning air was cold, but their temperature-controlled suits kept them warm.

Eagle Team was moving in nonstealth mode in order to save power. The hills were covered in pine trees, which helped to hide the team's approach to the objective. "Hold up here. Everyone take a knee," Travis ordered over his comm net. He wanted to focus his complete attention on General Krauss's answer.

Eagle Team stopped. DuBois was at point, his XM-29 rifle at the ready. Powczuk was right behind him, followed by Greene, Barrett, Wong, Olsen, and Blake.

The seconds passed, and Travis saw his warm breath cloud in the cold air. The snow glistened, and the glazed pine branches reflected flecks of moonlight. The sky was slowly turning gray with the approach of dawn. If he wasn't on his way to battle terrorists, Travis thought, he'd say it was a beautiful night.

"Barrett, good decision, son," Krauss announced over the comm net. "We can't let them take N1-2 out of North Korea. N1-2 is one of a kind. The destruction of that pathogen is a Code One priority. You have to find it. What makes you think that N1-2 is in that compound?"

"It's been less than twenty-four hours since they gained control of the virus. The terrorists headed directly here after their assault on Rybacky. This compound is an ideal place for them to safely study and operationalize the N1-2."

There was another short pause. Travis could hear the general talking in the background to someone else.

"We concur," Krauss answered. "What's your plan?"

"We can be in position in a few hours. I'll conduct a reconnaissance first, and then we'll position ourselves to designate the critical structures inside the camp for your precision munitions. I recommend that you strike them as soon as your weapons are in position. I'm hoping that you have something in the area of operations that can take this out."

"Wait," Krauss ordered.

Travis crouched silently in the snow, listening to his own breathing. If everything went right, they would identify the exact location of the pathogen, and Krauss would have a special Air Force strike blast it to kingdom come. Once the samples of N1-2 were vaporized, he would lead

Eagle Team to the coast and TFV-22 Super Ospreys could pick them up.

"I can have twelve Bunker Busters in the air, ready to deliver, in eleven hours," Krauss replied. "That will make it right about sunset."

Twelve Bunker Busters! Travis smiled. In most cases, one or two were all that was needed. The NSC wasn't taking any chances on this one.

"You have until then to verify the location of the N1-2 agent," Krauss continued, "or we'll have to use another option. There can be no weapons release without verification."

Travis didn't like the term *other option.* He could only guess that it was a worst-case option, the use of a small, tactical nuke to take out a potential weapons-of-mass-destruction threat to the United States. "Won't that be an act of war against North Korea?"

"You let us worry about that. If Eagle Team does its job and the damage is confined to Terrek's camp, we think the chances are pretty slim of the North Koreans escalating this affair."

"Roger that, sir. Anything further?"

"Yes, I've just sent you the latest intelligence update. It has been confirmed that Lee, on Terrek's orders, led the Rybacky assault. There is a good chance that Terrek is in North Korea, too."

"Sir, do we know if the North Koreans are behind Terrek's plans for N1-2?" Travis asked.

"No. You know how difficult it is to find out what is going on in North Korea, but we think Terrek has left the North Koreans out in the cold on this one. Our intel indicates that Terrek is running his own, personal war against the United States, and that the North Koreans are just renting him sanctuary. You may be able to exploit that."

"We'll do our best," Travis said, looking at the data scroll down his BSD screen. "We'll see if we can get Terrek for you in the bargain."

"No, it's too risky. I want you to verify the location of the N1-2 virus, and then we will destroy the Brotherhood base. We can't afford to lose any of you," Krauss answered. "Let the missiles do their work. However, there is one more thing."

Travis waited. The rest of the Eagle Team listened carefully.

"He may have taken the hostages from Egypt to North Korea. We don't know why, but there's a good chance they may be part of this N1-2 plan."

"What if the hostages *are* there?" Travis asked.

"Too many lives hang in the balance," Krauss replied. "Your mission is to destroy N1-2, not rescue hostages. You're lucky that the North Koreans haven't found you, let alone the terrorists. You must pinpoint N1-2 and then let the missiles do their work. After the missile strike, we'll pick you up by V-22 at the rendezvous point shown in the reports I sent you. If you can't pinpoint the exact location of N1-2, then the Eagle Team has until 0300 hours tomorrow morning to be at the rendezvous point for pickup."

"And then the NSC will authorize the other option?"

"Affirmative," Krauss answered tersely. "We are running out of alternatives. N1-2 is too dangerous. It's in your hands. Is that clear?"

"Roger, sir."

"Good luck. Krauss out."

Travis paused as Krauss's transmission ended; the thought of the other option sent a chill up his spine.

"Well, team," Hunter said, "it looks like it's us or Armageddon."

Stan turned toward Travis and said, "Do you mean to tell me that those bastards have American prisoners in there?"

"We don't know that for certain. It's a possibility until verified," Travis replied. His mind raced as he considered the courses of action he might take in the next few hours. If he decided wrong, there would be worldwide implications. His first duty was to the mission and his team. But what if they came across the hostages that Krauss mentioned?

"Why would Terrek go to the trouble of bringing hostages all the way to Korea?" Stan said. "A human shield? It doesn't make sense. He must know that hostages wouldn't stop us from taking him out."

"Hell, so far, he thinks he's in the clear," Jack said. "He don't know we're onto him. He thinks he safe as a bug in the rug, nestled up here in the wilds of North Korea."

"Well, it's about time he found out he's not," Sam added.

"Major Barrett, are you thinking what I'm thinking?" Sarah asked Travis over the comm net.

Travis suddenly knew the answer. "Yeah . . . if there are Americans here, they're not here as a human shield. They're lab rats. To operationalize N1-2, Terrek needs guinea pigs to test the pathogen on before he scatters it across the United States."

"So what do you want to do, boss?" Stan asked.

"You all remember Wong's Last Stand, right?" Travis said.

Sam had been following the conversation and was at a loss for words. "What are you talking about, Major? Sure, we remember. What does that have to do with anything?"

"I'll tell you later," Travis declared, a deadly determination in his voice. He felt the presence of the shadow, but he was too pumped with adrenaline, too focused on his next move, to care. "Okay Eagle Team, let's move out."

1100 hours, the Citadel, in North Korea

"Helga, did I ever tell you about my godson?" Elizabeth Douglas asked.

"*Nein,*" Helga answered. "I vould like to hear. Please tell me."

"His parents were our best friends, and my husband and I were chosen as his godparents. His father was in the military, and while he was posted overseas for several years, we raised him as our own."

"What does he do for a living?" Helga asked. The sound of heavy boots coming down the stairway directly in front of their cell interrupted the conversation. The stairway in front of them led up to the ground level of the Citadel. To the left of her cell was a concrete wall. To the right was a long corridor that contained more cells like her own. Anyone coming down the stairs first saw the cell in which Elizabeth, Helga, and the others were held.

Elizabeth stood up, looking through the bars at the stairway. Three black-uniformed soldiers walked up to her. Beverly sat on the thin-mattressed bed, with her back to the wall and her knees at her chest. Helga sat on the center bed, looking like an immovable spirit, solid and composed. Next to her was Rachel, with a brown wool blanket draped over her shoulders and her young baby in her arms. Mary Uley, the elderly Canadian woman, sat on the bed against the left wall, quietly praying.

The men stood menacingly in front of the cell and gawked at the women without saying a word. Elizabeth saw the look in their eyes, and she knew what they had come for. One man, an African with a dark black face and cold, savage eyes, stared at Beverly. The man next to him, a wide-faced, hawk-nosed European, fidgeted with a set of keys in his hand. The third man, a Turk with curly black hair, gaped at Rachel.

The men smelled of liquor. They were obviously just getting off duty and were searching for some off-duty pleasure.

Elizabeth leaned over to Beverly and whispered. "Don't ask questions. You are very sick. Start coughing and stick your hand down your throat without letting them see you, and try to vomit. Act like you are dying."

Beverly looked at her with incredulous eyes. Elizabeth met her gaze with a determined glare that said, *Do it!* Helga saw what was about to happen.

The black man nudged the Turk in the ribs. "It's about time we had a woman. I've been pulling guard duty every day for a week."

"I, too, am tired of these North Korean whores they send us. They're so damn skinny. But are you sure that we can take them? Didn't Terrek say that they were to be used for the project tomorrow?"

"When the bastards in that lab are finished with them, no man will want them," the European answered. "Hell, we're doing them a favor by letting them party a little before Terrek has no more use for them."

"Well, I know what to do with them." The Turk chuckled and said something obscene in Turkish.

The three men laughed. The black man passed a pint of whiskey to the Turk. The Turk downed a quick swig and then handed the bottle back.

"Stands back from der door," the European ordered in gruff, heavily accented English. He put the key into the lock.

Elizabeth stepped back but put her hands up in protest. "We are very sick in here. I think this girl here has a disease. We may all be infected. We need a doctor."

The European hesitated and looked up at the cell block designation as if to check the number. The Turk looked at the black man and again said some obscenity in Turkish.

The black man shrugged. "Maybe they have started on this group without telling us?"

Beverly leaned over on the bed, away from the men, and forced herself to gag. She fell off the bed and onto her knees on the cold concrete and vomited a cup of water, rice, and fish soup on the floor.

"This one is sick, too. She has a high fever," Elizabeth announced, pointing at Rachel. Rachel played the part, swinging her baby in her arms as if she were possessed and rolling her eyes around the room. "She's delirious. It's a serious virus."

"Smallpox?" The European took a step back. "A virus like smallpox?"

Elizabeth didn't answer at first, but she could see from the shock on the man's face that she had stumbled onto something. Could there be an outbreak of smallpox in the compound? She thought that smallpox had been eradicated. Had she caught on to something that she could use?

She felt her heart beating hard. She tried to play on the terrorists' fears, but she didn't know if they were buying the charade. "I am a nurse. Yes, it's the initial stages of smallpox. We need a doctor. She is developing pustules on her legs and under her arms. I know smallpox when I see it. Do you want to see the pustules?"

"Um Gottes willen!" the man with the keys cursed. "If zey are infected, we had better leave zem alone." The European turned to his two comrades.

"What about this one? She doesn't look sick," the Turk answered, pointing at Elizabeth.

The black man looked at Elizabeth and shook his head. "Too old," the black man said. "There are some younger, juicer ones down the hall in the next cell."

"Not too old for me." The Turk grinned a toothy smile. "I could use her. She was pretty once."

Elizabeth stood silent and still. Her heart felt as if it would leap out of her chest. She avoided looking at the Turk and stared at the European.

"Are you out of your minds?" the European said as he slammed the door. "Zey could all have za virus. Ve'll try another cell."

"Yeah, these bitches are not worth the effort," the African said.

The three men walked away, laughing. Beverly started to cry as she realized how close she had come to being raped. Rachel sat in silence and held onto her baby. Helga stood up and put her arm around Beverly's shoulders for comfort.

Elizabeth breathed a sigh of relief and turned to Beverly. Down the hallway, out of sight, they heard the sound of a cell door opening. A young woman's voice cried out, and they heard the men laughing. Then Elizabeth heard the sound of the cell door slam shut, and the three men dragged two young women past her cell. One of the girls was a teenager, possibly fifteen, and another appeared to be in her late twenties. The older woman looked at Elizabeth in terror as the Turk pulled her up the stairs by her long, brown hair.

"These bastards will pay for this," Elizabeth whispered, her body tight with rage.

She stood there for a long moment, holding onto the bars and trying to calm herself. Elizabeth heard one of the girls who had been taken up the stairway scream. *We won't be able to fool them much longer,* she thought. *The next time they come, I may not be able to stop them. How much more can we take? Please, God, send someone to help us.*

"What did they mean by going to the lab tomorrow?" Rachel asked, interrupting Liz's silent prayer.

"I don't know, honey," Elizabeth said, still standing and facing the bars of the cell. "I don't know."

1245 hours, headquarters to the 2nd Brigade, 121st Infantry Division, ten kilometers southwest of Aojin, North Korea

Colonel Kang Sok Ju, the commander of the 2nd Brigade of the 121st Infantry Division of the North Korean People's Army, put down the cup of soju and frowned at the young captain who stood above him. The colonel sat at a low table, his tunic unbuttoned, in a room that mirrored his Spartan view of life—containing only a sleeping mat, a table, and a wooden trunk for his uniforms. He was a soldier, with no family except his regiment. His only vice was his love of a stiff drink after the duty day was done. Sunday afternoons were considered off-duty hours, even in the North Korean Army. Now, even this small luxury was to be denied him.

"What is the meaning of this intrusion? How dare you disturb the brigade commander in his quarters!"

The young captain didn't flinch. He stood ramrod straight and looked into the commander's eyes. "Comrade Colonel, I am following your orders. All messages marked Critical that concern the Aojin Camp must be presented to you immediately."

The captain stuck his hand out and presented the report to the regimental commander.

Kang didn't like receiving reports on the weekend. Coded, high-priority reports never brought good news. He opened the report and read the contents quickly, then stared at the paper and read the report again.

"Have these codes been verified?"

"Yes, Comrade Colonel, I verified them myself."

Kang shook his head, then jumped from his chair and knelt down next to the safe to the right of his desk. He quickly dialed the combination, opened the heavy steel door, and withdrew his own code book. Turning to the proper cipher page, he carefully verified the authorization code.

The code was correct. There was no doubt about the authenticity of the orders. He was to set his command radios to the frequency stated in the orders and ignore all other transmissions until his mission was accomplished.

The colonel folded the report and tucked it into the inner pocket of his tunic. "What arrogance!" the colonel shouted. "How dare these running dogs set foot in the People's Republic!"

"Colonel, what are your orders?"

"Alert the brigade immediately, Captain. We have a nest of Americans to wipe out!"

Chapter Thirteen

Never bring a knife to a gunfight (law of gross weight and heavy caliber).

—TALON Force Rules to Live By

November 15, 1720 hours, the Citadel, near Aojin, North Korea

The guard shouted in Korean and waved the trucks forward.

"They told the trucks to park near the Citadel," Wong whispered over Powczuk's comm net.

Stan didn't answer. The rest of the TALONs could view everything that he saw. His BSD acted like a television camera, providing a front-row seat to the action for every TALON Force member. This was the beauty of being interconnected, not just internetted. Sam was safe, hiding in the trees on Hill 350, slightly south of the enemy compound. From there, Wong could keep a secure uplink with the satellites and stay in touch with TALON Force headquarters.

Stan was much closer to the enemy. He checked the view from the thermal image taken by a micro-UAV hovering over the camp. The big, square building in the center of the camp must be the Citadel that Wong was talking about.

The sun had sunk below the western horizon, and the light was withdrawing to the inexorable dusk. In the twilight, the two guards standing in front of the main entrance to the Citadel saw the lights of the weekly supply convoy approaching the main gate.

Seven trucks, each filled with meat, vegetables, and rice, formed a long queue in front of the entrance to the Citadel. The drivers, warmer inside their poorly heated cabs than outside in the cold air, looked straight ahead.

They did not see the shadowing shimmer that clung to the left side of the third truck in line.

Stan's heart skipped a beat as the truck moved past the man in the black uniform who was guarding the entrance to the compound. The tango was close—he could have reached out and touched him—but Stan moved past the unknowing guard like a gust of cold wind.

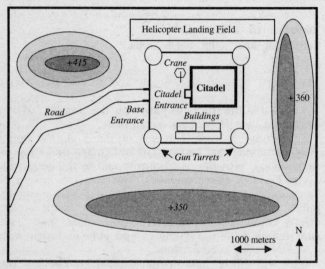

Map of the Brotherhood Base

The inside of the compound was surprisingly busy with activity. A huge crane, on the ground next to the Citadel, dipped down and lowered a ten-foot-square platform to ground level. A group of men labored to load the platform with heavy crates. The crane then pulled the heavy crates up and extended its long arm to the roof, where another group of men stood ready to unload them.

Inside the compound, the trucks took a left turn, and Stan hopped off, taking cover to the east of the big crane next to the wall of the Citadel. He then headed south, along the edge of the wall, moving like the last glimmer of sunlight glistening against the ice. None of the terrorists saw him as he made his way toward the central building in the compound.

So far, Stan's plan was working. Travis ordered Powczuk, Wong, and Olsen to reconnoiter the compound while the rest of Eagle Team set up on Hill 360. Powczuk and his three teammates moved to Hill 350 to find the entrance to the camp. From the western edge of Hill 350, Olsen and Wong launched Dragonfly UAVs, palm-sized robotic aircraft that quietly buzzed over the enemy positions without being noticed. Each UAV sent back different information. Wong's Dragonfly provided a thermal view of the compound from the air, identifying the location of the entrance to the fortress, the entrance to the Citadel, and the locations of buildings, fixed defensive weaponry, vehicles, and troops. Olsen's Dragonfly sniffed the air for specific human signatures, counting the number of defenders in the compound. The sniffer on her Dragonfly was able to register human scents and could differentiate between friend and foe by mere peculiarities in diet.

The initial reconnaissance had instantly sent valuable information about the terrorist camp to Travis and the others, who viewed the data in real time through their BSD. Travis saw that the camp was heavily guarded, with at least 120 men. The wall was twenty feet high and quite thick—too thick to blast through with the explosives that the team carried. Each of the round turrets at the four corners of the compound were armed with machine guns, automatic cannon, and surface-to-air missiles: in short, a formidable defensive position.

But the UAVs couldn't show Travis what was inside the central building, which the guards had called the Citadel. To get close enough to find where the N1-2 pathogen was kept and to destroy it, someone would have to get inside the large building behind the twenty-foot walls.

Characteristically, Stan Powczuk volunteered for the most dangerous mission. While Wong and Olsen lingered in lookout positions on Hill 350, south of the camp, Stan worked his way to the wall in stealth mode and headed

for the entrance of the compound. Stan was never a man
to do things in half measures, and there seemed no other
way inside than through the front door.

"Careful, Stan," Travis said over the comm net. Stan
was broadcasting a continuous stream of video to Travis
Barrett's BSD. The major and the rest of Eagle Team
could watch every move through Powczuk's eyes. "Don't
push your luck. Let the bug do the work."

Luck. Powczuk remembered the first time he had commanded a special operations mission. During the Gulf
War, SEAL Team 5 was given the mission of destroying
an Iraqi radar site the day before the air war was scheduled to start. They had flown nonstop from Diego Garcia
to a water drop zone just southeast of Basra in the Ara-
bian Gulf. The weather grew progressively worse as his
team closed on the jump point.

Stan remembered the Air Force jumpmaster report:
"The winds and sea state are marginal. Do you guys still
want to drop? It's your call."

Stan knew how important surprise was to the success
of the first day of the air war. No one knew how effective
the Iraqi air defense system would be, but it was a simple
fact that it would be more effective if the radar systems
were operational. Powczuk knew that the lives of U.S.
and coalition pilots depended on the destruction of those
radar sites, one of which his SEAL Team had to knock
out. Besides, his team had been pissing in their rubber
suits for four hours and had already cammied their faces
and checked their gear. This was the big night, and they
were ready. Nobody wanted to miss this party.

Powczuk replied, "Fuck yeah, let's go!"

As Murphy would have it, the wind at the drop zone
was blowing at fourteen knots. The six SEALs landed in
at least an eight-foot sea state. Because of their excellent
training and superb physical conditioning, all six managed to ditch their parachutes and swim toward the
beach without mishap.

They arrived on the beach at 0400, two hours late.
With the sun coming up in two hours, Powczuk decided
to head toward the radar site, then lay up nearby, and

attack the enemy radar installation at dusk. After the tough swim, every man needed a rest.

The SEAL Team occupied an abandoned oil drilling station, two kilometers from the Iraqi radar. Stan set up his SatCom radio and called in their location to headquarters, then settled down for a short nap.

Less than thirty minutes later, four trucks pulled up to the nearest road and off-loaded troops. The Iraqi infantry immediately formed a skirmish line and began walking toward the shack where the SEALs were hiding.

Powczuk remembered his heart racing as he alerted the team. He looked to the north and saw nothing but open desert. There was no place to run.

The skirmish line grew closer, and the SEALs charged their weapons. The seconds ticked by, and everyone waited, silently, desperate but determined, for Powczuk to give the order to fire.

He could make out the faces of the Iraqis. There were almost sixty men coming at them, their rifles at the ready. He knew that his SEALs were good men—the best special operations warriors in the business—but the odds were fierce. This was it.

Then, suddenly, a whistle blew, and the soldiers turned around and headed back to their trucks. Luck saved him that day, and he pushed his luck and used it against the Iraqis. That day, Murphy was on his side.

After dark, Powczuk's team moved down to the target area paralleling the nearest road. An Iraqi truck traveling with blackout lights slowly moved down the road in the direction of the radar station. Powczuk saw the truck, realized how open the terrain was, and decided to make a slight change in plan. He ran up to the cab and hopped on the running board, surprising the terrified Iraqi driver and pulling the truck over at gunpoint. The SEALs gagged the two Iraqis and bound them hand and foot, then dropped them off at the side of the road. Powczuk's SEAL Team then climbed aboard the truck and headed toward the radar site.

Stan pulled right up to the front gate of the barbed-wire compound. He opened the door to the cab, walked out in front of the truck, and rapidly shot the two Iraqis at the gate with his silenced .45 caliber pistol. No one else in the compound stirred. The sound of Arabic music from a local Baghdad radio station echoed from a bunker to the right of the large, oval radar dish.

His demolition team jumped out of the truck and ran toward the radar. With the other members of the team providing security, two SEALs placed explosives on the dish and set a digital timer.

Quietly, moving in short bounds, the men moved back to the truck. Within seconds, they were all in the truck and driving south, toward the beach and their pickup point. In another ten minutes, they were in the water and headed out to meet the pickup boat when the explosions went off. Almost simultaneously, an Iraqi armored column moved down the road toward the radar site. Powczuk looked back and saw the radar site in flames and the Iraqi tanks rushing toward the perimeter. Mission accomplished, but it had been a very close thing.

How many more close calls had there been since then? How many near misses had he survived? Stan didn't want to think about it. Were his chances running out?

Hell no. He grinned to himself. "I've just begun to fight," he answered over his comm net to Travis. "I've got to get closer, or the bug won't work."

The North Korean trucks that entered the compound stopped in a long line outside the Citadel. The drivers exited their cabs and moved to the back to lower the tailgates. A platoon of men left the entrance of the Citadel to unload the supplies.

Powczuk moved along the wall toward the entrance to the Citadel, unnoticed by a dozen men working in the open courtyard. Two men with automatic rifles guarded the open entrance of the Citadel. Powczuk recognized that he couldn't slip by those guards—stealth camouflage or not, they would feel his presence.

This is as far as I can go, he thought. *Time for the bug.*

Powczuk opened a pouch on the right side of his belt and took out three finger-sized, six-legged, micromachines. The bugs were small, almost transparent robots made completely of clear plastic and thin, silver wires. Powczuk placed them on the ground and activated them with his comm net. "Forward," he commanded.

The tiny machines raced toward the entrance to the Citadel, scurrying remarkably fast for their small size. Powczuk switched his BSD to see the view from the microbot. In a world that seemed all out of scale, Powczuk moved the tiny scout past the guards and into the Citadel.

"Okay, Stan," Travis's voice sounded over the comm net. "Mission accomplished. Sam will take it from here. You get your ass out of there."

Powczuk suddenly received a warning signal over his comm net. A pleasant female voice announced, "Power failure. Three minutes to stealth mode shut down."

Stan, in near panic, turned off his microbot view and quickly scanned the courtyard. Enemy soldiers were all about, some as close as twenty feet from him. He was safe, kneeling flat against the wall of the Citadel, as long as his stealth camouflage was on. As soon as his power failed, he'd stick out like a naked woman on the floor of the Senate.

He activated his auxiliary power pack. Nothing happened. The system had either malfunctioned or discharged.

"Shit, shit, shit! I'm moving to the compound entrance now," Stan whispered.

"I've got the front door covered," Wong announced. "If you need to run for it, I can support by fire."

"Two minutes and thirty seconds to complete power failure of stealth mode," the sweet feminine voice announced.

"Shut up!" Powczuk whispered. He was trapped. The guards in front of the compound were standing in the entrance. There were too many tangos all over the courtyard. He wouldn't be able to slip by, even in stealth mode.

Stan moved to the compound wall, still unseen, but knowing that his stealth power was draining. *Just my luck,* he thought. *Why the hell are these bastards so busy this evening?*

His mind raced. He wasn't going to make it. Then he saw the crane, filled with heavy boxes, beginning its move up to the roof. Quickly he aimed his left wrist at the control cab of the crane and fired a burst from his HERF gun.

The crane suddenly jerked to a stop, swinging the pallet violently to the left against the wall of the Citadel. The heavy boxes on the pallet spilled to the ground, smashing among the men in the courtyard.

"One minute until complete power failure of stealth mode," the unemotional feminine voice announced over Stan's comm net.

Men scurried all about the courtyard, trying to get away from the objects falling off the pallet. In the confusion, Powczuk sprinted for the entrance like his hometown football hero Mike Ditka rushing to tackle a fullback. Still in stealth mode, he hit the two guards at full speed and split them like a running back going for the goal line. They never knew what hit them, as they crashed to the ground. Powczuk, running at top speed, made it to the cover of the pine trees without being detected.

1900 hours, inside Terrek's control room in the Citadel

Lee passed the black-uniformed guards and entered Terrek's inner sanctum. As he walked toward Terrek, Lee heard a muffled, squeaking noise. He looked around but saw nothing.

"You are just in time," Terrek said as he turned to watch the latest live television broadcast from the lab. An unemotional Russian scientist looked on as a terrified young man, Rachel's husband, strapped to a table in an isolation lab, was exposed to the N1-2 virus. "I love the Ebola virus. It kills ninety percent of its victims in little more than a week. Connective tissue liquefies; every orifice bleeds. In the final stages, Ebola victims become convulsive, splashing contaminated blood around them as they twitch, shake, and thrash to their deaths."

Lee nodded to Terrek, then looked at the big screen on the wall.

"But N1-2 is even better. It kills in hours, not days or weeks. For N1-2, there is no cure, no treatment," Terrek announced. "It will spread through close contact with victims and their blood, bodily fluids, their remains, or by just breathing the surrounding air. Some researchers speculate that the Plague of Athens in 425 B.C., which devastated the city and ended Athenian control of Greece, was an isolated Ebola epidemic. N1-2 will be a thousand times more devastating."

Terrek grinned. "Just imagine what will happen when we infect millions of Americans with a new, virulent strain of N1-2. It will make the Plague of Athens look like a pleasant summer's day. It will be the beginning of a new world."

Lee smiled. "No one deserves it more than the Americans." Lee walked over to Terrek's side and glanced at the screen. The man strapped to the gurney in the isolation room was shaking violently. Even though his hands and legs were tied down, he pitched and screamed. Blood drained from his eyes and ears. In less than a minute, he was dead.

Dr. Kashkin's face filled the screen. "The problem with Ebola as a weapon is that it kills its victims too rapidly. But I believe we have solved the timing issue. Our computer simulations show that for some reason N1-2 kills men quickly, as you have seen, but may take several days to kill a woman. We believe that infected women will act as incubators for the spores. Their women, then, will become the carriers of the virus that will allow us to keep N1-2 active long enough to cause the contagion to spread across the entire American continent."

"How will we introduce the virus to America?" Lee asked. "Will we release the hostages, already infected?"

"That would not produce the results we need," Terrek said.

He pushed a button on his console. A computer-generated map of the United States appeared across the large screen on the wall, replacing Dr. Kashkin's image. "Timing is everything. I don't want to give the Americans a chance to isolate the contagion or develop an antidote. We must strike like lightning. We want to release it in a dozen cities in the United States at the same time. Observe."

Twelve cities on the East Coast of the United States were illuminated with a red dot. As the red dots grew in size, each representing the spread of the virus, the date and time registered above the map. As the hours turned into days, the red grew to cover most of the East Coast. In three weeks, the entire United States was consumed in red.

Terrek turned to Lee. "I want you to have twelve of your best men ready to fly to the United States. I have arranged for the appropriate passports, papers, and security clearances."

Lee bowed. "It will be done!"

"When will the virus be ready for transport?" Terrek asked Dr. Kashkin.

"Today we will complete our final test. After that, we can manufacture the virus in two days and have it packaged in less than twenty-four hours."

"Packaged?" Lee asked.

Terrek grinned again. "We can put enough N1-2 in an aerosol container the size of a can of shaving cream to start the process. Imagine, twelve cans of shaving cream will begin an epidemic that within three weeks will change the face of the world."

"Brilliant," Lee answered. "No customs official will be looking for shaving cream!"

"What about the hostages?" Lee asked.

"They are of no consequence. Tomorrow, we will infect them all as a final test of Kashkin's new weapon."

Suddenly, an alarm went off inside Terrek's control room. He heard a loud explosion outside. Terrek looked at the screen, then punched up a view of the front entrance to the compound. He stared at the scene, angry at what he saw. "We've been betrayed!"

A column of North Korean tanks were rambling down the road, firing at Terrek's defenders. Terrek's lightly armed guards returned fire and were gunned down.

"I should have never trusted these North Korean bastards!" Terrek screamed. He punched another button on his console, and the view from the 30 mm automatic cannons on the west wall of the fortress filled two sides of the screen. The two cannons fired at the lead tank, ripping its turret to pieces. The tank rolled to a stop and caught fire. "Is this how your country keeps its promises?"

"It is no longer my country. I belong to the Brotherhood!"

"If I didn't believe so, you would be dead!" Terrek pointed at the screen. "Assemble your men and stop that attack. I am too close to completing my plans to let anyone stop me. Don't let them into the compound!"

Lee bowed hurriedly and rushed out of the control room.

Terrek's gaze suddenly caught a strange movement on the floor against the wall of the control room. He stared carefully and beckoned one of the guards to come. Slowly, Terrek stood up and pointed at the seam where the wall and the floor joined. "What is that?"

The guard saw the object that Terrek was staring at and rushed toward it. In a scurry of moving legs, the tiny microbug moved quickly along the wall toward the door. A second guard, anticipating its move, smashed it with the heel of his heavy boot.

1905 hours, on Hill 350 near the Citadel

Sam Wong frowned as he realized that the first bug was gone. "Bug One just got stomped on," Wong announced over the comm net.

Sam sat among the fir trees on Hill 350, listening to

the sounds of the battle echoing in the hills below. Bursts of machine gun fire and the blast of 30 mm cannon answered the blast of North Korean 82 mm mortars falling inside the compound from the defenders.

"That's all right," Travis replied to Sam. "We've heard enough. How about Bugs Two and Three?"

Jenny Olsen, safe on Hill 350, scanned the valley to the northwest. Pillars of black smoke rose in the late-afternoon sky.

Travis's plan was a new version of Wong's Last Stand. Using his link with the NSA supercomputer, Sam had faked a coded North Korean message to the local military commander. The message ordered him to attack Terrek's men at the Brotherhood base on the orders of the Great Leader of North Korea himself. The message also stated that Terrek and his men were American agents. No one in the North Korean People's Army would dare disobey those instructions. At the same time, Krauss's wizards back at TALON Force headquarters redirected the Russian satellites that had blanked out the Russian Radio-Electronic Combat Node 75 of the Vladivostok Regional Command to jam the North Korean radio waves. Without any further instructions from Pyongyang, the North Korean commander would be honor bound to fight on until his mission was accomplished.

It was a perfect example of information warfare at its very best, Olsen mused. She switched her view to Bug Three, which she tracked through her BSD screen.

Sam sat right next to Jen, looking into his own BSD screen as the battle played out in the Citadel. He was already "living" Bug Two, moving along with it as it crawled along the floor of the Citadel, recording everything that its tiny video receptors could see. It was like jumping into the microbug's skin. "Major, this is Wong. Bug Two is in the lab now. I'm passing you a layout of the Citadel, as we know it. The pathogen lab is three floors below ground level, north side of the Citadel . . . and we also have the location of the hostages."

"Where are they?" Travis Barrett asked.

"Bug Three found them one floor below ground level,

east wing of the Citadel," Jen announced. "Looks like eighteen women, three children, and eight men."

"Roger. I'm designating the coordinates for four Bunker Busters," Travis Barrett said. "Sam, send a message to get five V22s to the pickup point."

"Major, we have to help these people," Jenny pleaded.

"Trust me, Olsen," Travis Barrett replied.

Olsen viewed her BSD screen and saw the major's target sequence depicted on a three-dimensional view of the Brotherhood fortress. Travis Barrett designated one to hit Terrek's control room, one to burrow deep and hit the lab, one to blast the twenty-foot wall on the east side of the compound, and one for the east side of the Citadel. With luck and the excellent precision from the makers of the Bunker Buster cruise missiles, Barrett and his assault team could blast their way into the compound from the opposite side than the North Koreans were attacking.

"Olsen, you and Wong stay in position and laser designate for the Bunker Busters," Travis continued over the comm net. "Once we've completed our mission inside and are clear of the fortress, designate the eight remaining bombs as I have indicated. Then get the hell out of Dodge and meet us at the pickup point."

"Roger, Major," Olsen replied. "We've got it."

"Sam, have you received confirmation on the pickup?" Travis Barrett asked.

"Affirmative, sir. You can pull up the plan on your BSD now."

"Okay, TALON Force," Travis Barrett answered. "In fifteen minutes, we rock and roll."

1930 hours, the Citadel

Two Dragonfly UAVs flew 150 feet above the Citadel, recording the battle between the North Koreans and Terrek's men. The North Koreans were advancing in waves of riflemen, supported by tank and mortar fire from Hill

415. The North Korean infantry were brave but as green as grass. They attacked in banzai charges against the guns of the defenders, and their losses were heavy. Terrek's veteran killers were cutting them down like a very grim reaper harvesting wheat with a scythe, but the North Koreans kept on coming.

Wong realized that the North Koreans needed some help. He requested a Bunker Buster on the gun turret at the southwest corner of the fortress and designated the target with his BSD. Within two minutes and forty-five seconds, a screaming arrow of flame fell from the sky and smashed into the gun turret.

"Bull's-eye!" Wong exclaimed.

The 30 mm cannon on the southern wall was suddenly a mass of jagged metal and flames. With this turret gone, a surge of firing swelled from the North Korean side. Without this heavy cannon support, the Brotherhood fighters couldn't stop the North Koreans from breaking into the compound.

Lee raced through the exit of the Citadel and arrived in the courtyard. Pandemonium had broken out among his defenders. The Brotherhood fighters were outnumbered and outgunned, and they sensed it. Their only consolation was the remaining 30 mm cannon on the north corner of the fort hammering away at the attackers.

"Damn you all!" Lee screamed. He realized that the North Koreans must be stopped from breaking through the entrance, or all was lost. If he kept them at bay outside the walls of the fortress, he and Terrek still had a chance. "Stop them from entering the compound!"

Everything was happening too fast, Lee thought. He smelled defeat in the air. He stood in the courtyard, a pistol in his hand, throwing his men into the fight. A dazed terrorist, who was wounded in the left arm, dropped his rifle and staggered away from the entrance. Lee pointed his pistol at the man and ordered him back into the fight. The wounded man just stood there, staring at Lee. Lee shot him where he stood and shouted, "I'll kill any man who doesn't fight!"

Mortar rounds fell inside the compound at the same

time, scattering their steel fragments in a shower of death. A dozen terrorists fell. One man was blown apart, and his torso fell against Lee, covering the lanky North Korean commando with blood. Lee staggered back and ran into the Citadel, closing the heavy blast door behind him and dooming his surviving men to a bloody fate.

The northern 30 mm gun continued to plaster the advancing North Korean infantry. A platoon of North Korean tanks maneuvered into position on Hill 415 and fired a volley of 115 mm cannon rounds at the gun turret. One of the tank rounds scored a hit, knocking Terrek's automatic cannon out of action.

The defenders' return fire was now reduced to a trickle of small arms. With a loud shout, the North Korean tide surged forward.

One of Terrek's men, a Brazilian named Montoyez, knelt behind a sandbagged position, alone at the entrance of the compound. He fired one magazine after another at the advancing North Koreans. As the mortar shells rained down, he blasted off his rounds. Two North Korean soldiers went down, hit by his rounds, but a group of twenty more riflemen charged forward. Montoyez looked to his left and right and saw that he was alone. His comrades lay in the snow, their blood splattered all over the ground. This is not what he had joined the Brotherhood for. Ducking behind the wall, Montoyez dropped his rifle and ran toward the Citadel.

As Montoyez ran away, a North Korean tank lunged forward through the entrance and fired. Piles of dead tangos lay in front of the entrance to the fort as the North Korean tank burst through the entrance and into the courtyard of the compound. The tank then pivoted and aimed at the blast doors of the Citadel.

Montoyez ran up against the blast door, pounded in vain on the steel surface with his fists, and shouted in desperation. He turned to see the North Korean tank, and was chopped in half by the tank's cannon blast.

"Keep moving," a North Korean major screamed, waving a 9 mm pistol. A company of North Korean infantrymen were clustered around him, rushing into the courtyard, shooting at Terrek's men who were running in all directions. "Wipe out all these vermin!"

1935 hours, Cell Block One, inside the Citadel

Elizabeth Douglas heard the explosions and the rattle of small arms from inside her cell. She stood up and walked to the bars, cupping her hand to her ear to listen. After a few seconds, a grin spread across her tired, dirty face.

"Oh my God," Beverly gasped. Tears filled her eyes and she dropped her head in her hands and fell back on the bed. "They are killing people. We are all going to die."

"*Nein,* I don't zink so," Helga announced. "Zere is trouble up above."

"She's right, honey," Elizabeth said, turning around. She pried Beverly's hands away from the young woman's face. "I think somebody's trying to rescue us. We need to be ready."

"Do you really think so?" Rachel asked, holding her young baby in her arms.

"Yes, I think that—"

Before Liz could answer, the tremendous, deafening blast of a Bunker Buster cut through the wall of the Citadel behind them. The explosion threw them all to the ground and covered them in dust and dirt. The lights flickered and went out.

Rachel screamed. Liz Douglas groped in the dark, trying to stand up. She suddenly found herself next to someone. It was Rachel. The young mother was lying under the bed on her side with her baby well protected in her arms.

Two more huge explosions tore into the foundations of the Citadel. The ground shook as if an earthquake was occurring. Everyone in the cell was choking from the dust. Suddenly, the emergency battery-driven lights sputtered on, dimly lighting the hallway.

Liz looked toward the center bed. She saw two ladies hiding under the bed. "Helga, Beverly! Are you all right?" she shouted.

"Ya! We are alive!" Helga's strong voice shouted back, cracking slightly as she stared across the room. "Mary. Mary is hurt!"

Elizabeth Douglas looked across the room. A hunk of concrete had fallen from the ceiling and struck Mary dead. The old woman lay sprawled out on the floor, lifeless and covered in concrete dust.

Beverly started to cry again.

1940 hours, Terrek's control room in the Citadel

Two powerful explosions rocked the Citadel. One explosion blasted into the outer eastern wall, creating a man-sized breach. The second explosion smashed into the eastern wall of the Citadel, burrowing into the reinforced concrete and exploding another hole in the wall.

"I have underestimated my enemies," Terrek announced out loud as he watched the missiles strike the Citadel on the big screen. He picked up the plastic microbug that his bodyguard had smashed with the heel of his boot. Who could make such a device? Who had weapons with such precision? Not the North Koreans. The North Koreans could barely feed their own people. The reclusive, incompetent regime in Pyongyang was holding onto power by its fingernails.

"Only the Americans have the ability to create such a device," he announced. He moved the controls of his surveillance camera to the east side of the fortress to observe the damage caused by one of the explosions. There, in a hole in the external wall of the camp, he saw a ghostlike shimmer. Intrigued, he set the camera to maximum resolution and magnification.

Terrek watched as two of his men ran toward the opening in the wall and were shot dead by an unseen enemy rifleman. A soldier abruptly materialized on his screen where moments before Terrek had seen the shimmer. The man was covered in a special suit and wore a helmet like a fighter pilot's. The man lifted the shield on the helmet. Terrek zoomed in on the man's face and saw the face of his foe.

Travis looked up directly at the camera and appeared to stare straight into the eyes of Terrek. Then the American raised his left arm, pressed a button on the sleeve of his forearm, and the camera went blank.

The big screen dissolved momentarily, then reinitiated in the simultaneous surveillance mode, with multiple boxes arrayed across the big screen to show the view from all the surveillance cameras at once. Half of the boxes were black. The rest showed scenes of Terrek's men raising their hands in surrender.

"It is the Americans," Terrek sneered. "It has been them all along."

The lights flickered in the control room. The computers that were lined up in a row in front of the big screen went blank. The sound of the radio transmissions in the control room ceased and was replaced by the echo of the battle raging outside.

"Sir, I have lost communications with the rest of our forces," one of Terrek's officers reported. "We are losing the battle below. We must abandon our position here."

Terrek stood up from his chair and grabbed the man by the throat. "Take every available man and get down there and fight them!" Terrek screamed.

The officer struggled for air and blurted out as best he could, "As you wish."

Terrek let the man go, then drew his pistol. The man staggered toward the door. "All of you, out! Hold them off, and I will pay you ten times your yearly salary for this one day's fight."

The dozen officers who manned Terrek's control room dropped their headsets and moved toward the door. Few believed that they would live to reap the benefits of Terrek's latest pledge.

Terrek's four personal bodyguards remained in position near the exit, their assault rifles held across their chests positioned at port arms. Terrek motioned to the leader of his guards. "Get the HIP ready to fly."

An explosion erupted on the big view screen on the wall. Terrek looked at the screen and saw a North Korean tank running over his men inside the compound. All at once, three of his cameras went blank. He had lost the battle and could no longer manage anything from his control room. It was time to exit.

1951 hours, Cell Block One, inside the Citadel

Helga moved carefully out from under the bed and stood up.

A man suddenly appeared in front of the bars. "Stand back!" he shouted, then placed a small device on the lock. The device fizzled, then burned with a brilliant flash, melting the metal. With a quick kick against the bars, the man opened the cell.

"We're Americans. We're here to get you out. Everyone out!"

Elizabeth Douglas couldn't believe her eyes. "Travis. *Travis!* Is that you?"

Major Travis Barrett stood awestruck as his godmother stood up a few feet in front of him.

"Aunt Liz? What are you doing here? Are you okay?"

She rushed to his arms, tears of joy in her eyes. "Help us! *For God's sake, son, help us!*"

Travis swallowed his surprise. *Focus on the mission,* he thought. "Where's Uncle Jim?"

Elizabeth Douglas shook her head.

Jim Douglas was the man who had been there for him when his father was away. The Douglases had taken care of him when his parents had been stationed in Germany during his last two years of high school.

A white-hot rage fell over Travis Barrett's soul. This was personal now. This was family. *By God,* he swore to himself, *I will get this motherfucker if it's the last thing I do.*

"Sir, we need to move these people out of here," Stan Powczuk announced into his comm net.

Travis looked down the hallway and saw that all the cells were open. Jack stood guard, looking north as Hunter helped the dazed American civilians toward the gaping hole that the Bunker Buster had smashed in the east side of the Citadel's wall.

"Powczuk. Blake. DuBois. Move them out, ASAP," Travis ordered. "Take them to the pickup point. Greene, you're with me."

"Major, we only have twelve more minutes of coverage for the remaining Bunker Busters," Sam Wong reported over the comm net. "You have to get everyone out by then, or I'll have to call off the bombs."

"You will not—I repeat, *not*—cancel the Bunker Busters. They go in as scheduled," the major ordered. "Do you understand?"

"I understand," Wong answered. "I'm still monitoring Bug Two in the isolation lab. The lab is two floors below you to the north. There are five technicians and two armed guards in the lab right now."

Travis hugged his godmother tightly, then passed her to Powczuk. "Stan, this one is special to me. Get them all out of here, safely. No matter what happens, get them all to the rendezvous point. Then make sure they are quarantined immediately! Radio ahead for a complete medical exam of everyone evacuated, including us, to see if anyone is infected with N1-2."

"Roger. Where are you going?" Stan asked.

"I've got to verify the destruction of the germ," Travis said. "And with any luck, I'll run into Terrek."

Powczuk nodded. "Please come with me, ma'am," he said, and pulled Elizabeth Douglas away. Blake and DuBois guided the other dazed Americans down the hallway to the hole in the Citadel's wall.

"Activate countdown, mark eleven minutes twenty-six seconds," Travis Barrett said, activating the voice command for his helmet computer system to remind him of the passing time. "Greene, follow me. Stealth mode."

Travis lowered his face shield and saw Sarah do the

same. The two TALON Force troopers turned invisible as their stealth camouflage registered the exact color and texture of their surroundings. In the dust-filled hallway they appeared as a misty vapor in the dim light.

Travis's mind raced with anger. The sense of foreboding that had followed him from the start of this mission began to lay on him like a heavy blanket. *Stay cool,* he thought. *This is not the time to lose it. The mission is almost complete. Verify the pathogen, drop a designator in the lab, get out of here, and bring out as many of the Russians as you can. We'll need them to create an antidote for this germ.*

But what about Terrek? Was that animal still in his control room? Would the Bunker Buster get him? I'd love to see his face as I put a bullet into his forehead, Travis thought, *but there's not enough time.*

He raced down the hall. A terrorist with an assault rifle suddenly turned the corner and moved in his direction. Travis aimed, fired and dropped the man before the terrorist could raise his weapon.

"Ten minutes, thirty-eight seconds," the uncaring female voice of his helmet announced.

Moving like a tornado down the hallway, Travis jumped over the body of the downed Tango and raced down the stairs. He came to a door on the third floor and kicked it open. A black-uniformed terrorist stood guard with his weapon at the ready and fired as the door flew open. A half dozen slugs from the terrorist submachine gun smashed into the wall, missing the major by inches. Travis fired his pistol instinctively, putting two shots into the man's chest.

Travis raced on and stopped at the locked door to the isolation lab. He opened a pouch on his belt and placed a small charge on the door and tapped the timer. As he stood back against the wall, the charge exploded, and the door burst open. A stream of automatic weapons fire blasted out and smashed against the concrete wall. The terrorists fired furiously at the open, empty hallway. When their ammunition was expended, Travis Barrett stepped inside and dropped the guards with two quick shots.

"Eight minutes and thirty seconds," his computer warned.

Travis Barrett looked around. Five Russian scientists cowered in the corner of the room. Travis Barrett turned around and scanned the hallway. In the excitement, he had lost track of Sarah.

"Greene. I'm in the isolation lab," he said into his comm net.

Sarah didn't answer. He heard shots down the hall.

Damnit, I'm running out of time, he thought. *I'm not going to make it.*

"Stealth off," Travis announced. The Russians stared in amazement as he appeared in front of them. He turned to the nearest scientist and, in perfect Russian, pointed his pistol at the man and demanded, "Where is the N1-2? Tell me and you will live."

The Russian pointed sheepishly at the dead American on the gurney in the isolation room. "I swear to God. All of our samples are in there."

Barrett raised his face shield. The look of rage and disgust on his face scared the Russian scientist more than the pistol that was aimed at the Russian's head. "Tell me quickly. Are you sure? Is there any more N1-2 anywhere else?"

"Nyet," the Russian said, as he looked over Barrett's left shoulder. "I swear on my mother's grave."

Travis Barrett tried to turn around, then heard a series of loud bangs behind him. Before he could react, he was flung to the floor by a powerful force. Bullets smashed against the wall. Kashkin was hit twice, spun around, and crumpled to the ground. Travis felt as if a dozen hammers had hit him in the back. Dazed, he lay facedown on the cold floor of the isolation room.

He tried to move, but the force of the blast had stunned him. The body armor that every TALON trooper wore had saved his life, but the force of the rounds striking against his back had temporarily immobilized him. Helpless, he tried to move to reach his weapon but failed. In that instant, Travis Barrett realized that this was it. He was certain—as certain as he had ever been about anything in his life—that this was how it would end. His time was over. He had cheated death one time too many, and now the Grim Reaper was coming to collect the bill.

Lee Chu Bok walked over to Travis Barrett and kicked him over with his right boot. A wide-eyed anger filled the North Korean's face. Lee aimed his 9 mm pistol at Travis's head. "I should have known that an American was behind this attack. I don't know by what magic you have survived, but now is your time to die.

"It was you who helped the Russians take out my men at Rybacky, wasn't it?" Lee snarled.

"Fuck you," Travis spit out.

Lee smiled, aimed at Travis's face, and prepared to pull the trigger.

Suddenly, two shots went right through Lee's chest. Lee Chu Bok's face was a mask of confusion and disbelief as his mouth filled with blood. He dropped the pistol and crumpled to the ground, falling on the hard floor next to Travis.

Sarah Greene materialized, her pistol at the ready. "You okay, Major?"

Travis Barrett felt the strength return to his limbs. Sarah reached down to help him up. Awkwardly, he raised up on his elbows and then sat up. "That's the second one I owe you."

"And don't forget it," Sarah said with a smile as she knelt by his side. "You're too valuable to lose."

"Six minutes and thirty seconds," the major's helmet announced.

Sarah pulled Travis up and put his arm over her shoulder. "Let's get out of here."

Travis nodded. He felt stronger now and stood on his own. "I'll be all right. One more thing to do here." He reached into the cargo pocket on his pants leg and activated a silver-dollar-sized target beacon by pushing in a small notch on the disk. He dropped it on the floor, then pointed to the remaining four Russians. In Russian he announced, "If you want to live, follow me."

Travis Barrett, Sarah Greene, and the four remaining Russians ran out of the building. They climbed the stairs and raced down the hallway to the opening in the wall. Hearts pounding, they cleared the hole in the eastern wall of the compound just two minutes before the remaining Bunker Buster bombs hit the Citadel.

Travis, Sarah, and the scientists lay belly down in a deep ravine as the bombs hit the compound. The outer wall and the ravine sheltered them from the blast.

With his face in the dirt, Travis couldn't see the Bunker Buster that burrowed through seven floors of the Citadel to explode inside the isolation room and vaporize the N1-2. He couldn't see the other Bunker Buster bomb smash into Terrek's control room and devastate the Citadel headquarters. And, most critically, he didn't see the Russian-made HIP helicopter fly from the roof just seconds before the bombs hit, lifting Terrek and his four bodyguards away toward China and safety.

Chapter Fourteen

He clasps the crag with crooked hands;
Close to the sun in lonely lands,
Ring'd with the azure world he stands.
The wrinkled sea beneath him crawls;
He watches from his mountain walls,
And like a thunderbolt he falls.
—Alfred, Lord Tennyson, "The Eagle" (1851)

**November 19, 1630 hours,
the Senate Building, Washington, D.C.**

General Buck Freedman nodded to the young lieutenant colonel standing next to a stack of three-foot-by-four-foot charts. The officer pulled up the last chart and placed it on the easel in plain view of the distinguished audience.

"Mission accomplished." General Freedman looked at the four senators sitting at the other end of the table and emphasized his words to drive home his last point. "As you can see from this map and the corresponding event sequence, the TALON Force's Eagle Team then moved the surviving hostages to a nearby pickup point. We extracted them and the Russian scientists by TFV-22s to an aircraft carrier steaming off the North Korean coast in international waters. One hostage was shot by Terrek's men in Egypt, and seven died in his experiments. N1-2 and the Brotherhood base were destroyed, and the North Koreans never even knew we were inside their borders."

The four elderly senators, three men and one woman, sat at a long, oval table in a quiet room normally reserved for secret sessions of the Senate Armed Services Committee. A stenographer sat to the right of the senators at a small, separate square table. Opposite the senators sat the Honorable Jeffrey Craig, the Secretary of Defense; Mr. Robert Jordan, the director of the Central Intelligence Agency; the Commander-in-Chief, Special Operations Command (CINCSOCOM), General Buck Freedman; and the Commander, Joint Task Force, TALON Force, Brigadier General Jack Krauss.

The room was bare except for a large picture of General George Washington, in full Revolutionary War military uniform, leaning against the barrel of a muzzle-loading cannon, which adorned the wall behind the senators.

"And that's the full report, distinguished senators," General Freedman concluded. "A remarkable and very successful action by America's most effective special operations force."

"It looks like we have stared into the abyss once again," the portly, immaculately dressed, silver-haired Senator Watkins announced. "If the thought of a nuclear or chemical attack is frightening, this kind of biological weapon attack is our worst nightmare."

Senator Dodge, a thin, elegantly dressed lady from Virginia, looked at Senator Watkins and received his nod to ask a question. "Has this ended the Brotherhood threat? And what can we do to prevent similar attacks in the future?"

"To answer your question, Senator Dodge, unfortunately, the threat is still out there. This latest Brotherhood attack is significant and will cause us to rush the development of several new defensive measures," the Secretary of Defense, a man with dark hair and wearing an expensive gray, Italian-made suit, answered. "First, we've increased awareness and security procedures at the national level. Security has been tightened in a dozen cities on the East Coast, and we are developing a full-time, twenty-four-hour-a-day Terrorist Situation Room in the Pentagon to coordinate our counterterrorist efforts."

"I see," Dodge replied.

"Internationally, we are working with friendly security forces across the globe to counter Terrek's forces, find him, and bring him to justice. Russian authorities have cracked down on an estimated five-thousand-member Brotherhood branch in their country and have announced that they will cooperate with the United States at a diplomatic level on the issue. After Rybacky, the Russians are nervous about the Brotherhood."

"But didn't the Russian daily *Izvestia* publish a front-page story suggesting links between the Brotherhood sect and two prominent Russian politicians?" Dodge asked.

"Yes, that's true," Secretary Craig replied. "However, I received a report today that the *Itar-Tass* news agency later issued a statement that denies this, saying that no one in the government has any questionable connection with the Brotherhood."

"What about the equipment?" Dodge pressed. "First, the Russians jammed our supposedly unjammable communications. Second, as I understand it, at a crucial juncture, the stealth camouflage system for one of our troopers malfunctioned. Third, there is this report of problems with the X-37 rocket plane."

"Senator, let me let General Krauss answer those questions," the Secretary of Defense said.

"By all means," Dodge replied. "General?"

"Senator, there are bound to be problems with prototype equipment, no matter how many field simulations we run," Krauss offered, "but we were able to adapt, improvise, and overcome the problems. The jamming situation can occur again, but it is highly unlikely. It is only an issue when we go up against a major technologically advanced enemy. Even in the worst cases, we now believe that we can work through the worst jamming in a matter of minutes."

"And this stealth camouflage?"

"The Low Observable Camouflage Ensemble is a central part of our covert capability. We are working to improve the system. An analysis of Lieutenant Commander Powczuk's system detected a short in his power pack that reduced the power storage of his battery. We are working to harden that system to decrease the chances of future failures."

"And the X-37 rocket plane?"

"Madame Senator, the X-37 performed flawlessly for this mission. Without it, we could not have moved Eagle Team as rapidly as we did. Without it, the Russians would have detected us as we parachuted into the Rybacky complex."

"But I understand that the X-37 fleet has been grounded."

"Yes, that is correct. After the mission, we discovered some serious structural flaws that are being investigated. It may be several months before we can get the X-37 back into the air."

Senator Dodge nodded, then turned to Senator Watkins and relinquished her control of the questioning. "No further questions."

"I see. Thank you, Mr. Secretary," Senator Watkins responded. "But I'd like to hear from the CIA director on an issue of concern to me. What do you think are the repercussions for our use of the TALON Force, invading another sovereign country, and the destruction of the Brotherhood base in North Korea?"

The CIA director, a thin, sharp-faced man in his mid-fifties, picked up a ream of paper in front of him and read from the top page of the stack. "I think that they are negligible. Our choices were few. We must always be willing to preempt terrorism by any means or suffer horrible civilian casualties and infrastructure damage."

Senator Watkins nodded in agreement.

"In particular, the TALON Force deception seems to have worked very well," the CIA director continued. "We have been carefully monitoring the North Koreans ever since the incident. The North Koreans are too embarrassed to tell each other the truth. They are reporting that this Brotherhood sect went renegade and had to be destroyed. Their official story is that North Korean forces destroyed the Brotherhood base. There is no mention of U.S. forces. I think that it is safe to assume that Terrek's use of North Korea as a sanctuary is over . . . at least for now."

"General Freedman, do you agree?" Watkins asked.

"Yes, sir. But I want to caution that this fight is just beginning. If there is a fog of war, there is probably a more dense smog of terrorism. The Brotherhood is just one organization, although it is a very large, well-organized, and lavishly financed one. The small nature of terrorist groups, their close interpersonal communications, and their predilection for soft targets of opportunity will make it difficult to predict their future operations."

The senator nodded. "Well, it looks like we got damn lucky this time."

"I'm bothered by the expense of this new force," Senator Dodge interjected. "When it comes to big budgets, I'm a skeptic. I'd like to ask the commander of the TALON Force a question. Can't we find a more cost-effective way to counter these threats, General Krauss?"

General Jack Krauss looked over at General Freedman and the Secretary of Defense. Both men nodded. "Madame Senator, you are right to be concerned about the costs of this force, but to my mind, the TALON Force is a bargain. Yes, the creation of this elite, high-technology special operations force has been very expensive. It will also be very expensive to continue to train and deploy. We must decide, however, whether we will choose to pay to maintain this force now, in order to preempt terrorist attacks, or pay the butcher's bill and suffer the loss of a city or a wrecked economy later."

"Very melodramatic, General Krauss," Senator Dodge said cynically. "But the truth is, we were just lucky this time. Am I right?"

Krauss's jaw tightened. "The driving factor in our success during our mission against Terrek in Russia and North Korea wasn't luck, it was the excellence of the TALON Force. Their superb leadership, training, technology, and teamwork made the difference this time and will make a strategic difference in the future."

"General Krauss, I think we can agree with you that we are thankful for the courage and sacrifice of your organization. A horrible terrorist plot was disrupted, and open warfare with a major power was averted," Senator Watkins interjected, trying to control the tone of the hearing.

"Yes, sir," Krauss continued. "But I want to make it clear that the capabilities that TALON Force offers make this possible. We have forged a thunderbolt of great power by creating the TALON Force. This is a perfect example of a situation where a small band of well-trained, superbly equipped special operatives made a strategic difference. The TALON Force provides the National Command Authority with one more tool short of overt military action. In that respect, it offers the nation an alternative between surrendering to blackmail and major war."

"Yes, we can see that, but the mission wasn't completely successful. The leader of the terrorists . . . this Terrek fellow . . . the leader of this Brotherhood . . . he got away," Mrs. Dodge announced.

"Yes, Senator Dodge, Terrek got away this time," Krauss replied, nodding. "But *we* won this round. The TALON Force foiled Terrek's scheme to launch a devastating biological attack on the United States. We killed many of his operatives and set him back months, if not years. And I assure you, as sure as I am standing here before you, that if we are allowed to pursue Terrek, we will get him. We will not rest until the Brotherhood is captured or destroyed."

"By God, General, I believe you," Dodge answered, changing her cynicism to a smile. "And as far as your precious TALON Force goes, I think that it is clear to all of us that, *for now,* we support the investment we have made so far."

Senator Watkins nodded to Senator Dodge. "Well, it has been a very long day. We appreciate your briefing us and your dedication to keep terrorism at bay. And General Krauss, from all of us, and a grateful nation, please pass on our congratulations for a job well done to the troopers of the TALON Force."

"Thank you, Senator Watkins, I will," Brigadier General Jack Krauss answered with a grin. "And let me just say that with every new type of warfare comes a new breed of weapons and soldiers. The TALON Force stands ready to help guard America and prevent major wars through preemptive, special operations action. We stand ready, willing, and able, whenever called upon."

November 22, 1230 hours,
the Yukon Mountains in British Columbia

A deep blue sky and a brilliant sun hung overhead as the climber in khaki shirt and green shorts traversed the steep, rocky Yukon peak for the second time. Beads of sweat rolled down Travis Barrett's face as he worked his way up a jagged vee in the mountain, to hunt the ram that had eluded him on his first attempt only a few days before.

So much had happened in those few days. So much sadness. The thunderbolt had been forged, the TALON Force had become operational, and Eagle Team had succeeded in its first mission. From now on, the National Command Authority had a new and highly specialized tool to use to protect the peace and citizens of the United States, as well as American interests around the world.

He climbed with his trusty .50 caliber Hawkins rifle and a coil of nylon climbing rope slung over his back. His breathing grew heavy as the toe- and handholds became harder to find. The rock face became a sheer wall at this point, with only the small crevice to offer anchor points to support his climb. He placed a metal chock into the crevice, pulled hard to test the strength of the anchor and, finding it sufficient, inched upward one hold point at a time.

It was a long way to the bottom, but this time he climbed with a special confidence. He had made the summit before. He knew that nothing would stop him from making it again.

He raised his head and saw the narrow ledge up to his left and the goat track that led from the ledge to the top of the mountain. With sweat running down his face, he moved his right leg, found a toehold, and ascended another three feet. A few more feet, and he would be at the summit. He placed another metal chock into the crevice and pulled on the nylon cord attached to the chock. He rested the tip of his left boot on a lip of rock and pulled himself to the shelf. He reached the ledge, turned, and sat with his back to the cold stone mountain.

The view was just as beautiful as before: breathtaking, but somehow different. The clouds shrouded the tops of the taller mountains that lay in front of him as if they were hiding some secret resting place of the gods.

Emotion tumbled from his soul like water over a cliff. He thought of Jim Douglas, his godfather—a man who had meant so much to him—and the tragic circumstances that caused his death. In a whirlwind of nostalgia, he remembered Jim Douglas congratulating him the day he graduated from West Point, standing in the crowd and cheering during the victory parade in New York City after Desert Storm, and meeting him at the airport in Galveston after the grim, terrible experience of Mogadishu and Chechnya.

Now, this good man, who had worked so hard to make a life for himself and his family, was gone.

Then, out of the corner of his right eye, Travis Barrett saw a big stone ram, the same majestic round-horned sheep that he had hunted the first time he sat on this ledge. For a second time, he had a chance at the shot of a lifetime.

The wind was in his favor. Moving slowly, he brought the powerful .50 caliber Hawkins rifle to his shoulder and took aim at the ram.

The ram stood perfectly still, unafraid. Slowly, the sheep turned his head and seemed to stare straight toward Travis. Travis pulled back the hammer of the rifle. Carefully, he aimed at the sheep's heart.

The ram still did not move. Travis Barrett held his breath and felt his heart pounding in his chest. Nothing could stop him from bagging his prey. Nothing but the will to pull the trigger.

Travis lowered his rifle and fired the shot against the rock, ten feet below the proud ram. The ram jumped, startled by the blast, and then bounded off out of sight.

Travis smiled. *A life for a life,* he thought. He suddenly realized how much he owed the man who had been his godfather and how much of Jim Douglas was in his soul. Sparing that sheep wouldn't bring Uncle Jim back, but it gave him a quiet sense of satisfaction that somehow, he had made a life-sacrifice to the mountains. Too many times in the past few days he should have paid death's bill. Maybe this would even out his account for awhile.

My business is killing, he thought. *My knowledge of life is limited to death. In my unit, out there, we all think alike. When we are on a mission, no one worries about the meaning of life because it has no meaning. They depend on me and I on them.*

As long as humankind remains as it is, there will always be wars and rumors of war. All wars are evil, but not standing up to murder is worse than evil—it's slaughter. My sole consolation in this bloody business is that I use my talents to minimize the damage, to prevent the kind of wars where millions die and then, afterward, wonder what they were fighting about.

The shadow that had hovered over him so closely the past few days seemed to disappear. His soul was at peace. He thought about the ram. It suddenly felt good to take the alternative path, to protect a life instead of taking one. Maybe that was the major difference between men like him and monsters like Terrek. Travis smiled and shook his head. *I'm turning into a damned philosopher, a dangerous move for a man in my profession.*

His thoughts quickly changed and wrapped themselves in the cold steel spirit that consumed him when he was in action. He considered Terrek and the dark terror that the Brotherhood represented, the innocent people who had died in the airline bombings, the massacre in Rome, and the death of his godfather and the others at Terrek's hands. This war was far from over. There would be many battles yet to fight, and he knew that the conflict wouldn't end until Terrek was killed or captured. He also knew that the next time they met, Terrek would be ready.

He remembered a line from Shakespeare: "Come not between the Dragon and his wrath." Well, this time, the eagle had prevailed over the dragon. Major Travis Barrett, U.S. Army, commander of the Eagle Team, TALON Force, looked up at the clouds and vowed that the struggle would continue and that the Eagle would win.

Secretary of Defense
The Pentagon
Washington, D.C. 20301-3140

Subject: TALON Force (Technologically Augmented Low Observable Networked Force)

Authorization: Attached is the organizational design and operating concept for the TALON Force as outlined in TALON Force Manual 1-1. In light of recent attacks against the citizens and interests of the United States of America, the Congress has established the need for extraordinary action to deal with the present and emerging challenges. The Congress has observed an increasing dependency on the defense information infrastructure and increasing doctrinal assumptions regarding the continued availability of that infrastructure. This dependency and these assumptions are ingredients in a recipe for a national security disaster.

Today's technology allows small groups to do extraordinary things. Our adversaries will tap into this ability. The Department of Defense, therefore, has been tasked to create new forces that will defend against possible terrorist attacks and information warfare attacks on facilities, information, information systems, and networks of the United States that would seriously affect the ability of the Department of Defense to carry out its assigned missions and functions.

The military forces of the United States must have the capability to deal with crises before they grow into full-fledged conflicts. This capability will save lives and money. The Department of Defense, under the authority of Executive Order 15064, establishes a joint commando force to accomplish the missions listed in TF Manual 1-1. Accordingly, we have created the TALON Force.

Sincerely,
Dr. Jeffrey Craig
Secretary of Defense

Talon Force Manual 1-1

There are several paths to military advantage in war: organization, training, technology, timing, and political preparation. Today we live in a world where relatively small elements can cause terrible damage to our nation and our way of life. The TALON Force is a new weapon in America's arsenal. The TALON Force is a precision commando group organized to operate with speed and stealth. Its members are superbly trained—the best of the best. Properly employed, the TALON Force will prevent wars and terrorist acts by preemption.
—*Brigadier General Jack Krauss, Commander of TALON Force*

1. Purpose: TALON Force Manual 1-1 (TF1-1) outlines the mission, organization, and equipment of the TALON Force. Additional information is authorized for TALON FORCE, TOP SECRET-NOFORN-ULTRA, authorization only. Additional requests for information should be sent to Commander-in-Chief, Special Operations Command (CINCSOCOM). TALON FORCE, TOP SECRET-NOFORN-ULTRA group personnel reports are contained in separate annexes.

2. Mission: The mission of the TALON Force (Technologically Augmented Low Observable Networked Force) is to independently execute missions that are politically sensitive and require *decisive* action with minimum overt employment of conventional U.S. military forces. The TALON Force is expected to accomplish the following covert action tasks anywhere in the world:

Hostage rescue
Reconnaissance

Preemptive Strike
Other missions as required by the National Command
    Authority (NCA)

3. Organization: The TALON Force is the ultimate military special team. The members of the TALON Force (Technologically Augmented Low Observable Networked Force) are recruited from the best volunteers from all four United States military services and from selected civilian experts. All civilian team members hold the temporary rank of captain (U.S. Army) and are temporarily under the legal jurisdiction of the Uniformed Code of Military Justice. This joint, all-service, special commando team has been designated a TOP SECRET-NOFORN-ULTRA black book organization. No information concerning TALON Force operations or personnel will be released to the public.

The TALON Force is a commando regiment of seven seven-man teams. Each team is configured to operate independently or in conjunction with other teams. The organization of the TALON Force is listed below:

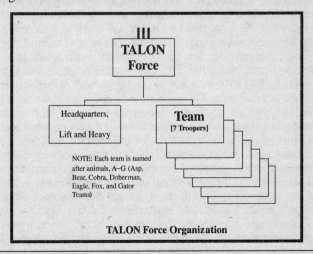

TALON Force Organization

Technology and Equipment:

Overview: The TALON Force is outfitted with ultra high-tech twenty-first-century battle gear. Most of the equipment is prototype. The equipment is so far out on the cutting edge that its capture and replication by enemies of the U.S. is unthinkable. The very latest weapons, such as directed energy, improved rifles, the latest explosives, sensor gear, built-in night vision devices, microdevices, UAVs (unmanned aerial vehicles), lightweight body armor, and improved straight-up-to-satellite minicommunications. The force is also armed with special parachutes, stealth gliders, and the X-37 rocket plane stealth reentry vehicle so that they can get anywhere in the world in hours rather than days.

The key to TALON Force survivability is the low observable camouflage suit that, for short periods of time, provides background scattering camouflage. The suit is actually a series of woven microcomputers that sense the color and shade of the background and exactly mirror the background image. When the Low Observable Camouflage Ensemble is turned on, this high-tech camouflage automatically blends in with the backdrop, making the wearer nearly invisible. The most that an enemy will see is a slight outline or shimmer. Although the Low Observable Camouflage Ensemble provides for near invisibility, it does not negate shadows nor make the TALON Force trooper bulletproof.

Each TALON member is equipped with a helmet that is the nerve center for his high-tech battle equipment. The helmet acts as a communications and sensor device that enhances each trooper's ability to fight and communicate. Communication is by voice and holographic imaging. The helmet has a small eyepiece that covers the left eye when the eyepiece is extended to operate the holographic viewer. This eyepiece transmits visual information into the eye, creating a holographic effect—a virtual 3-D image with full depth, color, and lifelike appearance. Each TALON Force Trooper can activate this viewer capability, hands free, by the movement of the left eye, in a similar fashion as the movement of the mouse on a conventional computer. The screen will display briefings, the location of all friendly and identified enemy units, battle reports, and views seen by other members of the TALON Force.

Specific data on technology and equipment is provided below:

Diagram of TALON Force Trooper Battle Ensemble

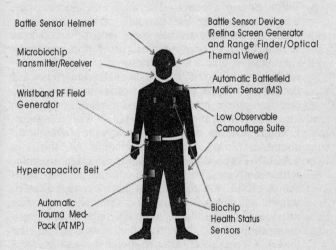

Battle Sensor Helmet

Microbiochip Transmitter/Receiver

Wristband RF Field Generator

Hypercapacitor Belt

Automatic Trauma Med-Pack (AT MP)

Battle Sensor Device (Retina Screen Generator and Range Finder/Optical Thermal Viewer)

Automatic Battlefield Motion Sensor (MS)

Low Observable Camouflage Suite

Biochip Health Status Sensors

1. The TALON Force Battle Ensemble—This uses the next generation beyond smart electronics. It is a "brilliant" suit that provides full body armor protection, immediate and automatic medical trauma aid, a body heat or body cooling capability, communications [voice, digital and holographic], thermal, ranging, laser designating and high-powered optical sensing. It also has a "brilliant camouflage" (Low Observable) capability. The suit is charged up before missions and has a normal power capacity of seventy-two hours without recharging, although the Low Observable Suite can only run continuously for six hours before draining the Battle Ensemble's charge. The ensemble is linked by proximity wave transmission to biochip sensors and transmitters surgically embedded just beneath the skin of every TALON Force trooper. The ensemble monitors life functions and regulates body temperature. It weighs only sixteen and a half pounds. Wearing this ensemble, a trained soldier becomes an enhanced fighter with extraordinary battlefield awareness, lethality, and survivability.

A. Battle Sensor Helmet—This high-tech helmet, outwardly resembling the standard combat helmet, is made of light but extremely tough microfibers, such as Kevlar. The BSH acts as ballistic protection, communications suite, and computer network station. Communications with Joint Task Force Headquarters, and between members, is routed by proximity burst to the communication biochips embedded under the skin near the right ear of every TALON Force trooper. Communications are directed skyward (straight-up communications) to a constellation of thirty-six TALON Force–dedicated satellites. Straight-up communications enables unlimited communications, position location and digital data transfer regardless of terrain and line-of-sight restrictions. This capability provides for continuous, virtually unjammable communications and data transfer anywhere on the planet. Caves, metal framed buildings and bunkers may degrade and negate the communications stream.

B. Microbiochip Transmitter/Receiver—The microcybernetic implant is a voice transmitter that allows TALON Force troopers to use the Battle Sensor Helmet Communications system to talk to Joint Task Force headquarters and members of the TALON Force without the need for an external microphone. The Microbiochip Transmitter can transmit and receive on its own, using line-of-sight transmissions, within a range of 1,000 meters, when the Battle Sensor helmet is turned off, damaged, or missing.

C. HERF Wristband RF Field Generator—This device is a nonlethal weapon that uses a short, intense burst of directed radio frequency energy (RF) to disable electronic devices. In the twenty-first century, radio frequency weapons employing electromagnetic pulse bursts have come of age. High-Energy Radio Frequency (HERF) guns direct a blast of high-energy radio signals at a preselected target. The HERF gun works on the principle that electronic circuits are vulnerable to electromagnetic overload. A HERF gun is nothing more than a radio transmitter that shoots enough energy at its target to disable it, at least temporarily. A HERF gun can "shoot" down a computer, cause an entire network to crash, or make a telephone switch inoperable. The circuitry within computers and modern communications equipment is designed for low-level signals, 1s and 0s, which operate within normal limits. The HERF gun is designed to overload this electronic circuitry so that the information system under attack will become, at least temporarily, a meaningless string of bits and bytes.

The Wristband RF Field Generator is woven right into the fighting ensemble and is activated by voice command via the Microbiochip Transmitter. The range of this wrist HERF gun is about 200 meters, depending on intervening obstacles, and must be aimed by pointing the left arm at the target. The radio frequency waves from this generator will not penetrate thick metal plate, as that of a tank, armored personnel carrier, or most fighting ships; but it will fry the ignition on an unarmored modern automobile or motorcycle and can short-circuit most electronic devices including computers.

The Wristband RF Generator is ideal for stopping vehicles, disarming computer-aimed weapons, and turning off computers, radios, radar and unprotected electrical devices. However, a misaimed burst will also blank out a TALON Force trooper's Battle Sensor Helmet and Low Observable Camouflage capability for one to two minutes, depending on the charge level left in the ensemble. Electromagnetic pulse safeguards in the TALON Force Ensemble protect each trooper from catastrophic electronic failure.

D. Hypercapacitor Belt—This belt contains charged lithiated carbon cells using Polymer Multi-Layer technology, which provide emergency power for the TALON Force Battle Ensemble. The Hypercapacitor Belt can power all systems on the ensemble for two hours, or selected portions of the system, like the Battle Sensor Helmet, for longer periods. The most power-hungry system, the Low Observable Camouflage Suite will operate for only thirty minutes on emergency Hypercapacitor Belt power. Hypercapacitor Belts can be detached and exchanged for use by other TALON Force troopers.

E. Automatic Trauma Med Pack (ATMP)—The ATMP is a microengineered medical system that provides the body with life saving drugs, fluids, and stimulants during battlefield trauma situations. If a TALON Force trooper is hit with a bullet in the arm, for instance, the embedded biochip will transmit vital lifesaving information to the ensemble's health sensors. These sensors will then direct the ensemble to automatically seal the wound, preventing catastrophic loss of blood. The ATMP will then apply the correct fluids and bioenhanced drugs to keep the TALON Force trooper alive. In extensive testing, this system has shown it would save a TALON Force trooper for 76 percent of all battlefield wounds. It will not, however, have any effect on catastrophic wounds, such as being crushed by a tank, falling off a twenty-story building, or having one's head blown off.

F. Battle Sensor Device (BSD)—The BSD folds down from the Battle Sensor Helmet over the left eye like a monocle. The device generates a laser pathway that paints images into the eye of the trooper, using his retina to produce the illusion of holographic images. This holographic capability can be used to display status reports, maps, and battlefield telemetry from distant locations. Linked by the Battle Sensor Helmet's communications system via satellite, the TALON Force trooper can see what the satellite sees in the form of a realistic, three-dimensional holograph that appears before the trooper's eyes. The BSD also acts as a laser range finder to determine the range to and the location of a target. The BSD can also laser-designate targets, up to a range of 3,000 meters, for attack by precision guided munitions. Finally, the BSD has a thermal viewing capability which allows the user to see in the dark, and through smoke and haze, out to a range of 2,000 meters.

G. **Automatic Battlefield Motion Sensor (MS)**—This device detects millimeter wave changes in movement out to seven hundred meters and automatically alerts the trooper with a minor electric tingling sensation to warn the wearer of danger, in addition to a voice description of the threat and visual sensor information in the Battle Sensor Device. The MS is the equivalent of having a sixth sense and is part of the TALON Force protective suite. If the thermal viewer of the Battle Sensor Device is malfunctioning or damaged, the Motion Sensor can pick up the slack and warn the TALON Force trooper of danger.

H. **Low Observable Camouflage Suite**—This is the slickest part of the TALON Force Battle Ensemble. Microsensors woven into the tough, bulletproof fabric of the ensemble (suit, gloves, boots, BSD helmet, and weapon sheath) automatically determine the visual qualities of the background and copy the exact shade, color, and luminosity of that background. In essence, the wearer becomes the background, blending in with the surroundings like a chameleon. A transparent, slidable shield in the Battle Sensor Helmet covers the face and generates a virtual camouflage face shield. Plug-in gloves and a plug-in sheathe will cover the XM-29 rifle. The only thing seen by the naked eye is a slight shimmer as the TALON Force trooper passes by. The Low Observable Camouflage Suite is the most power-draining device of the Battle Ensemble. The camouflage suite can be operated for short periods of time throughout the seventy-two-hour charge of the Battle Ensemble, or for no more than six continuous hours without recharging. Using emergency Hypercapacitor Belt power, with a fully charged belt, the camouflage suite can operate continuously for an additional thirty minutes.

I. Biochip Health Status Sensors—In addition to cybernetic implants in every TALON Force trooper, the Battle Ensemble has multiple Biochip Health Status Sensors to monitor vital body functions and report injuries. These biochips will also direct the immediate closure of any puncture wounds to the ensemble wearer through brilliant fibers within the ensemble. In essence, the Biochip Health Status Sensors of the Battle Ensemble execute immediate first aid and direct the activation of lifesaving drugs and fluids from the Automatic Medical Trauma Pack (ATMP) whenever required.

2. TALON Force Weapons

A. Missiles

1. Cruise Missiles: Cruise missiles can be launched by U.S. Air Force aircraft and U.S. Navy ships in support of TALON Force operations. All cruise missiles that support the TALON Force are armed with conventional high-explosive brilliant munitions. One cruise missile will take out an area the size of a football stadium, destroying exposed personnel and vehicles. Normally, only four or five cruise missiles carrying brilliant munitions will be available for each mission.

2. Hard and/or Deeply Buried Target Defeat Capa-

bility (HDBTDC) Weapons (also known as the Bunker Buster): Conventional explosive-filled penetrating weapons are often relatively ineffective in destroying large underground reinforced-concrete facilities. Even if the weapon detonates inside the facility, substantial interior walls or floors can confine the blast and fragmentation to a small area. Bunker Busters are designed to completely destroy underground facilities.

When these facilities protect WMD (Weapons of Mass Destruction), the random use of conventional weapons greatly increases the risk of NBC (Nuclear, Biological, Chemical) agent dispersal that may result in extensive civilian or friendly force casualties. Agent neutralization is the key aspect of HDBTDC weapons. The Bunker Buster is a precision, GPS, satellite- and laser-guided missile that has a Hard-Target Smart Fuse (HTSF). The HTSF is a microcontrolled, in-line fuse designed to be physically and electrically compatible with many bombs in the U.S. inventory (GBU-10, GBU-15, GBU-24, GBU-27, GBU-28, AGM-130, and general purpose MK-80 series weapons). The HTSF burrows deep to destroy NBC weapons and vaporize WMD with minimal collateral damage.

B. Aircraft

1. X-37 rocket plane: The Boeing X-37 Reusable Advanced Hypersonic rocket plane will rapidly deliver a TALON Force team anywhere on the planet in only a few hours. The X-37 is a manned, dual-engine rocket plane that carries seven fully equipped TALON Force troopers in specially designed entry packages. The entry packages, nicknamed eggshells by TALON troopers, protect the jumpers from the shock of exiting the aircraft at high speed and altitude.

The X-37 is approximately seventy-five feet long, has a twenty-eight-foot wingspan and is twelve feet tall from the bottom of the fuselage to the top of the tail. Two Fastrac rocket engines, which were developed by NASA at its Marshall Space Flight Center in Huntsville, Alabama, power the X-37. The rocket plane is carried piggyback style to high altitude by an L-1011 carrier aircraft. The rocket engines are ignited, and the rocket plane separates from the L-1011. The X-37 can achieve altitudes of up to 250,000 feet (almost 50 miles) and speeds of up to Mach 8, or eight times faster than the speed of sound. Following the exit of the eggshells, the X-37 accelerates to Mach 8, achieves low earth orbit, and returns to a designated runway where it lands horizontally, like an airplane.

2. TFV-22 Super Osprey: The TALON Force V-22 Super Osprey is the special operations version of the Osprey tilt-rotor aircraft, an entirely new breed of aircraft that is neither pure airplane nor pure helicopter but has features of both. It was developed by a joint venture between Bell Helicopters and Boeing. The Osprey takes off and lands like a helicopter, lifted by two huge rotors on the tips of its wings. Once in flight, the rotors can tilt forward, turning the aircraft into a high-speed turboprop.

Over the years, many have attempted to develop such a hybrid, but the Super Osprey is the first aircraft offering sufficient reliability and utility to be of practical military value. The aircraft is about half the size of a C-130 transport. The rotors can be tilted forward ninety degrees for either a vertical landing or a rolling landing if heavily loaded. The Osprey is able to take-off and land in the same space as the H-53 Super Jolly series of helicopters and is more stealthy and quieter than any previous large rotor craft.

The TALON Force V-22 Super Ospreys have the latest electronic antiradar and antiSAM jamming systems. They are fast, reliable and stealthy, capable of getting past most radars undetected. The Super Ospreys can carry an entire TALON Force action team. Under certain conditions, the TFV-22 can sling load a light vehicle, but only in the vertical lift mode and only for short distances.

C. Ground Support Vehicles

1. XM-77 Wildcat Armored Car: This light armored car built by General Dynamics is air transportable by the four special heavy lift C-117 Globemaster transports of the TALON Force Air Squadron. The Wildcat has special electromagnetic armor that acts like a force field to deflect the heaviest tank and antitank rounds. There are only four of these special vehicles in the TALON Force. The Wildcat is armed with a forward-mounted 7.62 mm machine gun and a commander's .50 caliber machine gun. Between the two conventional machine guns is a retractable directed energy weapon (DEW) that can blast holes in the strongest rock, reinforced concrete, or steel. The retractable DEW cannon has the capacity for ten shots before its energy pack runs out.

2. Improved Armored High Mobility Multi-Purpose Wheeled Vehicle (HMMWV, Humvee, or Hummer): AM General's Humvee has been the workhorse of the military since the late 1980s and is used by the TALON Force for special missions. This has an electric hybrid fuel cell engine that allows the vehicle to travel great distances without refueling. Armed with a special armor and bulletproof glass, the Improved Armored HMMWV is impervious to small arms fire less than 12.7 mm (.50 caliber). This vehicle is armed with a .50 caliber machine gun with improved ammunition. The improved ammunition is capable of penetrating the armor of most armored cars and armored personnel carriers.

D. Individual and Crew Served Weapons

1. The Offensive Handgun Weapon System (OHWS) .45 Caliber Special Operations Forces Pistol with Silencer: The OHWS is a new .45 caliber pistol specifically created for special operations forces. Manufactured by Heckler & Koch and Colt, the OHWS consists of three components: a .45 caliber semi-automatic pistol, a laser aiming module (LAM), and a removable sound and flash suppressor attached to the barrel. Holds a seven-round clip and is effective up to fifty meters. Has a match grade accuracy (2.5-inch maximum extreme spread in a five-round shot group at 25 meters). The SOF .45 offers the shooter great stopping power and superb accuracy.

2. 9 mm Baretta: Standard U.S. military pistol. The Baretta M9 is a lightweight, semi-automatic 9 mm pistol. It weighs 2.55 pounds fully loaded and holds fifteen rounds in the magazine. The maximum effective range is fifty meters. Carried by female TALON Force troopers.

3. XM-73 Pistol: This experimental pistol fires a 15 mm shell that launches half a dozen smart bullets at targets within an 800-meter range. The pistol is made of the same special alloys as the XM-29 Smart Rifle and is remarkably light, weighing only two pounds. The submunitions are combustible cartridge (no brass) 2.22 mm. These projectiles will penetrate most bulletproof vests. Each XM-73 carries a basic load of seven rounds in the box magazine near the trigger.

4. Heckler & Koch 9 mm MP-5 submachinegun: The H&K MP5 has a thirty-round magazine and is geared for close-quarters battle.

5. XM-29 Individual Combat Rifle: This rifle provides an enhanced capability over all other individual weapons, combining a 20 mm grenade launcher with a 5.56 mm rifle. It is aimed by a smart fire control system that includes accurate laser range finder, ballistic computer, direct-view optics, video camera, electronic compass, thermal mode, and automatic target tracker. This combination weapon system provides decisively violent and suppressive target effects out to 1,000 meters in rural, urban, and desert terrain. The 20 mm airbursting ammunition includes a miniature electronic fuse that permits the projectile to airburst at the appropriate target range. This capability enables the successful defeat of both exposed and defilade targets (individuals behind cover, within trenches, on rooftops, etc.). The XM-29 carries eighty-five 5.66 mm rounds of brassless ammunition and ten 20 mm high explosive (HE) rounds ready to fire. The special ammunition casings for both the 5.66 mm rounds and 20 mm grenades disintegrate after firing so there is no brass ejected from the weapon, a necessary stealth feature. This combination rifle weighs fourteen pounds.

6. Lightweight .50 Caliber Sniper Rifle: The .50 caliber sniper rifle is a one-man special sniper rifle with eight-power scope and ten-round magazine. Although this weapon may be designated as lightweight, it weighs twenty-one pounds.

7. M-30 Crew-Served Weapon: The M-30 is a next-generation combination crew-served weapon that replaces the .50 caliber machine gun. The weapon is two-man portable and backpackable. The M-30 delivers decisively violent, long-range, high-explosive fire that is considerably more lethal than conventional heavy machine guns or grenade launchers. The M-30 fires a high explosive (HE) or armor-piercing (AP) 25 mm round. The 25 mm HE precision airbursting round can explode about the target, scattering hot metal in all directions on the targets below the burst. The soft recoil system and advanced fire control system (laser range finder, thermal sight, and airburst fuse setter) make this weapon extremely accurate up to 2,000 meters in day or night operations. The M-30 weighs twenty-three pounds. Each ammunition can contains thirty-one rounds and weighs fourteen pounds.

E. Artillery

1. Arsenal Boxes: These special rocket-launched munitions are parachuted or air-landed and left in remote areas to provide immediate fire support for TALON Force teams. This system provides immediate, accurate, brilliant fire within twenty to forty-five seconds of the initiation for the call for fire. Arsenal Boxes are completely autonomous and require no personnel to activate and fire. Each arsenal box has eight shots. Although the munitions in each arsenal box can vary by the requirements of the mission, the usual load is a brilliant bomblet cluster that covers the area of a football field with personnel- and armor-killing detonations.

F. Robots, Unmanned Aerial Vehicles (UAVs) and Nonlethal Weapons

1. XM-11 Robot Sensors: The TALON Force is equipped with a number of robot sensors, all about the size of a cigarette case, that can be left in position and will report movement or visual data directly to team members.

2. XM-12 Bug: A sensor that crawls, linked to a microvideo high-frequency transmitter. The bug is a small, almost transparent robot made completely of clear plastic and thin, silver wires.

3. Unmanned Aerial Vehicles (UAVs): There are three UAVs at the disposal of the TALON Force. The larger the UAV, the greater the capability. In every mission the team will probably have two Predator 5's flying overhead at critical mission times. Hummingbirds and Dragonflies are carried by team members or are dropped by parachute in special containers and can be assembled and sent skyward in a matter of minutes.

a. Predator 5: Pilotless aircraft like UAV with wings and propeller that can carry a large electronics payload.

Size: Large; the size of a motorcycle with long wings.

Range: Long orbit and high altitude; almost invisible in the air at long range.

Purpose: Tactical communications relay, thermal and video imaging, and laser designating for targeting.

Noise: Loud, but flies high enough to minimize sound travel. As heard from the ground, the Predator 5 is relatively silent.

b. Hummingbird: Pilotless helicopterlike UAV that can carry a small electronics payload.

Size: Medium; the size of a model airplane.

Range: Short orbit and low altitude (two-hour flight time, thermal and video imaging).

Purpose: Thermal and video imaging.

Noise: Can be detected by sound within 100 meters.

c. Dragonfly: Pilotless microaircraft (aircraft-like) UAV with delta wing and pusher (rear-mounted) propeller that can carry a microelectronics payload.

Size: Small, palm sized.

Range: Low altitude, thirty-minute flight time. Excellent for use inside a building. Invisible in the air at long range, but can be detected at short range.

Purpose: Video imaging only.

Noise: Very quiet humming sound.

4. Nonlethal Generators (NLGs): These devices are the size of a small trash can and can be parachuted, air-landed, or carried in a rucksack for special missions. NLGs produce a low-frequency RF Field that causes unprotected personnel within a range of 600 meters to become uncontrollably sick. Within several seconds, the victim is rendered temporarily helpless on the ground, vomiting, and with pronounced loss of muscle control. Prolonged exposure over five or six hours can cause permanent damage. NLGs are used to deter civilian personnel or in situations where casualties are to be avoided.